For Damian, who made it possible

About the Author

Helen J Rolfe was born in the UK and moved to Australia in 2000 where she worked in I.T. After leaving the industry Helen studied writing and worked as a freelance journalist, volunteered as a media assistant, and finally began writing fiction seriously in 2011.

After fourteen years of living in Australia, Helen relocated back to the UK in 2014, where she now lives in Bath with her husband and their children.

The Friendship Tree is Helen J Rolfe's first novel.

You can find out more about Helen J Rolfe at:

www.helenjrolfe.com
https://www.facebook.com/helenjrolfewriter
https://twitter.com@hjrolfe
http://thewriteromantics.com
www.goodreads.com/helenjrolfe

Acknowledgements

Thank you to my husband and my children who have patiently allowed me to pursue my dream of becoming a writer. I am forever grateful for their endless encouragement, support and unwillingness to let me give up.

To the Romantic Novelists' Association (RNA), without whom I would've probably still been lost and working on my first attempt at a novel, going round in circles and torturing myself in the process. Through the RNA I have met many writers, and more importantly, friends, and found the encouragement and industry knowledge that enabled me to go on to achieve publication for The Friendship Tree.

Thanks to a great group of girls known as The Write Romantics who have been a tower of strength since we formed back in 2013. All ten of us have had our moments of triumph, moments of weakness, and have held each other up when the going got tough. We have also been able to celebrate one another's success, and long may the friendship continue, girls!

To my beta reader, and friend, Alison, who critiqued The Friendship Tree and is never afraid to tell me what she thinks. I'm secretly hoping that by mentioning her in these acknowledgments, she will be happy for me to pass her my next novel to read…

Thanks to my editor, Christine, who patiently waited for me to get the hang of Track Changes and worked with me to move my book to the next stage. It was a pleasure working with you.

And finally, a huge thanks goes to Laurence and Steph Patterson, of Crooked Cat Publishing, who loved The Friendship Tree enough to accept it for publication. You are a joy to work with. Thanks guys!

The Friendship Tree

Chapter One

Tamara Harding wondered how she had managed to get roped into this when she had only been in Australia for ten days. She looked down at the friendship tree – a hand-drawn, landscape-oriented picture that held the details of every resident who shared the Brewer Creek postcode. Her task, as co-ordinator, was to update and redistribute the tree.

"I think there are already some updates waiting for you," her mum explained. "I know that Jake Manning's details still haven't been added, and he's been in town for a while now. I'll leave you to it." Katherine Harding kissed her daughter's cheek. "I'll see you after work."

Tamara waved as she watched her mum head off to her part time job at the local post office, but her smile soon faded when she thought again of Jake, the man who had come to town and set up a second veterinary practice. Tamara was fiercely protective of her stepfather, Bobby, and suspected that the new competition in town was making more of an impact than he was willing to let on.

The warmth of the tangerine sun that hung in the sky filtered through the fly-screen door as Tamara looked out over the garden, the orchard, and the paddock. She glanced back at the picture of the friendship tree which had been maintained in Daphne Abbott's miniscule Mrs-Pepperpot-style handwriting. It had a thick trunk and sprawling branches heading up towards the top of the paper. More branches spread from those, holding up boxes containing the names and contact details of Brewer Creek's residents.

When Daphne had handed over the reins of the friendship tree to a still jet-lagged and bleary-eyed Tamara, she had done so with a look that left no doubt about the high standards expected of her from now on. But Tamara was ready to rise to the challenge; sitting around gave her too much time to dwell on the reasons why she had left London. Focusing on something new, like the friendship tree, would help her to settle in and feel a part of this town.

With her work hat on, she decided that her first task should be to bring this friendship tree into the twenty-first century. She booted up the computer in Bobby's study, and as the machine whirred into action she leant back in the leather chair and gazed out of the window. This sleepy town was as far removed from the London lifestyle and her job as a Public Relations Account Executive as you could get, but it also had the added bonus of being ten thousand miles away from Bradley Cox.

And that was exactly why she had come.

Since Bobby and Katherine Harding emigrated eight years ago, visits had been few and far between, with Tamara visiting Australia once and her parents making the trip home twice. The original plan had been for them all to emigrate as a family, but when Tamara's career took off in her early twenties she had made the heart-wrenching decision to stay in the UK. It had been her best friend Beth who had supported her in the early weeks when Tamara wondered whether she had made a mistake in staying put, but then Bradley came on the scene and everything in her world had been rosy… for a while.

Tamara studied the friendship tree with its scribbled alterations: one resident had married and changed surname; another had left the area; another looked as though he had moved with the times and added a mobile phone number. Daphne had also scribbled job descriptions: Bill "GP"; Derek "Mechanic"; Matthew "Dairy Farmer"; Len "Local Pub"; "Plumber" against a man named Flynn on the highest branch. She had never seen anything like this before. In the block of flats where she'd lived in

England, you were lucky to know anyone else's name let alone their personal details.

Tamara found an image of the outline of a tree with a wide canopy and saved a copy onto Bobby's computer, then she added boxes to the branches and transferred all the details from Daphne's diagram. Once they had been triple-checked, she bumped up the number of copies to forty-five – the exact number of squares that she had on the tree to represent each property – and left the printer to do its thing.

Since her arrival on Christmas Eve, Tamara had functioned in a jet-lagged haze, falling asleep on any unsuspecting couch and fixing snacks in the middle of the night. But today her body seemed to have adjusted. Today was the first day that she could fully appreciate how different life was in this town, compared to London. She poured a glass of orange juice and looked out at the waxy sheen of the tops of the trees, the pineapple-like trunks, the rambling open spaces with an infusion of greens, mustard-yellows, and reds injected into the landscape. Her mum's Instagram photographs simply hadn't done Brewer Creek justice. It was a small town nestled in the Central Coast of New South Wales, and the feeling of space along with the vast expanse of seemingly limitless blue sky left Tamara satisfied that she had made the right decision.

Tamara checked her watch and quickly calculated the time difference, then reached for the phone and waited for the international call to click through. She hadn't spoken to Beth since she left the UK, and it was lovely to hear her voice again. They chatted about the perils of jet lag, sun versus snow, the latest night out in the trendy London bars that Tamara hadn't thought she'd ever miss until now. They joked about being thirty and living with your parents all over again.

"Bobby painted the annexe, so at least I'll be semi-independent in there," said Tamara. "I've been roped into organising a friendship tree for the town, too." She explained the intricacies. "I thought that sort of thing went out with wind-on cameras."

"Hey," said Beth, "*never* underestimate the power of the friendship tree."

"That's true. We probably would never have been friends if it hadn't been for the one at school."

"Exactly," said Beth, not bothering to conceal a yawn. "So come on," she groaned, "tell me what the weather's like? Do I really want to know?"

"It's sunny, twenty-five degrees and climbing."

"Oh be quiet," said Beth. "I'm so jealous! Surprise, surprise, it's freezing here. It snowed on New Year's Eve, too, not a bloody taxi in sight…"

Tamara wondered whether Beth had bumped into Bradley on New Year's Eve – they frequented many of the same bars and pubs. Did he even know yet that she had left the country? Somehow she had successfully avoided all contact with him since that awful night when she had realised she needed to get away once and for all.

As though reading her mind, Beth asked, "Have you heard from Bradley?"

The breeze outside picked up, and the rustling of plants and trees instilled a sense of calm in Tamara. "Not a thing," she said.

"Good." Tamara could imagine Beth's trademark glossy red lips and her serious frown, her razor-cut bob as she recited her sermon. "No offence, Tamara, but it's a good thing you're there, away from him. It's time to think of your own needs for a change."

"I know." Tamara still didn't understand how it was possible to love someone one minute and be so wary of them the next. Leaving the UK had felt like ripping off an extraordinarily stubborn plaster: quick and hugely painful, but ultimately for her own good. Leaving Bradley, with his classic dark hair and film star good looks, had been the easy part; the part that made sense. Leaving the solidity of her close friendship with Beth, which had stood fast for more than twenty years, had been the hardest thing of all.

"Promise me something, Tamara?" Beth's tired voice came from the other side of the world. "If Bradley does get in touch, be careful. He seems to know how to wangle his way back in every time."

"I know what he's like."

To Beth, Bradley was a manipulative arsehole; to Tamara, he was a thirty-year-old man who had lost his way in life's maze, and at every turn he seemed unable to find his way out. Leaving him hadn't been easy. He had been through his own hell with his family, and until Tamara came along it had all been bottled up tighter than a jar of pickles. His past didn't excuse his behaviour, but it did give him a complexity to his personality which Tamara had tried her best to understand.

When they ended their call Tamara wondered briefly how long it would be before Bradley heard on the grapevine that she had left London. It was highly unlikely that he would jump on a plane and follow her. A London boy through and through, even the thought of relocating to the south coast last year when Tamara was head-hunted by an up-and-coming PR firm had rattled him.

She picked up the printed copies of the friendship tree and left them in a stack on the hutch in the hallway before trotting upstairs to get ready for the day. Unlike the world of PR where everything had to be done yesterday, the distribution phase of the trees wasn't urgent, and thanks to modern technology she was probably already well ahead of the game.

"Good morning, Bobby," she called chirpily as she passed the bathroom.

Bobby poked his head around the door, one half of his face freshly shaven and the other covered in the whipped-cream-like shaving foam. "Good morning, love." He still held the razor in his hand, a towel slung over his shoulder on top of a black dressing gown. "Were you talking to yourself again?"

She gave him a playful shove which barely registered with the tall, solid man whose head skimmed the door frame. Quite by chance, Bobby Harding had the same emerald green eyes as Tamara and Katherine, and aside from the fact that she always called him Bobby it was only Tamara's cocoa-coloured skin – a blend from her London-born mum and her biological, Nigerian father – that gave away the fact that he was her stepfather.

"That was Beth on the phone," giggled Tamara. "She says hello, by the way."

"Ah, that explains it. So I don't need to call the men in white coats yet then?"

"Not yet."

"So what's the news from London? Any snow there yet?"

"A bit on New Year's Eve apparently."

Bobby leaned against the door jamb, unconcerned that Tamara had interrupted his shave. "Still feeling a bit homesick, love?"

She rolled her eyes. "It's only been a couple of weeks. People go on holiday for longer than that."

He ruffled her shoulder-length, wavy hair with his free hand. "I know, but moving around is hard; I've done it enough in my time to know that you'll have some ups and downs. Remember this is your home for as long as you need."

Tamara hadn't revealed the reasons behind her sudden relocation to Australia; as far as her parents were concerned, she was here on an open-ended visit and nothing else.

Bobby caught the trickle of white, watery liquid that began creeping down his throat. "I'd better finish up. Those trashy UK magazines that you were after are still in the car, on the passenger seat."

"Thanks, Bobby." Tamara trotted downstairs in her pyjamas and slipped on a pair of flip-flops at the back door. Getting ready could wait; celebrity gossip and problem pages couldn't.

Outside, she aimed the remote at the small red hatchback to wake it up. She leant over to the passenger side to grab the pile of glossy magazines, but as she pulled her body back out she felt a firm hand swipe across the bare skin of her shoulder blades.

She screamed. The pile of magazines launched like confetti in the air as she clasped her chest, gasping for breath as she turned to meet the person responsible. "What on earth do you think you're doing?"

"Whoa, take it easy," said the man. He held up his hands as though he was the victim rather than her. "You had a spider on your back," he said matter-of-factly.

Tamara spun round on the spot like a dog chasing its own tail. Her arms chopped through the air like blades on a windmill as she attempted to detach any cobwebs that might still be lingering. Oh God, was there something in her hair? She swished at that, too; she felt itchy all over.

Cornflower-blue eyes looked down at her, a hint of amusement disguised beneath a wide-brimmed Crocodile Dundee-style hat, and a smile played on the man's smooth, pale pink lips which were surrounded by a light layer of manly stubble.

"G'day, I'm Jake Manning." A hand extended towards her as she looked up at him, moving into the shade created by his body so that she wasn't squinting in the sun.

"Tamara Harding." She found the warmth of Jake's rough, hard-working hand, which dwarfed her own and contrasted against her dark skin.

She bent down to gather the magazines from the dirt below and took one from Jake when he crouched down to help her. Suddenly aware of her barely-there pyjamas, she folded her arms in front of her chest when she stood up, using the magazines as added protection. She locked eyes with him, unsure whether she was more embarrassed by how little she was wearing, or the fact that he was drop-dead gorgeous and totally unexpected.

The corners of Jake's mouth curved upwards and parted enough to show a row of neat teeth. "Spiders sometimes sneak in that gap around the door frame," he said, gesturing towards the car. "Huntsmen aren't poisonous, but they could give you a nasty bite."

"Thanks. I'll try to remember that."

It was still early enough in the morning for the air to carry a chill despite the glow of the sun and the promise of an Australian summer's day, and Tamara felt her body showing outward signs of being cold. She hugged the magazines even tighter against her chest.

"I'm here to see Mr Harris's horse," said Jake, the same persistent grin on his face as he pointed to the fields running adjacent to the Harding property.

"Well don't let me keep you."

"Don't let me keep you either." He tipped his hat, smirked at the picture of Jennifer Aniston on the front cover of the magazine. "You look busy."

She walked away, frustrated at letting him have the last word. Up until her recent redundancy, she had worked incredibly hard and this was her first real bit of relaxation in eighteen months. She wanted to ask why he was here to see Mr Harris, who was one of Bobby's clients, but that wasn't something she wanted to tackle whilst wearing skimpy pyjamas. Instead, she stalked back into the house and turned around in time to see Jake saunter past the swaying branches of the eucalyptus tree at the foot of the garden, his faded Levis perfectly capturing his masculinity.

This wasn't why she had come to Australia; she didn't need another man to complicate things.

Chapter Two

Jake passed through the gate to Mr Harris's property. He couldn't shake off the image of Tamara, her skin silky-smooth to the touch as he'd knocked the spider away. He let out a breath as he thought of her dark hair that caught highlights from the sun and hung down between delicately-boned shoulder blades, and that sexy little toe ring that glistened in the light. As pleasant and well-meaning as Daphne was, she certainly wasn't a patch on this girl from London who had taken over control of the friendship tree, and he looked forward to coming face-to-face with Tamara again if she was as serious about keeping it up-to-date as Daphne was.

With noticeable hourglass curves, and cute, seductive, heart-shaped lips, Tamara was a welcome distraction in the midst of all the trouble in Jake's life right now, although he didn't doubt her ability to land a decent punch on him should he put a foot out of line. When she'd caught his gaze drop to the silky pyjama top which left little to the imagination, he'd averted his eyes quickly.

He knew he'd also raised Tamara's suspicions the second he mentioned that he was here to see Mr Wilson, and he admired that in her; looking out for your family was something very close to his heart. But if Tamara thought that he was here to cause trouble or muscle in on Bobby's clientele, then she was wrong. His reasons for being in Brewer Creek were far less callous than that, and he had chosen a place with country town safety that couldn't be mimicked elsewhere.

Soon after he'd arrived in town, Daphne Abbott had cornered him in the milk bar that she ran and requested his personal details for the friendship tree. From that moment he had been hooked on the place. It felt as though he had stepped into the pages of a children's book rather than an insignificant town.

Jake closed the gate to the paddock and waved over to Mr Harris, who was fitting a saddle to one of his horses. A quick glance at his watch reminded him that he didn't want to be out for too long, because April hated being left alone in the house.

Mr Harris pushed his greying hair back over to the other side of his head and Jake didn't have the heart to tell him that comb-overs really were a thing of the past. He followed the man past the stables and into the rear paddock where Solomon looked happy enough.

"The medication to clear up that abscess must've worked its magic," said Jake, gently inspecting the hoof which had been treated. When he patted Solomon and felt the horse tense, he took a closer look at the coat beneath the mane. "What's this?"

Mr Harris's face dropped when he peered at the injury. "He must've caught it on the fence; I can't believe I didn't notice."

Jake rummaged in his bag, deftly cleaned the wound, and then stitched the small area. "He'll be fine, Mr Harris, but you need to sort that fence out over there before any more animals get hurt." Jake pointed to a section of exposed barbed wire which had most likely been the culprit. "If there's grass over the other side, then Solomon's going to put his head over the fence to eat it. And next time he could do more damage."

"I'll get to it straight away. Thanks, Jake." Mr Harris shook his hand enthusiastically, an action which conveyed how welcome Jake was in this town. Already he felt part of the small community, and knew he and April had made the right choice in coming here.

With his bag repacked, Jake made his way across the paddock and looked over at the Harding property. He was settling in just fine in Brewer Creek, but Tamara Harding was a complication that he wished he felt ready to handle. In those few moments they had shared today, she had crept well and truly under his skin.

Chapter Three

"Here you go." Tamara plonked a pile of mail down onto the kitchen table beside Bobby. Despite the early morning wake-up call from the kookaburras, followed by a lengthy Skype call with Beth, she was full of energy.

"Thank you. Any creepy crawlies get you out there this morning?" Bobby teased.

"There was a nasty big cockroach scuttling across the lid of the mailbox; it must've seen me coming. God bless English postboxes, where the mail just lands on the mat."

Bobby ripped open a couple of utility bills and left them at the side of the table. "What did you think of my painting in there?" He gestured towards the annexe.

"I love it. Thanks." Tamara planted a kiss on his cheek.

The custard-coloured walls of the annexe were bare except for a framed picture of concentric circles in shades of reds and oranges, and some shelving above the bed. The annexe had its own kitchenette equipped with a fridge, toaster and a kettle, as well as a small shower room. "I really appreciate you making me feel so at home."

"No worries," Bobby replied in his best Aussie accent. "The paint smell will go in time, and feel free to put up some more pictures."

"You don't want to make me too comfortable," Tamara smiled. "I might outstay my welcome."

"Twaddle," Bobby slurped his tea. "We don't see enough of you anyway, so make the most of it. And you've got those concertina doors along part of one wall so you can open them up and enjoy the garden when you feel like it."

Tamara hugged him tightly. He had shown her the grand plans for the house renovations whilst she was still wobbly-legged from her flight, his enthusiasm bubbling over about the pool he wanted to put in, the cabana, and maybe a home theatre, too.

"Don't you have to get to work?" She looked at the clock as the big hand took it past ten o'clock. Bobby was still munching on the last mouthful of peanut butter on toast.

"Soon," he shrugged.

"Where's Mum?"

Bobby tipped his head of short, greying hair back to get the dregs of his tea in the bottom of the cup as he headed to his study, calling over his shoulder, "She's on the morning shift today, back at lunchtime."

Tamara pulled out a fresh loaf from the breadbin – why they couldn't buy bread pre-sliced she would never know – and cut a slice. When the slice tried without success to pop out of the toaster, she switched the machine off at the wall and used a knife to rescue it.

"I hear you met Jake the other day." Bobby reappeared in the kitchen and grinned at the sight of Tamara's toast, cut so unevenly that it looked like a ski run.

Trying to ignore the unexpected tingle that had zinged all the way up her spine at the mention of Jake, Tamara spread a generous helping of jam across the toast's bumpy, golden surface and said, "I thought Mr Harris was your client."

Bobby stashed a bowl and his empty mug in the dishwasher and sighed heavily. "Tamara, it's good of you to worry about me; about us. Jake is healthy competition, nothing more, nothing less. Times are tough for anyone these days and I'm no exception, and I'm guessing neither is Jake. Don't you worry, I still have my loyal customers."

"But some of them have left, according to Mum." Tamara knew that her stepfather wasn't the Rottweiler that he needed to be to keep his client base. Instead, he was the dog that rolled over and let you tickle its tummy, and that could threaten what he had built up over the years.

He smiled at her now. "When I'm booked up, some of them drift over to Jake and unfortunately it means that sometimes they don't come back. I expect Jake was here to check on Mr Harris's horse. I couldn't get out to him last week as I was dealing with Peggy Thompson – a litter of kittens arrived as a surprise one night in the corner of her laundry; she'd thought her cat was getting fat." His rounded belly jiggled as he laughed. "She had the poor thing on all sorts of diets before she even realised."

Tamara grabbed hold of his arm before he had a chance to fob her off some more. "You look tired."

"That's because I'm old."

"You are not old!" She nudged him, even though she had noticed herself that his eyes were more sunken and lacked their usual clarity, and his words harboured a definite lethargy whenever he spoke.

"When you get to my age, Tamara, going out to work each day becomes much like having the same dinner every night of the week. It satisfies you and means that you can function, but the excitement has gone."

She hesitated a moment, not wanting to speak out of turn. "You could always retire, or at least cut back a bit."

"One day," he said, and with that he left Tamara in the kitchen to wonder what this usually relaxed, happy-go-lucky man was holding onto so tightly inside.

She wandered into the front sitting room and watched Bobby's car slowly reverse off the drive, leaving her alone in the house. It was so quiet she could almost hear the grass growing outside. Tamara was used to living on her own in a one bedroom flat in Watford, not far from London, but the general noise that came with living in the same building as others and in such close proximity to shops and local businesses, must have kept her company.

She sat on the edge of the armchair and sipped from a glass of iced water, wondering how her parents could face their morning cups of tea or coffee when the weather outside was so warm. She looked out of the window at the landscape which her mum had provided a passionate rundown of when she arrived. Dappled with vibrant purple splashes of the jacaranda trees, and the creamy white sprays of fragrant flowers on the Fiddlewood that sat to one side of the driveway, it was the epitome of country living.

Restless, Tamara headed to the study and flicked on the computer. As it went through the motions of starting up, she let the sun warm her through the open window and carry the scent of the outside to the desk. She moved the mouse and prepared to live her life vicariously through the wonders of the worldwide web, flicking through her emails, deleting spam that asked whether she wanted to get laid more, something from EnlargeIt-Fast, and an invitation to have non-surgical fat reduction.

Her emerald green eyes played with the screen as she opened Facebook, unable to resist the opportunity to check-in with what was happening in the city she had left behind. She scrolled down the News Feed, giggling at Beth's post showing a photo of her on a narrow boat travelling along the Norfolk Broads with her brother Heath. Beth was the skipper and she looked as though she were driving a car in the Grand Prix rather than a vessel that was moving slower than a push bike.

When Tamara left the UK, she didn't think she'd miss her drab flat with its tatty Formica kitchen floor and the slightly torn wallpaper beneath the lounge windowsill. She never imagined she'd miss the smell drifting up to her paper-thin windows every morning from the cafe across the road, or the sound of the twin toddlers upstairs wailing as their mother tried to get through the witching hour. But now, seeing such scenes with only the whirring sound of the computer for company, she yearned for that type of familiarity.

The leather chair creaked as she leaned into its backrest and smiled as she saw her message inbox receive a new mail. It was from Beth:

*Really missing you, mate, but DO NOT COME HOME YET! (I'm
writing this because I know you'll see Facebook posts that make you
feel as though you're missing out. Believe me, you're not!)*
*Trust me; I've always had your back, haven't I? Ever since that Darren
Wallis picked on you by the friendship tree. Blimey, wonder what he's
up to now? God, who cares!*
Anyway, gotta go. I've got an early meeting in the morning.
Say a big hello to the parents. Love and hugs!
Beth x

Tamara manoeuvred the mouse ready to reply, but her eyes
jerked to the other side of the screen. She felt her body go cold as
she froze, because there staring back at her was a Friend Request,
from Bradley.

She wondered why she hadn't seen this one coming.

"Pah… I thought Facebook was for *Losers!*" She held her
thumb and forefinger against her forehead in an 'L' shape,
remembering how he had used those very words when she'd
signed up to the social networking site. She realised then that she
was rubbing her temple, and even though the bruise had healed
pretty quickly, the memories still lingered of that night.

She shuddered as her mind flitted to Bradley's solemn
confession about his family a couple of weeks into their
relationship: "I hid under my bed like a coward," he'd said, as he
described his father's rage. "I should've protected my mum."

The breeze from the open window made Tamara shiver now.
She couldn't deny that she missed Bradley, and she wondered
whether things could've been different if she'd made him get help,
or if she had supported him more. The answer from Beth would
be easy: a resounding "no"!

Sometimes Tamara fought to forget the good times so that she
could open her eyes to the bad. Was that what she needed to do
now?

Of course Bradley had a nice side, but not everyone got to see that. Sometimes he'd bought her flowers "just because"; he'd driven around for hours one night to get her flu tablets when she couldn't sleep and her temperature had gone through the roof; he'd cooked her breakfast in bed when she had the hangover to end all hangovers.

Bradley had kind eyes, a soft voice, and all the vulnerability of someone with a shaky past which Tamara had found herself responding to. Could she really push him away when he was reaching out to her, the girl he described as his "best friend"?

Two rectangular-boxed options waited on the screen for her to make her choice:

Ignore.
Confirm.

Her eyes looked first at one and then the other, unable to settle on either. She rubbed her hands against her bare legs, biting her lip as she refused to let her hands anywhere near the mouse. This was her chance; her chance to let him know that it was really time for them to go their separate ways.

Her hand returned to the mouse, moving it from side to side as though it were some kind of Ouija board:

Confirm, Ignore, Confirm, Ignore.
Click.

Chapter Four

In the early days of their relationship, Bradley had dropped his Jack-the-lad pretence and shared his past with Tamara. Her childhood had been a fairytale in comparison to one where Bradley had learned firsthand that his father could only express his emotions with his fists. Growing up in that environment had left its mark, and Tamara soon became Bradley's only confidante, the one person he could lean on.

Now, in the kitchen at the Harding property, Tamara made a strong black coffee despite the heat of the day. She needed it. She sat at the kitchen table with her hands clasped around the mug and tried to justify her actions to herself, but she got nowhere. She wondered what Beth would make of her decision. With the time difference, she couldn't even call her best friend to talk so had to settle for sending her a text instead. She checked her phone again, but it was the middle of the night in the UK so there was no reply. Tamara had nothing but her own thoughts to help her right now.

She thought back to her last day in her flat, sitting on the grubby carpet with Beth, sharing a bottle of champagne.

"We've come a long way from the two schoolgirls who used to arrange Hula Hoops on each finger and sip from bottles of ice cold milk," Beth had said, as she helped herself to another piece of Marks & Spencer's quiche. "Do you wish you could turn back the clock sometimes?"

"All the time," answered Tamara. "Life was far easier as a kid; life was easier before we discovered men."

"I'll drink to that."

"Skipping ropes, games of elastics, and sleepovers were all we had to worry about," Tamara mused.

Beth giggled. "Remember our first sleepover?"

"Do I ever? Everything had to be red: red plates, red cups, red fizzy drink…"

"I'd forgotten about those revolting soda stream concoctions! My mum was so unimpressed at the sound of the gas being pumped into those bottles in the middle of the night." Beth's champagne slopped out of her glass when she fell back laughing.

"Just rub it into the carpet," Tamara grinned mischievously.

Both girls collapsed onto the floor in fits of laughter as they continued reminiscing about sleepovers, taping the Top 40 every Sunday night, and generally having a great adolescence until they discovered boys.

"It definitely was much easier back then," Beth concluded sombrely, upending the champagne to get the final drips. She stood, held her glass high in a toast as Tamara followed suit. "Cheers to you, Tamara. My best friend, no matter how near or far you are from me. And here's to some time in Australia, away from he-who-shall-not-be-named. May it bring you the happiness that you deserve."

Tamara wondered whether having such different personalities was the key to their lasting friendship. Beth oozed a confidence that sometimes Tamara wished she could emulate. Beth was a fighter in her personal and professional life, climbing the ranks at work, and never letting a man get the better of her.

With the champagne bottle empty, they both knew that it was time.

"I know you need to do this, Tamara." Beth shrugged on her faux-fur coat. "And who knows, maybe you'll fall in love in Australia?"

"I think I need to steer clear of men for a while," Tamara countered. "I've had enough. And anyway, I'm going to a quiet, country town where I'm going to lay low with nothing but green space and animals to keep me company."

Beth's look heavenward voiced her doubts.

"I'm serious. The thought of embarking on another relationship after Bradley, is pretty much on a par with how I felt going in to sit my finals at University: sick, shaky and utterly exhausted after the long haul."

"That's very dramatic for one so young." Beth hugged Tamara and stood back to look at her. "You could meet Hugh Jackman's double, or the man himself. Or you could meet Chris Hemsworth in the flesh. Or what about the *Bondi Vet*?"

"Nice idea, but I don't think any of them are likely to be strolling around somewhere like Brewer Creek."

Her illusions shattered, Beth said, "Ah well, just enjoy it." And with that she'd pulled her friend into a final tearful hug.

Finishing her final crust of toast, Tamara thought back to her friend's parting words: "Enjoy it." She rinsed her plate and stacked it in the dishwasher, and tried not to dwell on whether she had made a huge mistake in accepting Bradley's friend request. She was far enough away from him that he couldn't manipulate her now, and she tried to convince herself it was right not to completely cut him off and rub his nose in the fact that their relationship was over.

Befriending Bradley on the social networking site might even work in her favour: he would see her going about her new life without him, and perhaps it would help him to finally move on knowing that she had done just that.

Tamara went out to the back veranda with a tall glass of iced water. The tops of the trees swayed in the distance, and the sound of sheep frolicking reminded her of her freedom. She pulled her sunglasses over her eyes and gazed up at the clouds playing peek-a-boo with the sun.

When her phone bleeped into life, she knew it was a text message from Beth and could almost predict the words even before she read:

I should've confiscated all use of social media for the duration of

your time in Australia.
   For selfish reasons, I didn't.

Tamara smiled. Beth would be annoyed, she knew, but at the same time she would stand by her regardless of whatever decisions she made. That was what true friends did, after all.

Beth didn't wait for a reply text before she added:

He's not your responsibility. Put yourself first for a change. Now no more texts, I really need some sleep. We'll talk at a more sociable hour!

Tamara grinned at the thought of Beth with her eyes half closed and the phone about to topple from her palm, and decided it was time to get out and explore. Instead of hiding away feeling like a victim, she pulled on her runners and applied some sunscreen to her face. She hoped that the outside noises emanating from the countryside would blow away any feelings of seclusion here in Brewer Creek.

***

Kenny Jackson stood ankle-deep in mud in his gumboots, which looked to be the only thing holding him upright and stopping him from falling apart with panic. The nineteen-year-old had been standing out front of his family's homestead at Brewer Creek Dairy when Jake drove past that afternoon.

"Where's Bobby?" Jake asked, as Kenny led him around the side of the house and across the gardens to the fields beyond.

"I've left him a couple of messages," said Kenny. "I was waiting out front for him when I saw you. Sorry, perhaps I should have –"

"You did the right thing, Kenny." The Jacksons were Bobby's clients – had been for a long time – but Jake wasn't about to let an animal suffer, or risk putting other livestock or farmhands in danger because of the competition. He'd back off when Bobby arrived and not before.

22

"She's separated from the herd," Kenny explained as they approached Tess, the heifer he was so panicked about. "This is her first calf and I know she's due any day now."

Jake didn't know the herd but he could see that Tess was restless. Mature cows coped a lot better, but with this being Tess's first time she was no longer chewing the cud; she swaggered as though contractions could have started already. The poor animal was probably wondering what on earth was going on.

"She's not doing anything too out of the ordinary, so try not to worry," said Jake. Kenny would do well on the farm once he'd learnt the ropes properly, but right now Jake knew the boy wasn't ready to cope with Tess alone.

Jake moved alongside the cow. When he crouched down, he could see that she was bagging up and her udder was enlarged and the teats had started to secrete liquid. "Where's your dad?"

"He was up and out the door before I even woke up today." Kenny's gumboots stuck firm in the mud.

Jake suspected the first step of learning the ropes for Kenny should be that early mornings came with the job.

"He's gone to pick up a new part for the milking machines." Kenny spoke nervously as he tried to soothe Tess.

With no sign of Matthew Jackson or Bobby, Jake made a judgement call. "I'll see how she's progressing." He pulled on a long glove and checked Tess. Sure enough, he could feel the feet of the calf in the birth canal.

"What happens now?" asked Kenny.

"Now, we wait."

When Bobby and Matthew arrived, Jake packed up his bag and moved aside to let the other two men take over. "You did a good thing, flagging me down," he told Kenny. "Farmers know their cattle better than anyone else possibly can, and that comes from frequent observation. You knew that Tess's behaviour wasn't normal for her and you asked for help. You'll make an excellent farmer."

Jake started to walk away but stopped when he heard Bobby.

"What on earth is Tamara doing?" The older vet's hand shielded his eyes as he watched a figure climbing over the perimeter fence of the farthest field.

"I've no idea," said Kenny, "but she'd better watch out for Fergus."

As soon as Jake heard that the bull was in the field, he dropped his bag and ran. "Bloody city chicks," he muttered, running alongside the fence next to where the rest of the herd had gathered. City slickers were clueless when it came to farm life, even more so than he was.

Tamara was almost in the middle of the field by now and hadn't heard him yelling her name. Her clothing choice wasn't going to help her much either: Dressed in denim cut-offs, she couldn't have chosen a worse colour today with the red gingham shirt that tied at the front and skimmed her navel.

"Tamara, stop!" Jake yelled, as he saw Fergus on the opposite side of the field. The animal had stopped grazing and looked pretty interested in this new-looking specimen trespassing on his territory.

She still hadn't heard him and Jake knew that any bull – even one as old as Fergus – could move fast and should always be viewed as dangerous and a potential killer.

Tamara had her back to Fergus as she crossed the field diagonally, and the bull continued to advance slowly, intent on investigating. Jake calmed his breathing, trying not to panic. He hadn't seen a bull attack anyone before and he hoped that today wouldn't be his first time. He skilfully leapt over the fence and into Tamara's line of vision, but when he yelled her name the wind blew his voice away.

Fergus closed the gap some more.

Tamara stood oblivious, iPhone in one hand, her other hand on her hip, until finally she noticed Jake.

"There's a bull." Jake spoke low and calm.

"What?" Tamara turned and that was when she saw the shiny black coat on a hulk of a bull, its nose ring glinting in the sun. She froze.

"Keep watching him," Jake continued in a low voice. "Don't turn your back."

"Why?"

"Don't ask why, just do as I say. Jeez, you had to be wearing red, didn't you?"

"What?"

"It doesn't matter. Now walk slowly back towards me."

She did as she was told, her slim, brown legs lost in the great big pair of Blundstones.

Fergus stopped still. He let out a long, deep throaty groan in protest at these intruders in his field. When Jake saw him lift a foot and scrape at the dirt, he knew there was no time to do this calmly any more. He yelled, "Over the fence, quick!"

Almost there, Tamara turned, put one foot on the lowest rung and swung her other leg over, with Jake following close behind. Fergus's pounding hooves made the ground vibrate beneath him but Jake didn't turn back. He followed Tamara's lithe body over the fence, landing face first on top of Tamara in a ditch of mud.

Jake's Levi-covered leg looped across Tamara's bare skin and he panted, trying to get his breath back as he realised how close they'd both come to being Fergus's next plaything. Face-to-face with Tamara, he pushed himself up onto his forearms. She lay beneath him, a look of horror on her face. Her shirt was an interesting shade of muck and before she could scream at Jake to get off, Fergus let out a long, lasting groan to tell them that he was still the boss.

"You're an idiot!" Tamara yelled, now that the shock had passed.

Jake pushed himself up and offered his hand to help her to her feet. She didn't take it. She plonked her own hands in the mud quite happily instead.

"Is that the thanks I get for rescuing you?" he asked.

Tamara harrumphed as she squeezed mud from the bottom of her shirt, then more that dripped from the back of her hair.

"Fergus could've killed you." Or Jake reckoned he might himself, if she couldn't at least thank him.

"Don't be so ridiculous, he wasn't interested in me."

"City chicks," he muttered.

"What did you say?"

"You heard me. You're a city girl and you've got no idea about life in the country."

She looked as though she was considering what he said, realising that he actually made sense, but then, "I think you're being a tad melodramatic."

Fergus retreated farther away now that his work was done, but Jake and Tamara stood facing one another, each covered top-to-toe in mud.

"Did you hurt yourself?" he asked, calmer now.

"When you landed on top of me, you mean?"

"That wasn't intentional," he smirked. "Don't tell me that you think it was?"

She didn't answer but instead bent down to retrieve her iPhone from a nearby clump of grass which had saved it from the mud bath.

"What were you doing in the field in the first place?" he asked.

"What were you doing here?" she countered.

He pointed over to the Jackson property. "Your dad spotted you from over there. And before you ask, I was checking out the heifer until Bobby arrived." He loved how protective she was over her family – it was an admirable quality – but he didn't want to give her the chance to accuse him of trying to steal Bobby's clients. Sometimes he wondered whether Tamara had just simply decided not to like him.

"I got lost." Tamara held up the iPhone as part of her answer. "The map function doesn't really help much either."

"No, it wouldn't." Ah, a truce. "Next time, stick to the outside of a fence; don't try to take a shortcut. And maybe next time, don't wave the red flag." He nodded towards her shirt, which had more brown than red now.

She pulled at the front of the red gingham which clung in places that pulled in his gaze no matter how hard he tried not to let it. "Thanks, I'll try to remember that."

"Are you thanking me for the fashion advice? Or are you thanking me for getting you out of the field before you became Fergus's new toy?" He leaned against the fence as the sun began to dry the mud on his forearms.

"Just… thank you." She held his gaze for a moment. "They should put some signs up to warn people."

"They should, and I've told the Jacksons that myself. Not everyone knows the dangers out here." Especially not city chicks, he wanted to say, but decided to keep that to himself.

"I might go over and see Dad," said Tamara. She seemed as anxious to escape him as she was Fergus.

"I think he'll be busy for a while." Jake explained the situation with Tess as he walked with Tamara along the edge of the field – on the right side of the fence this time.

When they reached his pick-up, he asked, "Can I give you a lift home?"

"No, I'll walk, thanks." She started off down the road and Jake leaned against the back of his truck watching her. He doubted that grubby clothes, boots and muddied skin had ever looked so sexy, on anyone. He let her walk a few more steps and then, laughing, he jogged after her, put his hands on her shoulders and turned her to face the opposite direction.

"Are you sure you don't need a lift?" he grinned.

She walked off in the right direction this time, without saying a word.

"Watch out for livestock," he shouted after her.

Without turning around she called, "Thanks, I'll try to remember that."

As Jake drove home to check up on April, he felt content at this more sedate pace of life in Brewer Creek. But he couldn't let his guard down, not yet. He had spent too many years living under the same roof as his stepfather, Marty, and knew that the

27

only remedy for Marty's vendetta would be to find them both. And Jake would do everything in his power to stop that happening; he wouldn't let Marty hurt either of them ever again.

***

Tamara washed her hair – for the second time that morning – until the water in the shower recess ran clear. Satisfied that the mud had all gone, she dressed and took a book outside. Back in England her hair would've stayed damp for hours, but with the Australian landscape swathed in a sun stronger than anything she had ever seen, she knew that it would dry in no time.

When her bottom went numb and the thought of Jake falling on top of her became too distracting, Tamara ventured inside. She pulled a can of Diet Coke from the fridge as her mum appeared with an overflowing basket of wet washing.

"When did you get back?" Tamara slurped the top of the fizz as it escaped from the ring-pull.

"I've been back at least an hour." Katherine laughed. She had a traditional pale British complexion and her warm, deep brown hair, highlighted with the greys that had fought their way through over the years, hung loose around her shoulders. "You were so engrossed in your book that I thought I'd leave you to it."

"Here, let me help." Tamara took the basket out into the back garden and Katherine pulled out the washing line until its length stretched from the back of the house to the first gum tree.

As they hung out the washing together, Katherine said, "I see you haven't managed to deliver those updated friendship trees yet."

"I'll get to it." Tamara bent down for an extra couple of pegs. "Do you think it does much good? I mean, do people really value the tree or is it more Daphne's doing?"

Katherine paused, Tamara's red gingham top in her hands. "You know, I had my doubts when I first arrived in Brewer Creek, but I must admit the whole idea has rubbed off on me over time.

28

Apparently, the friendship tree has been a thing here for more than fifty years."

"Wow, that's a long time."

"Daphne's father started the whole concept years ago when Brewer Creek had a handful of residents and, of course, none of this newfangled technology."

"You mean, back in the olden days?"

"Less of the old, thank you very much," Katherine chided, as she slung a sheet over the line and deftly pegged each end before the breeze got other ideas. "Back then, the friendship tree was a means of getting the community together. It had names and addresses, but obviously no phone numbers or email addresses. And whenever there was a farmers' market coming up, Daphne's father would rally around and make sure that everyone was included, that nobody missed out."

"You know, Mum, I think that's one of the things that I really love out here; that sense of community. I can understand why you love it so much." Tamara wasn't surprised that Daphne was the instigator in the tree concept, either. Only minutes after they'd first met in town, the woman hadn't hesitated to give her the lowdown, including details of regular bake-sales, some adult classes that ran at the local community centre, and even the opening times of the pub.

"What else did they use the friendship tree for?" Tamara's curiosity had grown.

"I think they organised the odd dance at the community centre, fundraising events, that sort of thing. The farmers' markets were a big deal, though – that was how many of the town's residents made their income."

Tamara shook out a towel and pegged it on the line. "It sounds like something out of a Disney movie."

"It does a bit, doesn't it?" Katherine grinned. "Unfortunately, nowadays the friendship tree is little more than an emergency contact list."

"That's a shame."

"Well, you say that, but it has helped people. Take Mr Wilson, for example. He had a fall a few years back and, although he'd broken an ankle and had some serious bruising, he managed to pull himself to wherever he kept the friendship tree and called someone. It scares me to think how long he could have been lying there if he hadn't had a number to call."

Katherine picked up the last pillowcase and fixed it to the line. "There's the threat of bushfires, too, which thankfully haven't affected Brewer Creek for many years. But it's good to know that the town can come together if it needs to."

With all the washing flapping happily in the wind, Tamara picked up the box of pegs. "Let's hope it carries on for many more years then. I can't imagine anything like that back in London, can you?" She linked her mum's arm, marvelling at how settled her parents were in their new lifestyle. Whether she stayed on long-term in Australia or not, it felt good to know how happy they were.

"Some people dismiss people like Daphne Abbott and say that Brewer Creek suffers from small town mentality," said Katherine, "but there's a lot to be said for it. Bobby gets to know a lot about this town from having the odd beer with the locals. Apparently many small towns have lost their identities, with small, family-run shops and businesses being taken over by bigger and better names."

"Trust Bobby to get in amongst it with the gossip," Tamara giggled.

Katherine's next question came out of the blue. "Are you still in touch with Bradley?"

Tamara's jaw tensed. "He's a friend on Facebook, but that's it."

"Can I ask what happened between you two?"

"Oh, the usual scenario; it's no big deal. I suppose we grew out of each other."

Tamara had chosen to omit many of the details of her relationship with Bradley. It wasn't that her mum would tell her to stay well away; she had every confidence that her mum would understand why Tamara had stayed with him for so long and had been willing to give him the benefit of the doubt. But she hadn't wanted to worry her parents when they lived on the other side of the world, so conversations had been more in the form of general chit-chat and petty gripes that could be solved in an instant.

Katherine pointed at the red gingham shirt on the line. "Didn't I wash that yesterday?"

"Ah, there's a story behind that," said Tamara. "I met Fergus." She'd met Jake, too, but she wasn't going to share every single detail of that part of the tale.

Chapter Five

"It's a beautiful day, April." Jake knocked back the dregs of his morning cup of tea. He should've been out of the door by now and on his way to Mrs Baxter's property to vaccinate a horse, then onto Mr Wilson's to check on Solomon. "You should at least sit outside and enjoy the garden."

"I'd feel better doing that if you were here, or the next door neighbours were within shouting distance."

"Relax. Marty has no idea where we are."

"Not yet." April rinsed her own cup and slotted it into the dishwasher, as Jake gently reached for her arm.

"Living like a prisoner isn't healthy," he told her.

She sighed heavily. "Maybe we would've been better off telling the police our side of the story in the first place."

"That's crazy and you know it. He's cunning; a nasty piece of work. You and I both know that he'd have lied and made us out to be the bad guys. He's a conniving two-faced bastard–"

"Calm down, Jake. Maybe it's you who needs to relax in the garden today," she teased.

He picked up his bag. "We left Perth because Marty would've come after us, no matter what. Don't forget what he did to you."

"I won't, Jake, not ever."

He gave her hand a squeeze and left the house. He hoped that one day he would see April smile like she used to; smile without her eyes giving away that something was amiss.

***

Tamara began to realise that her social life amounted to Skype sessions with Beth and playing endless games of Rummikub and Boggle with Bobby. She had even gone along to the local bake sale at the community centre one afternoon, chatting with the locals over Lamingtons and Victoria Sponge and wondering what kind of parallel universe she had stepped into compared to London.

Outside on the rear veranda she swatted away a fly and lit the citronella candle on the table. It was the final month of summer and Tamara was about done with the heat; even at night it rarely dipped below the mid-twenties. As she relaxed into her chair she spotted Jake making his way across the muddy paddock from Mr Harris's place. She pretended to swish another bug from her leg but she hadn't got away with it: he waved in her direction. For a minute she thought he would come over when she raised her hand to wave back, but her breathing returned to normal as he swaggered over to his truck and threw his bag into the back. From behind the safety of her sunglasses she took in the sight of his tanned neck beneath that wide-brimmed hat, the jeans that showed off his sturdy physique, and the slightly dust-covered navy t-shirt that hugged the defined contours of his arms and chest.

Jake was so unlike her usual type. Her boyfriends had always been natty dressers, corporate types mostly, and definitely not the type to get their hands dirty. She smiled as she tried to imagine Bradley doing anything more laborious than picking up an Indian takeaway or nipping out to the local Pizza Hut.

A persistent breeze lifted the branches of the trees, sending some upwards towards the sky dotted with cotton wool clouds and others bending down towards the rich green blades of grass below. Tamara breathed in the familiar smell of cut grass, mixed with the fragrance of flowers that she was yet to identify. She looked out to the sprawling acres of land peppered with animals: horses grazing, heads hung and mouths nibbling; sheep drinking from a nearby water trough; and an orchard, which she was eager to investigate.

When the flies wouldn't take the hint, she blew out the candle and retreated inside the house, letting the screen door bang shut behind her. She had to get out and deliver those updated friendship trees before the serenity of the great outdoors and the deserted house drove her crazy, and before Daphne got wind that she wasn't doing her job properly.

"Hello, darling." Katherine was already in the kitchen unpacking the groceries and restocking the fridge.

"Hey, where've you been?"

Katherine gave her an "isn't it obvious?" look.

"It's been a bit quiet around here, that's all." Tamara grabbed the roll-on Aeroguard from the top drawer in the kitchen. She moved it up and down both legs before covering her arms in more slicks of the stinky transparent repellent; it was either that or build up a collection of unsightly red raised blotches by the end of the day.

"You okay?" Katherine watched her daughter.

"I'm just feeling a bit cut off from the real world, that's all."

"It's different out here," said Katherine, as Tamara helped her haul the last of the bags in from the hallway. "London and Brewer Creek are at two opposite ends of the spectrum, it'll take time for you to adjust. Any luck on the job front?"

"Not yet." Tamara thought about the many job applications she had fired off that morning. She had done the same last week and the week before, and the week before that, but hadn't heard anything. She knew that time away from the workplace had done her the world of good but she was starting to crave office politics the same way that some people craved *Ben & Jerry's* Chocolate Fudge Brownie ice-cream.

"You didn't shop in Brewer Creek, did you?" Tamara unpacked another stuffed-full shopping bag.

"No, I went out to Lake Haven, to Woolworths."

"Isn't Woolworths for toys and pens and stuff?"

"You're showing your English side now, young lady. Woolworths here is a supermarket. It took me a while to get my head around that, too." Katherine bent down to put a large bag of potatoes on the bottom shelf of the larder and then loaded the salad vegetables into the crisper section of the fridge. When she stood up, she said, "Don't stress too much about finding a job. You needed a break anyway, and I'm far less worried about you than I was when I first saw you at the airport. You looked strung out when you arrived."

Tamara felt guilty at having underestimated a mother's intuition. Sitting on the kitchen stool, her legs swinging beneath, it was almost as though she was back in the tumultuous teenage years, chatting about boys and trouble in the school playground. But she didn't want to confide about Bradley. Was there really any point when he was in the past?

"You know, if ever you do need to talk, then you know where I am," said Katherine.

Tamara watched her mum; this woman who had taken to life in this very different town as easily as she adapted to anything, from coping with a child as a single mother when her first husband died, to supporting Bobby and his ambition to run a vet's surgery. From the moment Tamara had seen her parents in the Arrivals hall at the airport, she'd realised how much she had missed them. Moments of her childhood, all the birthdays, all the scrapes she had gotten into, had all rolled into one delicious ball and swum before her eyes.

Hopping down from the stool, Tamara picked up the pile of friendship trees from the kitchen bench. "I'd better go and deliver these. I've been hibernating in the annexe far too much and sitting on my arse out on that veranda." She noted her mum's frown. "Sorry, excuse my language. For a moment I forgot that I was living with the olds."

"You're picking up the Aussie expressions already!" Katherine laughed.

"When in Rome... Anyway, let's hope I have more luck on this walk than last time."

Katherine sniggered. "I wish I'd been there to see Fergus looking at you like you were his next meal."

"It wasn't funny!"

"I beg to differ. I'm just thankful Jake was there to rescue you."

What was it with people who thought she needed rescuing? She was perfectly capable of sorting out her own problems, wasn't she? After all, that's what she had done by coming to Brewer Creek in the first place.

Katherine stowed a box of dishwasher tablets beneath the sink. "The friendship trees can wait until later, Tamara. How about we have a short stroll around here before I go and do the afternoon shift at the post office? I'll take you to explore the orchards that you somehow managed to miss last time."

Tamara dropped the pile of friendship trees back onto the bench. "That sounds like a plan."

Outside, Katherine couldn't resist tugging a few of the weeds out of the ground near the seating area. Tamara wondered if multi-tasking and running a home despite any obstacles that came your way was an integral part of being a woman, and she hoped that she would inherit those characteristics one day. Gardening, however, definitely wasn't in her genes.

They made their way along the edge of the paddock and waved to Bobby as he pulled up on the driveway.

"We're off for a quick stroll." Katherine called through a cupped hand.

He lifted a hand in acknowledgement.

"I worry about you, too. Both of you," said Tamara, as they carried on their way.

"Well you shouldn't; it's not your job, my love."

"Do you still think Bobby's hiding something?"

"I really don't know, but he's fighting the suggestion to retire and I've no idea why. Even Jake arriving and establishing another practice hasn't loosened his grip on working. I assumed that it would." Katherine looked out at the fields beyond, as though they held so many answers. "He doesn't talk about the financial side of things, so maybe he isn't in a position to retire yet."

"Do you want me to try talking to him?"

"I don't want to upset him."

"It wouldn't upset him, Mum. We're both worried."

Katherine dismissed the suggestion with a wave of the hand. "I'm sure he'll open up in his own time."

Tamara pointed to the stables on the Hardings' land as they reached the rear paddock adjacent to the Harris's place. "Who do those horses belong to?"

A horse hung its head over the stable door, nostrils quivering as it explored the fresh outdoors and Katherine's hand when she stroked its coat. "This Palomino is Saffy, and the other is Neptune, and they both belong to the Dolans. We rent out the stables, and the horses keep the grass in the paddock under control. We don't really need all the land that comes with this property, but we wanted the peace and quiet that Brewer Creek has to offer."

They passed through the gate at the far end and weaved their way towards the orchard. Tamara ducked under low-lying branches as Katherine found her way to one of the apple trees.

"I remember this backdrop," Tamara grinned. "You sent me a photograph with the stables in the background. See…" She positioned herself in the same place that she remembered seeing her mum. "You said you loved it here because the blossom on the trees reminded you of snow."

Katherine closed her eyes and inhaled the sweet scent of the fruits that now hung in place of the delicate white flowers.

"Do you miss it?" Tamara asked.

"What, blossom?"

"No, silly, do you miss the snow? Do you miss the UK?"

"In many ways I do, yes."

The grass was longer in the orchard and made a rasping sound beneath their feet.

"I love it here, though: the space, the climate, the easiness of it all." Katherine beamed, her smile a match for the sun. "You're the only thing missing."

Tamara squeezed her mum's hand. "If only Christmas were cold, eh?"

Katherine smiled. "Do you know that every year I secretly hope we'll have the coldest December day on record? Just for one day, you know?" She plucked a couple of helpless lemons from their branches, inspected the fruit, and sniffed at the skin.

"I always found it odd when you sent photos of you and Bobby sitting outside in the sunshine," said Tamara, "you with your Christmas bling, and him with that ridiculous Santa hat that he insists on wearing skewiff."

Katherine passed a lemon to Tamara for her to enjoy the aroma. "Christmas wouldn't be Christmas without that hat," she giggled, plucking another lemon from the tree. "Let's make pancakes later," she grinned mischievously.

"As long as you let me flip them," replied Tamara.

"I'm not sure about that. Have you been practising since last time?"

"Oh come on, I reckon it was your faulty batter that made it stick to the ceiling. I–"

"Don't blame me! You tossed it to kingdom come! It took me forever to get that ceiling clean."

Back at the house Katherine made the tea and Tamara pulled out a carton of milk from the fridge.

"Jesus Christ!" shrieked Tamara. She glued herself against the kitchen wall. "Okay, don't panic, Mum, but there's s-s-something above your h-h-head."

Katherine looked up above her to see what all the fuss was about, and then carried on pouring the boiling water into the cups.

Great. Tamara suspected she was about to finally put that first aid training to good use and treat her first burns' victim. Her mum had obviously failed to zoom in on what she'd seen.

"Mum!"

"Bobby," Katherine called with a smile, before she resumed humming.

He appeared from his office at the front of the house. "Did I hear you talking about pancakes?" He rubbed his hands together.

"Yes, you heard right. But right now we have a more pressing issue. Could you remove our friends from up there, please?" Katherine handed Tamara a mug and ushered her over to the table on the opposite side of the kitchen.

So Mum *had* seen the spiders. Funny, if anything that size had made an appearance in their house in the UK, Katherine would have been the first one to scream.

Tamara made sure she took the seat where the spiders were in full view; she didn't want one of the little buggers sneaking over unexpectedly.

"If I help you out, does that mean I get the first pancake?" Bobby climbed onto a chair.

"I'm sure you'll get no arguments from Tamara," smiled Katherine.

The two spiders were still moseying along towards the wall until Bobby skilfully knocked them into a large plastic bowl with a rolled-up newspaper. He laid the newspaper over the top to stop them from escaping, and stepped down from the chair. "They're only huntsman spiders, love. They're more scared of you than you are of them."

"Why do people say that?" Tamara pulled a face. "I don't think we can ever really know that, can we?" She gulped, unable to relax until they had gone. That was the second time the blessed things had taken her by surprise, although this time she hadn't had the pleasure of Jake coming to her rescue. She felt strangely disappointed about that.

"Don't you dare," she said, when she saw Bobby head in her direction.

A belly laugh rumbled away as her stepfather took the bowl outside and gave the spiders their freedom on the back grass. Tamara would have preferred to witness their execution but apparently you didn't do that with harmless spiders; only the deadly ones.

***

Driving to Jon Ramsey's place to vaccinate the latest litter of puppies, Jake couldn't get the picture of Tamara out of his head. He could still see her in those denim cut-offs and that shirt that tied just above her midriff; it had teased him as much as it had Fergus.

He pulled up a short distance from the property when he saw Aidan Ramsey getting a right rollicking from his dad; he didn't want to intrude. Jake couldn't make out the words even though Jon Ramsey was yelling at the teenager, who was dressed in Gothic black with one of those revolting piercings that enlarged the earlobe. Jake's own mind was involuntarily thrust back to his own teenage years, when it hadn't taken much to ignite Marty's temper which lay dormant like a disused, faulty firework, just ready to explode.

Marty had always been the creepy stepfather rather than a big, scary man. He was puny compared to Jake: a slim man, but a man whose fists certainly knew how to function, and a man who knew that he could overpower most women. But what Marty lacked in stature, he made up for with his mind games, taunting Jake with talk of what he would or could do if Jake upset him.

Until Jake turned sixteen, Marty hadn't put a foot wrong, although he always had a feeling of unease whenever he was around him. But the day after Jake's birthday, he had come home from school and made the mistake of mentioning the faulty sash windows that were an invite to any burglar.

Since he'd lost his job as a builder, Marty had made the local watering hole his full time job, and when he wasn't there he was at home, sitting at the kitchen table exactly as he was then, drinking at four o'clock in the afternoon.

"Hey." Jake had figured he'd grab a couple of pieces of toast and then scarper to his bedroom to study. He had no incentive to wait around with Marty. In fact, it was getting to the point that he rarely wanted to be within a hundred yards of him. His mum said that they had to give Marty time, because it was hard losing a job when you were in your forties. So Jake made an effort for her. She was working extra shifts to compensate for Marty's loss of earnings, so the least he could do was to be friendly to the man.

"Where are you going?" Marty snapped.

"I've got study to do."

"And what, you can't give your old man ten minutes of your precious time?"

He wasn't his old man; far from it. But Jake knew better than to say that. He sat at the table and ate his toast as quickly as he could, and made the mistake of attempting to make conversation.

"We should probably sort these windows." Jake pointed to the one in the kitchen hidden from view and the easiest access point for a burglar. "Anyone could get in, steal whatever they like. There was another burglary in Armadale last night."

Marty's empty beer bottle slammed onto the table and Jake jumped.

"All I'm saying is that you can't be too careful." Jake put his empty plate in the sink, anxious to get out of there. "You never know who's watching the place, planning another robbery."

Jake didn't see it coming but he sure as hell felt it. Marty's fist made contact with the side of his head, slamming Jake into the kitchen bench top and knocking a glass onto the floor.

The only words Marty said before he stomped over the broken glass and out of the front door were, "And you can clear that up before your mother gets home."

At first he'd thought that Marty was pissed because Jake had implied he wasn't pulling his weight around the house. But it was hours after the incident that he put two and two together and realised why Marty had snapped. Jake put the chain on the front door and the bolt on the back gate so that he could search the shed at the bottom of the garden without being interrupted. It was then that he realised Marty was up to his neck in this spate of burglaries.

Outside the Ramsey property now, Jake took his bag from the back of the pick-up. He'd promised April that he wouldn't be long, and then they could go and grab some supplies from the local shop. Damn Marty for instilling such fear in April that she wouldn't even take herself off for a walk.

Jon Ramsey's voice had lowered in volume as Jake approached, and Aidan looked pretty upset before he disappeared back inside the house.

"Is everything okay?" Jake asked.

Jon rubbed the tension in his neck with his hand. "The boy won't be told. His grades are slipping this year again, and he'll end up unqualified and bumming around. That's not what I want for him."

Jake wished he'd had someone to watch out for him like that – Marty certainly hadn't. Marty would've been quite happy for him to follow in his footsteps: a life of petty crime, too much booze, and basically a really unhappy bloke who took his frustrations out on the people around him.

Jon Ramsey led Jake through the house and into the annexe at the back, where six Labrador puppies waited for him.

"They've grown already." Jake crouched down to make a fuss of the entire mob waddling towards him. A chocolate lab sniffed at his hand and the mum came wandering over, too. He fussed over her the most, knowing how easy it was to go for cute and tiny instead.

"Aiden will sort himself out," said Jake. "Does he have any idea of what he wants to do when he leaves school?"

"Apart from get the hell out of here?" Jon sighed.

"Teenagers," said Jake, shaking his head as he started the vaccinations.

All those years ago when Jake had chosen the University of Sydney, he had been thinking along the same lines as Aiden Ramsey. The University's degree in Veterinary Science enjoyed an excellent reputation, but better than that, it took Jake far away from his stepfather. Now, he couldn't imagine leaving the women he loved in so much danger, but at the time he had been blinkered like Aiden Ramsey. At that age Jake's mind had been set on the fact that he brought out the worst in Marty, and because the man hadn't lifted a finger to him since, and because his Mum seemed happy, Jake had done what he thought best and left.

Marty had soon found another job contracting for a building company, and when Jake did some detective work on a weekend home and found the garden shed full with just junk and gardening tools, he decided that the man deserved a second chance.

What a mistake that had turned out to be.

***

After a cup of tea to calm her down after the latest "spider incident" – this was Australia, after all – Tamara set off with the bundle of friendship trees tucked under her arm. Delivery was easy: one to every house that she could manage on her walk, and the rest she could take later in the car. She could already put faces to some of the names: Mr Wilson, Daphne, Stanley and Mabel from the post office. It was a comforting thought to be settling in to this town, and already it felt like the perfect place to shut the Bradley-chapter of her life and start afresh. She hoped that this friendship tree would work as well for her as the tree back in the school playground had all those years ago.

The sun shone as Tamara rolled the friendship trees and pushed them into the mailboxes along the way. Brewer Creek was incredibly pretty; drier beneath her feet than she had expected yet still lush, thanks to the torrential rains from early January. Rich, green fields sloped away from her at either side as she walked, and the creek offered a tranquillity that she appreciated more than she had thought possible.

She passed the neighbour's property, its front door a good thirty metres from her own, and she wondered how these people would cope if they were picked up and placed in the centre of London with its bustling crowds, the noise, and the ten to twelve houses that would be crammed into the equivalent space of one of theirs. The comparison made her think back to her final days in

London and the series of "lasts", taking in everything from Oxford Street and Trafalgar Square to Boots and Marks & Spencer.

It had been more than three months now since she had set foot in the corporate world and over two since she had looked at her old workplace for the final time. She had caught the tube to Marble Arch and stood across the road from Wellington Smart, the firm where she had been employed for six years. Inconspicuous in ripped jeans, a simple plain white t-shirt, and sunglasses shielding her from further recognition, she had watched as people rushed past and traffic accumulated in gridlock. She watched office workers pass through the revolving door like hamsters on a wheel, balancing take-out coffees as they arrived or when they ducked out on their way to see a client.

She closed her eyes now as she paused on top of the rickety, white arched bridge that allowed people to pass over the creek. Grasping the rest of the friendship trees, Tamara walked onto the wide street dotted with small, characterful shops. It reminded her of the typical Australian country drama with its traditional frontages, many with brown signs and weather-beaten gold writing. Her tummy rumbled rudely in anticipation of the pancakes she would have later, and she crossed the road to grab a snack from Daphne's shop to keep her going. It would also give her the chance to prove that she was on the ball with getting these updated friendship trees into circulation.

"Damn." She cursed as she read the sign in the window: "Back in thirty minutes."

A car slowed to a stop beside her.

"G'day, Tamara."

"Hi." She cleared her throat, suddenly nervous at seeing Jake up close for the first time since that day he had fallen on top of her. Without his hat, his hair was a mix of dark blond and lighter strands, and he looked even better than she remembered.

"Need something from the shop?" He hopped out of the pickup and read the sign on the door. Tamara felt the warmth of his body as he leaned past her.

"I'm a bit hungry, that's all; I was going to grab a snack to keep me going." The walk under the glare of the sun had made her thirsty, too. "What about you?"

"We're out of milk." Jake eyed the friendship trees still firmly in her grasp. "What have you got there?"

She turned one round for him to see.

"Ah, I see you've already put a modern spin on those things. Nicely done."

"Thanks," she grinned. "Hopefully it'll be a lot less work next time a change needs to be made."

"I notice you're on there," he said, peering at the tree more closely. His mouth did that strange pulling thing at the corners again. "You must be staying for a while."

Was he asking her, or was he making an observation?

It was then that she noticed Jake wasn't alone. She tried not to make it too obvious that she was trying to discover his passenger's identity, but he was onto her straight away.

"Tamara, this is April."

A neatly-manicured hand stretched across the front seats as Tamara leaned in. "Nice to meet you, Tamara. Jake says that you're visiting from London."

She was momentarily thrown by the thought of Jake talking about her.

"I'd love to hear all about London sometime." April leaned on the open window of the driver's door. She had delicate strands of chestnut hair and eyes that were just as blue as Jake's, and she seemed fascinated to meet someone new.

"You should go over there," Tamara suggested. "It's very different from Australia."

"I'm sure it is. And I bet it's a lot crazier than this place." April gestured down the high street that looked about as busy as one of England's country lanes. "Mind you, I hear you had some action with Fergus the other day."

Tamara's cheeks grew hotter at the thought of Jake lying horizontal with her in that muddy ditch. She wondered whether

45

Jake had told April that he'd lingered in that position a moment longer than was necessary before he'd offered to help her up.

"You want to watch out for him," April giggled. "He's the randiest male in Brewer Creek, or so I've heard."

When Tamara realised that April was referring to Fergus and not Jake, she let out a relieved laugh. "Thanks for the visual. It's the best action I've seen since I arrived, but from now on I'll be giving Fergus a wide berth."

"Listen," said April, "a few of us are off to the pub tonight. Why don't you join us? We'll have a few drinks, a bit of a chat; maybe even play a few games of pool?"

"I'd like that." She ignored the surprised look on Jake's face; whether it was at the suggestion of girls playing pool or the invite itself, she had no idea.

"We'll introduce you to Danielle. She's lived in Brewer Creek her whole life and has made us feel really welcome since we moved here, hasn't she, Jake?" April didn't wait for an answer. It was as though the girl hadn't had such a long conversation in a really long time. "She's been away staying with her sister for a while."

Jake's stubbled jaw moved with his smile, and Tamara's insides flipped over. She noticed a light dusting of dirt that had settled on his sky blue t-shirt; the look that you came to expect of someone in his line of work. She tore her eyes away from the hairs on his golden biceps as they stood on end in the gentle breeze. Trying not to sound too desperate, she asked, "What time?"

April shuffled over as Jake climbed into the pick-up.

"We'll see you about seven." Jake smiled. He'd been strangely quiet for most of the conversation, and Tamara wondered whether he would carry on being the strong-silent-type when they met up again that evening.

"Aren't you waiting to get your milk?" she asked.

"There's a bottle shop up the road, they should have some." His eyes twinkled dangerously before he covered them with his sunglasses.

"Here." She handed him a copy of the friendship tree before he could drive away. "You may as well take this; save me popping one in your letterbox."

His fingers grazed hers as he reached out and took the sheet of paper from her hand. "We'll see you tonight." And with that, the engine obediently purred into action.

As she watched the pick-up drive into the distance, Tamara wondered how serious Jake and April were; perhaps pretty serious if they lived together. But that was a good thing, she decided. It would help her to compartmentalise Jake in her mind as an acquaintance rather than anything else.

The sound of jangling keys announced Daphne's arrival and interrupted any thoughts about Jake.

"I do apologise," said Daphne, shooing Tamara inside the shop as she removed the "Closed" sign from the window.

The glasses perched on the bridge of the old lady's nose gave her the air of a former school mistress, and her tightly-wound grey hair resembled a bread roll, not too dissimilar from those sitting inside the glass cabinet near the till.

"The post office is only open until two o'clock today and I really didn't want to wait until tomorrow," said Daphne, as she fixed the door open using the metal hook behind and then tied on a white apron. "Is that the updated friendship tree?"

Tamara handed over a copy to Daphne who enthusiastically took in the printed picture, a tiny smile on her lips.

"This is fabulous." Daphne shook her head at the wonders of modern technology. "You must have a whizz-bang computer to have done this so well." She fixed her copy to the wall beside the till as though she was hanging a valuable classic painting.

"Do you need another copy for home?"

"Oh yes, please, if it's not too much trouble."

"Of course not, I'll print another one out later today and pop it into your letterbox."

"Thank you. You know, I don't think I could've handed the job onto a more competent person, Tamara Harding."

With the remaining friendship trees under one arm, Tamara

grabbed a can of Diet Coke from the fridge. "I'll deliver the rest by the end of the day," she said.

Daphne tidied the packets of crisps on display, content to have someone to pass the time of day with. "It would be quite a walk to do them all on foot, Tamara." Next, she adjusted the confectionery at the counter in front of the till, lining up packets of Starburst fruits and neatening bars of something called Violet Crumble. "Mr Gilbert lives the farthest out, and Jake and April live in the old cottage way out past the station."

When Tamara dropped the correct change onto the counter, Daphne said, "You know, I'm not sure what to make of those two."

"Which two would that be?"

"Well, Jake and April, of course." Daphne distributed the coins into their appropriate sections of the till. "There's something odd about them, but I can't for the life of me figure out what."

Outside the shop, Tamara pulled back the ring-pull and took a thirsty gulp of the black, fizzy liquid. Daphne liked a chat; she liked company. But was she a gossipmonger? Tamara didn't think so, and that was what made her comments all the more intriguing. As Tamara made her way back home, she wondered whether she had underestimated innocent Brewer Creek with its pretty little friendship tree and strong sense of community. Perhaps the tiny town would take her by surprise yet.

Chapter Six

The sand-coloured and royal blue sign that read "Brewer's Inn" swung lightly in the breeze from two short rusty chains. A row of cars lined the street outside, and the same shade of blue from the sign matched the window frames that sat behind iron balcony railings on the top floor.

Tamara took a deep breath, pushed open the weathered midnight-blue door and let it creak shut behind her. The hum in the room stopped for a moment but, to her relief, picked up again just as quickly. For a small town, the place was surprisingly busy. Dotted around were wooden tables perched on a darker, wooden floor, with chairs sticking out at angles where they hadn't quite been pushed in as neatly as they should. A long bar lined one wall and curved round a corner with a brass rail, and at each end was a hinged section to allow access for staff.

As Tamara waited at the bar she noticed the grubby ceiling, presumably from years of thick cigarette smoke; thank goodness those days were over. A fireplace shone from the opposite end of the room, illuminating the faces of two elderly gentlemen who looked settled for the night on the tatty sofa in front of it, grabbing all the warmth. She stifled a giggle. These Australians had a strange sense of what "cold" was, to be able to justify lighting an open fire in the final month of summer. Still, it did add a certain ambience, and with the sun giving up much earlier these days, the fire would look less out of place later that evening.

"G'day. Now I bet you're Tamara, aren't you?" A portly man behind the bar introduced himself. "I'm Len, the landlord of this place. It's nice to meet you."

"Nice to meet you, too, Len-the-landlord." Tamara picked up the wine list and opted for a glass of Marlborough Sounds Sauvignon Blanc; she remembered that Beth – an expert in wine tastings, or so she liked to think – had recommended New Zealand wines, and she smiled at the thought of drinking something her friend would approve of.

Len poured the chilled wine and gestured to his left. "This is Hugo, my son."

Hugo raised a hand. "G'day," he said. Scruffy-looking, with ruffled, jet black Elvis- coiffured hair and tattoos up both forearms, he had a genuine smile and kind yet wary eyes. He was taller than his father – but only by an inch, if that – and despite Len's receding, grey hairline, you could see the resemblance: the same square jaw, the same forehead that jutted out a little.

"It's nice to meet you both," said Tamara, before she turned at a familiar voice.

"A Hahn Light, please, Len." The door fell shut behind Jake and he pulled up a bar stool.

When Jake's leg accidentally brushed against Tamara's as he sat down, she felt herself flush as she remembered the same leg lying across her in that ditch of dirt. She took a big gulp of wine but knocked it back too quickly and spluttered when it went down the wrong way.

"Hey, slow down. I'm not that bad, am I?"

April's arrival rescued Tamara from having to think of the perfect riposte. As she recovered, she watched the stubble that had started to appear on Jake's chin and jawline, and his hair that wasn't deliberately styled but somehow knew how to flop in exactly the right way every time.

"I'm glad you came, Tamara." April took the stool that Jake had already lined up for her, and Tamara couldn't help but admire his chivalry. "Danielle's running late but she won't be too long."

"I really appreciate the invite." Tamara twirled the stem of her wine glass between her fingers, unsure whether to risk taking another sip.

"I've been saying to Jake that I can't wait to ask you more about London," April continued.

Happy to have a topic for discussion rather than any awkwardness with two people she barely knew, Tamara launched into a familiar conversation, talking about where she'd lived, which landmarks she'd passed on a daily basis, the shopping, the restaurants. When the conversation about London reached a natural pause, she said, "Daphne tells me that you haven't been in Brewer Creek for long either."

"We arrived at the end of last year," said April. "It's a lovely place."

Tamara noticed that the excitement which had danced in April's eyes during their conversation about London wasn't quite there any more. She turned to Jake. "And do you like it here?"

"It's nice," he answered, and swigged his beer.

April was quick to change the topic of conversation. "It must be nice to spend some time with your parents. You look like your mum, too, although she has a much fairer complexion than you."

It was a politically correct way to ask Tamara about her skin, which in no way resembled Katherine Harding's. "I get my colouring from my dad. Bobby is my stepfather; my biological father was from Nigeria, and he died when I was four."

"I'm sorry," said Jake. "That must have been hard on you."

"It happened a very long time ago. Mum met Bobby a couple of years after my dad died, and I couldn't wish for a better stepfather." Whenever she spoke about Bobby, she felt the swell of pride in her chest at the man who had taken on a wife and a child in one package, and had handsomely filled his role as head of the family. It was the very reason she felt so protective over him.

"So where are you both from?" Tamara asked, anxious to find out more about this pair.

"Country Victoria," Jake answered.

Tamara hadn't missed the look which passed between the two of them, and when they fell silent again she tried to gee up the conversation. "How long have you two been going out together?"

"Four years." Jake tipped his head back to get the last remnants of beer from the bottle.

It was as though she'd asked them about their favourite sexual positions rather than a brief background on their lives. But if they didn't want to tell, then Tamara reckoned that was their prerogative.

When Jake disappeared to buy another round, April asked, "How are you enjoying Australia?"

"It's an amazing country."

"So you'll be staying for a while?"

"I'll be here for at least a year, but if I don't get work soon that may change."

"What do you do for work?" Jake appeared again and shuffled back onto his stool. His legs were precariously close to Tamara's, but it didn't appear to bother April.

"I was an Account Executive for a public relations firm, handling the publicity for different businesses that were either starting up or expanding. You know, restaurants, fitness centres, spas—"

"Oh, tell me about the spas." April stared into space. "What I would do for a spa right now."

Jake rolled his eyes at the feminine turn to the conversation.

"One of my clients opened a brand new spa in Hanover Square," Tamara continued, "and as one of the perks, we had freebies: facials, body brushing, scrubs." She smiled, remembering the blissful afternoon she had spent there with Beth a week before she left.

"Wow, it sounds like you had an awesome job." April finished her water save the slice of lemon lingering at the bottom of the glass. "You know, you'd love *The Golden Door*."

"What's The Golden Door?"

"It's this amazing place with healthy food and exercise programmes. Nothing but yourselves and total relaxation, from what I've heard."

"Is it expensive?"

April's eyebrows arched. "Why do you think I've never been?"

Bored of the current conversation, Jake asked, "Are you looking in Sydney for work, Tamara?"

"It's probably the only option."

"It'll be a bit of a commute from here."

"I don't mind; not in the short term, anyway."

Jake looked deep in thought. "Why didn't you just come to Australia for a holiday?"

His question hovered in the air like a dragonfly stationary for far too long. April dug him sharply in the ribs.

"What?" he snapped.

"That's rude!"

"No it isn't."

Tamara wished they would debate the point a little longer to give her the chance to think of an acceptable answer; one that was better than saying she was getting as far away as possible from a man rather than having to deal with him face-to-face.

"I was made redundant and it seemed like a good opportunity to spend some quality time with my parents," she said instead.

The word "redundant" always got that same head tilt of sympathy; not quite such a head tilt as when she said that her dad had died a long time ago, but it was still a noticeable movement.

"I'm sorry," said Jake. "I didn't mean to pry or be rude."

"No offence taken."

"Well, I think it's a great opportunity to see a bit of the world," April concluded. "Do you think you'll travel anywhere else before you go back to London?"

"Not unless I win the lottery, but it's too complicated even trying to buy a ticket over here. You guys have so many different types! And I don't much fancy the idea of backpacking."

Jake went off to chat to Hugo at the end of the bar while April and Tamara launched into a debate about the merits of a hotel versus the great outdoors.

"Do you work with Jake at the veterinary practice?" Tamara

asked, when they reached the conclusion that they both liked their creature comforts too much for camping and sleeping rough.

"I'm studying a business course via correspondence." The sparkle reappeared in April's blue eyes. "I'd really love to do what you're doing, and go and work in another country: London, or maybe New York."

"So what made you come to Brewer Creek? It's hardly Manhattan."

"We came here for Jake, to set up the practice," she said matter-of-factly. Tamara was left wondering what would happen when April qualified and grew out of Brewer Creek. Where would that leave her and Jake?

Throughout the evening, the constant flux of locals gave the pub a welcoming feel. It was noisy enough that people couldn't hear your every word, but not so noisy that you had to shout at each other to be heard.

"Hey, over here!" Jake called out to a girl with long red hair, who was coming into the bar. She seemed to know each and every patron in there, waving and nodding hellos in all directions. A plait ran straight down the middle of the girl's back, and she was grinning from ear to ear, her hazel eyes mischievous as she walked over to them. She was tall and slender with prominent cheekbones and freckles that ran in a delicate line across the bridge of her nose.

"I missed you guys." The girl hugged April and then Jake, before extending a hand to Tamara. "You must be Tamara; I'm Danielle, it's nice to meet you."

"I remember your name from the friendship tree," said Tamara, as she shuffled up to accommodate an extra stool.

Jake passed Danielle a beer. "Tamara is the friendship tree co-ordinator now."

"So I've heard." Danielle nodded approvingly. "That friendship tree has been Daphne Abbott's baby for years. You should feel privileged that she trusts you with it."

"I'm beginning to understand that," said Tamara.

"If anything changes in this town, she's onto it," Danielle continued. "She doesn't miss a thing. A girl called Marion used to help her out in the milk bar and Daphne found out that she was stealing from her. She fired her on the spot and the friendship tree was updated – minus Marion's details – almost before Marion had packed her bags and left town."

"Brutal." Jake teased.

Tamara sipped her wine, aware that Jake's eyes were upon her again. Why did he make her so nervous when he looked at her like that?

Already onto her second beer, Danielle asked Tamara, "Have you been into Sydney yet?"

"I haven't had a chance." That wasn't strictly true, but the motivation hadn't quite been there.

"It's a beautiful city," April enthused. "The harbour is amazing, and the bridge, the Opera House. Then you've got those markets where you can find some real treasures. There's the one at The Rocks, Paddington–"

Danielle nudged Jake. "She's off again."

"I'll get there soon," Tamara giggled. "So what do you do for work, Danielle?"

"I work on my family's farm at the moment. But as of next February…" Her eyes lit up.

"Oh come on, you can't leave us hanging." Jake swigged his beer.

"Yes, come on, Danielle," April urged.

"Well, as of next February, I'm doing a nursing course."

"That's great news," said Jake, wrapping her in an enthusiastic hug which left Tamara wondering what it would feel like to be in Danielle's shoes right now.

"Congratulations, Danielle," April and Tamara chorused.

"I didn't say anything before, because my family needed me on the farm, what with my sister flying the nest first. I thought they'd go berko, but it turns out that they're pleased. They've wanted to sell up for a while and downsize, so the timing is perfect."

For so long Tamara had lived and breathed London, with its inhabitants rushing from place to place, vigorously climbing the career ladder as though their lives depended on it. As she listened to Danielle rave about nursing and what she eventually hoped to specialise in, Tamara realised how refreshing it was to see such a down-to-earth attitude.

Jake stood abruptly. "I think I've chatted with you girls long enough. Does anyone want to be beaten at a game of pool?"

When he looked directly at her, Tamara shifted in her seat. Thankfully, Danielle hadn't registered the direction of his gaze and said, "I'll take that challenge." She blew on her fingers and clapped her hands together in preparation for that cue. "I grew up playing this game. You're toast, Jake Manning."

Tamara watched this what-you-see-is-what-you-get girl, as she pushed her plait over her shoulder and dusted the tip of the cue with the square of blue chalk. She watched as Jake pulled out a twenty cent coin from his pocket, flipped it into the air, and slapped it onto the back of his hand.

"Tails," said Danielle. "No, heads!"

"Women!" he said, as he revealed the outcome and Danielle stepped forward to break.

The pool table was visible from where they were sitting at the bar, and as Tamara and April watched the game begin, Tamara realised what it was that had been niggling her: it was the distance between Jake and April; not in the physical sense, but how far apart they seemed as a couple. They spoke to each other, they bantered like anyone else, but there were no hints at their relationship to outsiders; no holding hands, no secretively touching each other as they moved closer without anyone noticing. It was almost as if they were a couple facing an imminent divorce and were being amicable for the sake of the kids.

"Not bad." Jake smiled at Danielle's attempt and leaned towards the table, before skilfully sinking a red. He potted another and then another, before she had the chance to try again.

"That yellow, Danielle." April pointed to the ball hovering inches from one of the middle pockets.

"Jake's good, isn't he?" said Tamara.

"He is." April absentmindedly swilled the ice and slice of lemon at the bottom of her glass.

Jake had evidently won the game, judging by the look on Danielle's face. "Okay, who's next?" he asked.

"I think I'll go off and sulk at losing," Danielle told Tamara. "I've got to say some more hellos to the people I haven't seen since I got back to town."

Before Tamara managed to say that she would play, Hugo came over to join them. "I'm not interrupting, am I? The bar's pretty quiet so I thought I'd take my break while I had the chance."

"No worries, mate." Jake passed him the spare cue and Tamara tried to hide her disappointment.

"He's not bad, either," she told April, when Hugo got off to a winning start.

"What do you mean?"

"He's not bad at pool; why, what else would I mean?"

"Nothing, sorry, I'm a bit ditzy lately."

"Is everything okay?" Tamara probed.

"Yes, of course."

Hugo claimed victory for the first game, and they quickly began a second. It didn't escape Tamara's notice that April's eyes followed Hugo more than they probably should have. She certainly focused a great deal more attention on him than she had on her own boyfriend.

"How's the course going, April?" Hugo paused to chat as he dusted his cue with chalk while Jake lined up his next shot.

"Hard work, but I enjoy it," she explained.

"Well, that's the main thing." Hugo stepped forward to take another shot but missed. His focus appeared to have left the game.

"Do you think you'll need to move out to the city where all the major corporations are, once you're qualified?" Hugo was straight back over to them as Jake moved around the table to work out his next move.

"I'm not sure yet."

"Mate, you're losing your touch," said Jake, taking victory.

Hugo shrugged. "Thanks for the game." He nodded to Tamara and smiled warmly at April.

Tamara wondered if Jake had picked up on the spark between these two, but he seemed oblivious as he leant the two cues up against the wall. "You'll have to wait till next time, Tamara," he said, looking at his watch.

She smiled and felt like a try-hard schoolgirl pining after the captain of the rugby team, as she hoped she wouldn't have to wait too long for that next time.

Once they had rescued Danielle from Lily Archer, who was gabbing on about horse grooming and Olympic dressage, they filed out through the front entrance, calling out their goodbyes and thanks to Len and Hugo.

"I had a great night, thank you," said Tamara, tantalised by that feeling of belonging as they gathered outside.

"Who's up for next week? My shout, as I didn't get one in tonight." Danielle pulled her fleece tightly around herself as the evening cooled.

"That'd be great." Tamara gave a small wave and then turned in the direction of home.

"Whoa. Where are you off to?" Jake called after her.

She wished he wouldn't do that; she wasn't a horse that refused to do as it was told.

"I'm going home." Wasn't it obvious?

"You're not walking home on your own, I'll take you; I'm the designated driver tonight."

"Well, I don't know how it works here, but in the UK we don't approve of drinking and then driving home." She didn't mean to sound quite so uppity when she really had enjoyed his company tonight.

Amused, he said, "Despite what you may think of me, I don't

approve of it either. I was on light beer all night."

"He was." April backed him up.

"But I used to walk everywhere in London," Tamara argued.

Jake rolled his eyes and stood his ground, arms folded firmly across his chest, waiting. "And what happens if you stumble into a field and come face-to-face with Fergus again? He looked disappointed not to get you in the first place."

Tamara was glad that the darkness and the alcohol could disguise her embarrassment when she thought of how close her body had been to Jake's that day. Her eyes did the same one-eighty as his had done, before she followed all three of them over to his pick-up. She bundled into the back with April, whom she hoped hadn't picked up on the flirting from Jake. Then again, perhaps it worked differently in country Australia than back in London; perhaps he was just being friendly.

When Tamara saw how sparingly street lamps were used in Brewer Creek, she was glad that she had relented and taken a lift right to her front door. Tucked safely beneath her duvet in bed in the annexe, she gazed into the blackness of the room dotted by tiny flecks from the stars outside, as though they had been flicked up there by a gigantic paint brush. She didn't know Jake, April and Danielle all that well, but she did know that this was a start; this was the beginning of an entirely new phase in her life. But what that new phase would bring, she had no idea.

***

With Tamara and Danielle safely delivered home, Jake drove on to the small cottage that he shared with April.

"You know, it's harder to lie than I thought it would be." He didn't take his eyes off the road. "I mean, bloody hell, April, these people in town are becoming our friends. I feel like we're trying to take them all for a ride."

"Don't say that, Jake. We're not hurting anyone; we're protecting ourselves. They'd understand."

The longer he stayed in Brewer Creek, the more important his reputation became, and not just because of the veterinary practice. Every time he met someone new, he couldn't help thinking that if people ever found out that they were lying, he would never be trusted again.

When he heard a sniffle he turned to see April desperately trying to fight the tears pooling in the corners of her eyes.

"Sorry, must be premenstrual or something," she tried to joke.

When he reached out to grab her arm reassuringly, she gripped onto his hand for dear life.

"Do you think he could find us here?" she asked.

He dipped his lights as they approached the row of houses before their turn-off. "I doubt it. Remember he's not the cleverest bloke."

"You know, I think we can trust Danielle and Tamara to—"

The dirt slipped beneath the tyres as Jake came to a sudden halt at the side of the road. "He may be stupid, April, but Marty's like a dog with a bone! You know that, don't you?" He didn't wait for a response. "We need to be careful, wait till he makes a mistake, gets caught, and is safely locked up behind bars."

"But he'll always be there, lurking; even jail won't mean that we're safe."

As Jake pulled out along the dirt road again, he tried so hard to appear confident and stay strong for April, but he knew she was right. They'd woven lies to keep safe from Marty, but in doing so perhaps all they had done was to make things a whole lot more complicated. Jake couldn't see any way out of it.

Chapter Seven

Life in Brewer Creek meandered on as summer passed lazily into autumn. Outings to the pub became more frequent, and Tamara found herself ensconced in a tight friendship with Danielle and April, and even with Jake. The foursome went to the movies, out for dinner, on walks around town; as time wore on, Tamara settled into a different life.

She still missed London, particularly after her regular Skype calls with Beth, but she had stayed true to her word and hadn't messaged Bradley at all. As her thirty-first birthday passed without so much as a well-wishing message, she was convinced that he had moved on, too.

Tamara organised a church fete using the friendship tree and Daphne's expertise. And when she delivered the bread basket – won in the raffle – to the Barker farm that afternoon, Danielle greeted her in her typical farm uniform comprising dungarees and a tatty shirt. Only the gumboots were missing; in their place was a pair of luminous green fluffy socks.

"Thank you," Danielle grinned, taking the basket and peering through the cellophane. "That'll keep us going for the next month!"

Tamara followed her through the house to the kitchen at the back. "It sure will."

"I'd ask you to stay for lunch, but I really have to get going," Danielle explained. "Come on. I'll show you what a hard day's work is. Look how wrecked my hands are from all this manual labour." She displayed fingers and nails that desperately needed a makeover.

"I doubt it'll get any better with nursing," said Tamara.

"I expect you're right. Come on, I'd better get outside. I had a lie in after the late night at the pub."

"It was another great night, wasn't it? And thanks for the pool lesson, you're as good as any guy I've seen play."

"It comes with the territory." Danielle gestured out of the window to the great outdoors, then pulled on a pair of gumboots that stood waiting on the mat at the back door.

Out the back of the property they dodged the rooster and chicken welcoming committee and passed by the garage where an old car sat defiantly, surrounded by lawnmowers, gardening tools, and a couple of old bikes.

"That's a 1950's Hillman Minx." Danielle must have noticed Tamara's interest.

"It's certainly full of character."

"It was my parents' pride and joy. They've vowed to have a major clear-out when I start the course. They're downsizing, so they'll have to be brutal." Danielle winked, shutting the gate behind them so that the chickens couldn't escape.

Every day Tamara found another reason why people loved this town. People seemed to live less complex lives, not worrying about having the latest cars or most up-to-date gadgets. She wasn't sure that it was completely her, but it was refreshing all the same.

Danielle motioned for Tamara to follow her into one of the stables. "How's the job hunting going?"

Tamara, glad she had her Blundstones on to tackle the uneven, muddied outside and the debris in the stable, replied, "I applied for another one this morning, but it's pretty quiet. At this rate I'll still be living with my parents when I turn forty!"

"I'm hearing you, girl. I'm way too old to be at home, it's almost shameful. But it took me a long time to really decide what I wanted to do, and to have the guts to actually take action and do it."

"Will you stay here while you study?"

"It all depends on this place, and whether Mum and Dad can get things organised. I would hate to leave them in the lurch, but all being well I'll move to the city and rent an apartment while I study." She smiled. "Living in Brewer Creek has the perk of being quiet, so I've been saving for a long time and have enough funds to get through University and have my own place."

Danielle patted the deep chestnut horse that had begun nuzzling her from the moment they set foot in the stables. "Morning, Cap."

Tamara stroked Cap's mane as Danielle freshened up his water supplies and re-filled the feed bin.

"What was it like growing up here?" Tamara asked, as she stroked Cap's nose from between his eyes all the way down to his twitching nostrils.

"It was an absolute dream." Danielle led Cap out into the paddock. "These fields were my playground, and I had the kind of freedom that most kids dream about. I was never told off if I came home dirty; it was expected. There was more suspicion if you came home clean."

"It sounds amazing."

"It was. I mean, I know it's a different life here and I sometimes feel about as feminine as a cow that's just dropped a humongous pile of poo from its arse–"

"You're not that bad," Tamara laughed.

"Maybe not, but my point is that as much as I want to do nursing, I will always be proud of Brewer Creek and what it has done for me."

Tamara didn't doubt that.

"Cappuccino has been with us since she was a foal, you know," said Danielle proudly. "I named her, too."

"Don't feel guilty for pursuing your dreams, Danielle." She hoped her comment wasn't out of place, but she knew how difficult it could be to dare to try something new: a different career, a different country, a different life.

Facing the back of the horse and lifting its rear leg, Danielle scraped the dirt out of Cap's hooves and moved around to the front to repeat the procedure. She tucked a wisp of red hair behind her ear before she bent down again. "I don't feel that guilty, not when my parents are so happy about it. But you must understand more than most how hard it is to break the habits of a lifetime."

Danielle was referring to Tamara's change in location, but Bradley had been a hard habit to break, too, and it was him she thought about when she answered, "Yes, but I also know that once they're broken, it can open new doors that we never knew existed."

***

"Penny for them," said Katherine, ruffling Tamara's hair as she sat at the kitchen table that afternoon.

"I applied for five contract jobs last week but I haven't heard from any of them," said Tamara. The yearning for the corporate scene had reared its ugly head again, especially since talking to Danielle and listening to her excitement about getting out into the big, wide world. Brewer Creek was lovely to come home to, but Tamara desperately needed something else.

Katherine put a hand on her daughter's shoulder. "Something will turn up, I know it will. And a week isn't long. They're probably gathering in applications before they sort through the rubbish from the candidates like you."

"Thanks, Mum." Tamara hugged her and planted a kiss on her cheek. "You always know the right thing to say."

"You would let me know if you needed any money, wouldn't you? I don't want you to be stressed about that while you're here."

Tamara dropped a heaped spoonful of coffee granules into a mug, added a spoon of sugar, and inhaled the aroma as the boiling water from the kettle made contact. "Stop worrying, Mum. My redundancy payout was pretty generous, and my board here is way too cheap."

"Nonsense, you're my daughter and I hardly ever see you. It's my right to treat you and make the most of having you around."

"But I'm living at home at thirty-one!" She grimaced.

Katherine leaned past her and flipped open the lid of the biscuit tin, tilting it for Tamara to make a selection before taking one herself. "What's brought all this on? Are we driving you crazy?"

"Not at all," said Tamara, as she devoured the double-coat Tim Tam biscuit. "The annexe is fantastic, don't get me wrong. But if I end up staying in Australia long term, I'll get out of your hair and rent my own place."

The drizzle outside had turned into a downpour, as though someone had turned on a shower in the great skies above.

"Are you missing the convenience of London?" Katherine cheekily grabbed two more biscuits and gave one to Tamara.

"I guess so, although not necessarily London. I think that once I'm back at work I'll be so much better."

"Have you given the possibility of long-term much thought?"

"I bet you've been dying to ask me that, haven't you?"

"Ever since you stepped off that flight," Katherine admitted sheepishly, her cheeks flushed with guilt.

When the doorbell rang, Tamara opened the door to find Mr Wilson, a smile edged nervously across his face.

"G'day, Tamara." A quiet man, no taller than Tamara's five foot six frame, his skin was wrinkled and sprinkled with age spots, and he had a voice that was no bigger than he was.

"Hi, Mr Wilson," she smiled, not quite comfortable to pull off a "G'day" just yet. "Come in, please."

He stepped through the front door, shuffling his shoes on the mat to wipe them. "I'm looking for Bobby, is he here?"

"Sorry, he left an hour or so ago." Tamara took a gulp of coffee when she felt the coolness of the air outside meet her skin.

"I used both numbers on the friendship tree but he didn't answer either of them," said Mr Wilson. "I tried calling here, too."

"I'm sorry, Mr Wilson, we were all out this morning."

His voice broke into a canter. "It's my dog, Ada. She's in a bad way. And Bobby will know what to do; he fixed her up a few weeks ago. Took a lump out her side the size of a melon," he indicated the size with his equally wrinkled hands, before shoving them back in the pockets of his long, wax jacket.

Katherine emerged from the kitchen and Mr Wilson took off his cap, then ruffled his grey, pressed-down hair as he repeated the story to her.

"Let me see if I can get hold of him." Katherine picked up the telephone and dialled the surgery.

"You didn't walk all the way here, did you?" Tamara peered outside to see whether someone had given him a lift. She remembered delivering his copy of the friendship tree, and it had been one of the properties where she'd needed the car.

He nodded and his body shook with the cold and the damp, but he was unconcerned about himself. "I'm worried about Ada. She's been with me for fourteen years, you know, never left my side in all those days."

Tamara knew enough about the animal kingdom to know that fourteen was old for a dog.

"I'm sorry, Mr Wilson," said Katherine, "but there isn't any answer from the surgery. He could be with someone or he could be driving. He's not answering his mobile either."

Tamara held Mr Wilson's arm as he lowered himself onto the cushioned stool in the hallway. Katherine disappeared and Tamara heard the sounds of the fridge opening and shutting, the cluttering of the utensil drawer, and then her mum appeared with what looked like a cup of steaming coffee. At least that's what Tamara thought it was, until it passed under her nose and she realised that it was a great deal more potent than that.

Mr Wilson's eyes pleaded with the two women as he nursed his hot toddy. "She's lying there, breathing funny. I don't know what to do."

"Drink up," said Tamara, "and I'll go and see her." Tamara had been around animals long enough to be comfortable checking up on them and fussing over them until the cavalry arrived.

By the time she arrived at Mr Wilson's place, the shower overhead had been switched off and the sun was fighting for pole position in the skies.

"Bloody automatics," she swore at her mum's car, as her foot searched blindly for the clutch that she was so familiar with in the UK. She pulled up outside the dilapidated weatherboard cottage and grabbed an old blanket from the back. She walked up the path, swiping the brambles out of the way as they scratched at her legs.

"Ada? Ada?" She walked through the sun-drenched hallway, the musty smell and eau-de-dog mingling into one. She left the front door open and shut the fly wire to try and get some airflow through the place. Walking through the gloomy house, she spotted the many signs of an elderly person living all alone: the lone toothbrush in the pot next to the sink; the single cup, plate and bowl left to drip-dry on the drainer. It made her realise how important a friendship tree and a sense of community was to people like Mr Wilson.

The curtains were drawn throughout the house and Tamara pulled open the deep brown drapes in the lounge, narrowly avoiding stumbling on Mr Wilson's slippers which lay in the doorway. Dust particles danced in the stream of sunlight that sprayed across the room as she called the dog's name.

Through the door at the end of the kitchen, Tamara found Ada. "There you are." She bent down and stroked the head of the golden Labrador. "Mr Wilson's worried about you."

The dog was sleepy, its eyes half closed and sticky. Its mouth drooped at the corners but Ada's tail came to life as best it could when Tamara covered her with the blanket and stroked her head. This same confidence with animals had terrified her mum when Tamara was little; she would forever pet other people's dogs, and her mum had to pull her back and tell her to be more cautious.

Tamara found some dog biscuits shaped like bones and offered one to Ada, who sniffed at it, about as interested as a toddler being offered mushed-up vegetables.

"Huh, so you're not hungry?" She let the biscuit rest under the golden fur of Ada's chin. "Well we're going to get Bobby to look at you, as soon as we can find him. He'll know what to do." She ruffled the dog's head and felt the sting of tears in her eyes. Not just for Ada, but for Mr Wilson, too. This wasn't looking good at all.

As she locked the door behind her, Tamara pinched the top of her nose to stop the tears from escaping.

"What are you up to?" A voice made her jump and she almost dropped Mr Wilson's keys.

"You scared me," she said, her hand clasped to her chest. "I was checking on… er–"

Jake hopped down from his pick-up. "Checking on what?"

Tamara knew that Bobby and Jake co-existed in Brewer Creek as vets, but she had still cautioned her stepfather to make sure he kept his regular customers and they didn't defect. If he was having financial problems, then it was the only way. "Ada." She said reluctantly.

She felt his eyes taking in the sight of her in her familiar denim cut-offs; she had seen him do the traditional male scan of sizing a woman up from head to toe and all the way back up again, and it wasn't the first time it had happened.

She moved to open her car door.

"Hang on a minute." He laid a hand on her arm as she reached for the handle, and she froze at the feel of his touch. "I'm serious. What's wrong with Ada? Mr Wilson is a decent bloke, and if I can help I'd appreciate you telling me what's going on."

She exhaled. "If you really must know, Mr Wilson's over at our place with Mum, and they're waiting for Bobby to come home so that he can check up on Ada himself."

"Will he be there soon?" He crossed his arms firmly.

Tamara looked down at her boots. "He should be." She leapt in before he could speak. "He's Bobby's client, Jake."

"Forget about whose client he is for the minute. If the dog

needs looking at, then she needs looking at. There's no need to make her suffer because of your hang-ups."

She didn't appreciate the scolding, especially since they had become friends. She climbed in the car and revved up the engine as though it could match the emotional fireworks firing around inside of her.

Jake's voice trailed through her open window. "I'll follow you back to your place. If you still can't get hold of Bobby, then please let me help."

"Fine," she said.

The dirt sprayed in all directions from beneath Tamara's tyres as she drove away not bothering to wait for him.

***

"Women!" cursed Jake, as he jumped into his truck and matched the drama of Tamara's departure, sending mud all up the sides of his pick-up.

One of the qualities that attracted him to Tamara was her confidence, her loyalty, and her overwhelming sense of strength, but she was damn frustrating when she got on her moral high-horse about something; warranted or not. Her car still in sight, he imagined her slim, perfectly-formed legs operating the pedals, and her delicate city-girl hands turning the steering wheel. An "on" or "off" switch to control his feelings would be ideal right now; his life was far too messy to introduce another complication.

Chapter Eight

"You didn't have to speed off back there," said Jake, when he pulled up alongside Tamara. "You're a danger to yourself and everyone else on the road."

His words bore into the back of her head as she marched up to the front door. She had visions of him checking her out again like he'd done before; she'd swing for him if he was. She knew she was overreacting to the situation – no doubt that's what Bobby would tell her anyway – and maybe it was his flirting that riled her more than anything.

"Did you get hold of Bobby?" Tamara asked, as soon as she stepped through the front door.

Katherine looked above Tamara's head at the tall figure passing through the doorway. "Hello, Jake." She turned to Tamara. "I still can't get hold of him, no."

Jake looked at Katherine. "Can I help?"

She nodded.

Mr Wilson was relieved that Ada would get the help that she needed, but Tamara wanted to tell Jake to go easy when she saw his firm handshake startle the old man.

Tamara crouched down beside Jake and took Mr Wilson's cold, wrinkly hand in both of hers. "Jake is a good vet," she said. "He took care of Mr Harris's horse when Bobby couldn't. You should listen to him. I could drive you home; we'll follow Jake in his pick-up." She didn't bother to consult with Jake on the matter.

When they arrived at the house, Jake went straight to Ada's side and Tamara busied herself in the kitchen putting away the crockery which had been left on the drainer. She checked the fridge and noticed how bare it was; the larder, too. She wondered how Mr Wilson stayed looking so healthy if this was how he lived. She noticed her friendship tree pinned to a small cork board beside the cooker and felt a sense of pride.

Mr Wilson came into the room along with Jake. The old man looked more stooped than ever before when he pinched the skin between his eyes and said, "I'm really going to miss her."

Tamara gulped. Her throat felt as though it had narrowed in the last thirty seconds. The news was expected, but it didn't make it any easier. She put an arm around Mr Wilson's shoulders even though all she wanted to do was turn away. She didn't want Jake to see the tears in her eyes or hear the wobble in her voice.

"Can I take you back to our place?" she asked. "You don't want to be on your own."

Mr Wilson patted her hand. "No, dear. I'm happy to be here. I knew she didn't have long left. I wanted to make sure that she didn't suffer any longer than was necessary. I couldn't bear that." He pulled out a faded, burgundy cotton handkerchief and dabbed at his eyes. He looked out to the back garden and the sunshine that had finally emerged to grace the lawn. "Seeing her fall asleep was the best way," he sniffed.

Tamara could see the regret in Jake's eyes and knew that his task would've been punishing; she had seen the same melancholic look in Bobby's eyes often enough.

Jake crouched down beside the old man. "I need to know what you want me to do with Ada," he said.

Mr Wilson looked at Tamara, then at Jake, and in a small voice that only reminded them of his age, said: "I think I need some help."

**

Mr Wilson stroked Ada as she lay at peace in her basket on top of an old square of carpet which matched the threadbare one in the lounge. Tamara waited with him, watching Jake through the laundry window, taking in the powerful muscles in his forearms as he plunged the spade into the ground time after time.

When the hole was big enough, Jake signalled that he was ready and Tamara helped to carry Ada in her basket down to the burial spot. She felt as nervous as a pallbearer as she gripped the bunched-up edges of an old sheet which Jake had manoeuvred beneath the dog to enable them to lower her into the ground.

Mr Wilson knelt beside the hole and dropped in a piece of chewed-up rope. "She's had this since she was a pup," he explained. Then he sprinkled in the first handful of earth, and when Tamara placed a hand on his arm, his cold skin gripped hers as he wept quietly.

Tamara bit down hard on her lip, hoping that it would scare her own tears away while Jake filled in the hole. "Perhaps you could plant some grass seed on top, maybe even some flowers?"

"That sounds like a wonderful idea, Tamara."

When they had finished and were happy that Mr Wilson would be fine, Jake swung his bag into the back of the pick-up truck. "Well done in there."

She felt embarrassed at how she had reacted to his efforts earlier. "Well done to you, too." She looked down at her dust-covered boots. "Was it really awful?"

"It's always awful. And for the record, I wasn't chasing the client to get him for myself. Surely you don't think I'm that much of a jerk?"

"You're not a jerk." She couldn't look him in the eye.

"Truce?" he held out a hand.

Tamara put her hand in his, savouring the warmth of his skin. It reminded her of the first time they touched, when he shook her hand beside the car that morning.

"How about we go to the pub for a drink?" he suggested. "It's my shout, and I need one after that."

"You're on," she agreed.

***

Tamara found a parking space directly opposite Brewer's Inn and was about to push open the midnight-blue door, when another more masculine hand appeared a few inches above hers.

"Let me get that." Jake was close enough that she could smell the same heady aftershave that had wafted past her at Mr Wilson's. She felt her cheeks heat up at the closeness of his body, and only came down to earth when they reached the bar and placed their order.

Jake took off his hat and ran a hand through hair dappled by years of Australian sunshine. It was a gesture Tamara had come to realise meant he was thinking before he spoke. "I don't drink in the day very often," he said.

"No need to explain. I think it's more than justified this time." She took a beer from Hugo and they clinked bottles. "And same here, just the one and then water for me, or maybe a tomato juice if they've got any." She peered at the selection of bottles behind the bar.

"Does anyone seriously drink that revolting stuff?"

She thought for a moment and then said, "Dot Cotton."

"Who's that?"

"Never mind," she giggled, enjoying the smile that spread across his lips and made the skin at the sides of his eyes crinkle. "She's a character from a soap opera in the UK." She waved Hugo over. "Could I have a packet of salt and vinegar crisps, please?"

Jake laughed and his hair settled in that oh-so-sexy way. "Don't you mean chips?" His gaze flitted between her mouth and her eyes, like a bumble bee given so many sources for nectar that it wanted to buzz around and try them all at once.

"At least I don't say *thongs* for something I wear on my feet," she teased.

"What's wrong with thongs?"

"Where I come from, a thong is a skimpy pair of knickers that go up your bum."

73

His face twitched. "So what do you guys call thongs?"

"Flip flops."

"Flip flops," he repeated, tickled at the words. She heard him say it again as he excused himself and went off to the bathroom.

"No April today?" asked Hugo, pulling a pint of Guinness for Jack Calder who'd just arrived in the pub.

Tamara shook her head as she finished a mouthful of crisps.

"I expect she's studying hard for the next round of exams," he continued. "I did a business course myself so I know what it's like."

"Did you really?"

"Don't look so surprised that the barman has a brain!"

"No, it's not that…"

"I know. The tatts and the pulling pints all day don't really imply 'academic', but I wanted to get some kind of qualification. You know, in case I decide the pub business isn't for me."

"And is it?"

He thought for a moment. "I'm still not sure. I love Brewer Creek, it's my home, and I can see it as the place where I'd like to raise a couple of kids one day. What?"

"Nothing," Tamara smiled. "It's just that most men wouldn't be as open as you're being now."

"That's because you English are all so uptight," he teased, and turned to deliver the Guinness.

"What, stiff upper lip and all that?"

He shrugged. "I don't mind people knowing who I am, Tamara. I figure it's easier than playing games and making them guess what I'm all about."

Well, that was the truth if ever she'd heard it.

"The jury is still out on the pub business, though. I guess over time I'll know whether it's right for me. I wonder what April will end up doing when she's qualified."

Tamara knew that he wouldn't be able to stay off the topic of April for long. The boy had a serious crush. Mind you, she was one to talk.

"She seems to be dreaming of the big city life," he continued. "I can't see her settling down around here."

When Jake reappeared, Hugo disappeared to gather the empties from along the bar top. It was obvious to Tamara that Hugo was keen on April, but whether it was obvious to Jake, or even April herself, she had no idea.

"We could organise a working bee for Mr Wilson's garden," said Jake, as the stress began to melt away for both of them with every sip of beer. "It could use some work, and not just the patch where Ada is buried. I noticed the back fence is rotting, and weeds are sprouting up like there's no tomorrow."

"Well that's a job for me, I guess. I'll get the friendship tree and round up some volunteers."

He grinned. "You're enjoying being the new Daphne Abbott of Brewer Creek, aren't you?"

"You know, I actually am. In the absence of a real job, it's stopped me from being bored, and I've got to know most of the people around town, too."

"You sound as though you're quite taken with Brewer Creek."

"It's growing on me," she grinned. "When I saw how isolated Mr Wilson's place actually is, even though someone else owns all the land that sits behind it, it brought home to me how someone like him could be forgotten."

"Super Tamara to the rescue!" he joked.

"Hey, don't take the mickey. And I'll have you know that Brewer Creek isn't the only place that uses the friendship tree concept."

"What do you mean?"

"I've been best friends with Beth – she lives in London – for more than twenty years, and I owe it all to a friendship tree. When I started a new school the headmistress told me about this big, old oak tree that sat at one end of the playing field. She said that if I ever had trouble finding someone to play with, then I should stand under that tree and someone would find me."

Jake made a peculiar face.

"There, that's the face I made to the headmistress," she giggled. "I thought that I'd look like a complete loser, and the first time I stood beneath it I thought that I was right. Some boys teased me, called me names like 'darkie' and 'Scott-no-mates', but then Beth turned up."

She grinned now. "If you ever meet Beth, her bark is worse than her bite. But these boys weren't to know that. She scared them off good and proper, and ever since that day we've had each other's backs and been there for each other through life's ups and downs."

"The power of the friendship tree, eh?" He wasn't teasing her now. If anything, Tamara could've sworn he admired the whole concept, too.

"I'm still worried about Mr Wilson." She sipped her beer, and when Jake touched her arm it sent shivers down the back of her neck. His hand lingered and she wondered if she should pull away, but it seemed unfeeling and unnecessary so for a moment they stayed as they were.

"He'll be fine," said Jake, only removing his hand when the door behind them creaked open and in walked April. She smiled across at Hugo before she headed over to them.

"How's the course going?" Tamara's heart was still racing and her mind had to force itself to jump back to reality. She felt as guilty as a child caught smuggling chocolate after teeth had been brushed and lights turned out.

"I need a break," April pleaded.

Tamara recounted their day in detail, if only to explain what she was doing there at the pub with this girl's boyfriend.

"Oh, that's terrible," said April. "Mr Wilson is a lovely man. Daphne Abbott cornered me the other day when he left the shop, and she told me all about him. Apparently his wife died five years ago now."

Tamara could recall seeing a photograph on his bedside table, but hadn't wanted to pry. What she was growing to love about this town was that it didn't seem so small that people knew everything about everybody else, yet it was small enough that people still cared. The elderly people in her block of flats back in London could be incommunicado for days before anyone noticed, and then it would most likely be because of the stench of a dead body.

"We buried Ada in the back garden," said Tamara. "I thought my arms were going to break, she was so heavy."

"You must be stronger than you look," said April.

"She is." Jake's eyes lingered on Tamara as she shuffled uncomfortably on her stool, willing him to look at April instead.

April finished her drink and said her goodbyes so that she could return to her study. Odd that she didn't seem to be at all concerned that her boyfriend was at the pub, drinking with another girl.

Jake pulled out his wallet and waved to Len.

"Uh-uh... no more for me," said Tamara.

"Oh, come on. We've had a hell of a day. I'm leaving my truck here, that's for sure."

She hesitated for one more second, and then, "Oh why not?" She put her empty beer bottle onto the bar as she felt a rush of the flirty sort of fun she and Bradley had enjoyed before they ended up in bed together. And while she knew things couldn't go that far with Jake, she couldn't deny that she was enjoying herself.

Tamara lost count of how many beers they necked that afternoon, and as Jake did an impersonation of his old schoolteacher she threw back her head again and laughed. "You look like Quasimodo!"

When he had stopped laughing, his look turned serious. "So, Tamara, when are you going to stop giving me such a hard time?"

She felt her body stiffen. "What?"

"Oh, come on. You think you've got me all sussed as some arsehole who's trying to steal Bobby's clients, but that's ridiculous. I'm not like that, honest."

"Aha, there you go. Never trust a man who says he's honest."

"Who says so?"

She shrugged her shoulders. Whatever his motives in the

veterinary world were, the fact remained that he didn't seem to have any scruples when it came to his relationship with April. She hadn't imagined the flirting between them, she knew she hadn't, and it had been building from the very first day they met.

"Seriously, Tam, I–"

"Tam?" she giggled. "Since when have you heard me being called Tam?"

"We shorten everything in Australia," he explained. "Narelle is Naz; afternoon is arvo; sausages are snags; and so on, and so on."

She'd never been called "Tam" but something about Jake saying it felt different; it felt nice. "What else do Aussies say?" she asked.

He smiled that irresistible smile, with lips slightly parted and a deeper crease in his left cheek than his right. "Oh, we've got some rippers out here. Let me think. Rellies – relatives; dacks – trousers; two-pot screamer is a person who can't handle their drink; oh, and of course we're at the local watering hole, not the pub."

Tamara grinned. "Actually, I think it's time I left the local watering hole."

Jake downed the rest of his drink, and then as though it was the most natural thing in the world, he took her hand. "I'll walk you home," he said, "and I'll tell you some more Aussie slang. But be warned, some of it shouldn't be used by a sheila!"

Outside, Jake strode over to his silver pick-up to check that it was all locked up for the night and Tamara followed suit, surreptitiously touching her hand as though his touch still lingered. They met beneath the dim lights of the pub doorway and walked side by side, him with his hands firmly in his pockets as though he didn't trust himself, and her with her arms crossed for the same reason. They turned the corner and walked past the creek, the sound of trickling water audible in the stillness of the night, and paused at the top of the small footbridge as Tamara had done on her own so many times.

"So come on then, tell me some more Aussie-isms," she said.

Jake laughed and shook his head. "I don't think I know you

well enough yet, I wouldn't want to offend you."

"Spoilsport," she chided.

"Next time, I promise."

She looked up at the crescent moon. This was all getting so complicated, and far from what she had expected when she came to the other side of the world. Not only did she have feelings for another girl's boyfriend, but it was blindingly obvious that it wasn't one-sided.

"I love standing here," his voice broke her thoughts. "It's so quiet. I can think here, I feel free."

She cast aside her misgivings for now and leant on the white, worn fence, too.

"Did I just sound like a total girl, or what?" he asked.

She shook her head but couldn't meet his gaze, and instead looked out across the water and at the gum trees that ran along one side of the creek. "We all need time out, Jake; even men. I sit out on the back veranda all the time and stare at the palm trees, enjoying the sounds of the countryside and the odd gecko darting past my feet. There's something about all that fresh air and stillness that lets me process."

Jake's mouth twisted into a knowing smile. "I've seen you. Sitting out the back of your house, I mean."

Her heart leapt at the thought of him watching her unnoticed, and she felt the thrill cascade through her body as she wondered: When? How?

She changed the subject. "You know, you'd be impressed at my reaction to the Australian wildlife now. Geckos no longer make me jump out of my skin; even the resident blue tongue lizard doesn't send me into a crazy panic like it did the first time I came home and it was waiting there on the doorstep."

When he threw his head back and laughed she knew that she had never seen him quite so relaxed. He always looked as though he had a peculiar weight resting on his shoulders that he constantly dragged around with him. Out here, tonight, he seemed to have left that burden behind.

"But are you used to the huntsman spider yet?" he asked.

"Now, let's not push it. Lizards I can do, kookaburras, lorikeets, even the possums when they make that horrible screechy sound. But spiders are a different thing entirely."

"Just you wait. You'll happily co-exist with them if you stay here long enough."

"I can assure you, that'll never happen."

"What, the acceptance of spiders? Or staying here in Australia?"

Stumped, she looked down at the water, its trickling tune drowned out by the rising evening volume of the cicadas.

"Can I ask you something, Tamara?"

"Uh-huh."

"Why did you really leave London? I mean, you say you lost your job and you missed your family, but I think there was another reason."

"You're very intuitive." Her eyes followed the patchy bark of the nearest gum tree all the way up to the top and then back down again.

"Do you want to talk about it?"

Here, on this bridge, on this perfect evening with a man she was doing her best not to fall for, she didn't even want to consider Bradley Cox and the reasons why she'd had to get away. "Not really," she said.

They stood quietly for a while until she shivered.

"I'd offer you my top if I was a gentleman, but this is the only one I've got," said Jake, pulling at the single t-shirt on his back.

She smiled, blocking out the image that crept into her psyche of Jake stretching his arms up high and pulling his t-shirt over his head. She'd caught a glimpse of him a few times over in the paddock at Mr Harris's place when he'd got unexpectedly muddy trying to treat an unwilling animal.

The lights were still on at the Hardings' when they reached the house. Tamara knew that if her heart pounded any harder in her chest it was at risk of bouncing right out and off down the road.

She felt as though she was on a first date and that awkward goodbye-moment had arrived in which neither knew whether a kiss was the way to go. And if so, what kind of kiss?

"Thanks, Jake. You cheered me up this afternoon."

"No worries." He scuffed at the gravel on the driveway with his leather work boots.

She took a deep breath. "Goodnight then."

"Goodnight, Tamara."

Jake waited for her to go inside, and like a teenager Tamara waved back at him through the glass beside the front door before she crept out to the annexe. As she climbed into bed, she couldn't stop smiling at the thought of this man who had jumped unexpectedly into her life.

Chapter Nine

The sun hung bravely in the sky as Brewer Creek prepared to flip seasons from autumn to winter. Since the night that Jake had walked her home from the pub, he had been strangely distant. Nights out had tailed off, with Jake and April failing to turn up on more than one occasion. But perhaps it was for the best; Tamara had had enough mind games with Bradley to last her a lifetime, and she didn't need to play them with anyone else.

Using the friendship tree, Tamara organised a working bee for Mr Wilson's place. A few of them took the inside, cleaned out cupboards and restocked the larder; others got the garden ship-shape and planted flowers on Ada's grave that would make Mr Wilson smile far more than a dismal mound of earth. Tamara also made contact with the man who owned the land behind Mr Wilson's property, and between them they discreetly saw to it that the Brewer Creek resident was routinely checked on and helped out. Tamara visited a few times each week, and what started out as a sense of duty and community spirit soon changed. The pair enjoyed long walks chatting about anything and everything, and Tamara found an unlikely friend in Mr Wilson, one who left her believing in the greater good of humankind.

"How was Mr Wilson?" Katherine asked when she arrived home that afternoon after their regular trek from his place to town and back again.

"He's doing well; fit and spritely for an eighty-nine-year-old, I'd say. I stocked up his larder and left him for an arvo nap."

Katherine sniggered.

"What?"

"You said 'arvo'."

Tamara grinned. The previous day Bobby had teased her about saying "G'day" to Daphne Abbott, and this morning Mr Wilson had picked up on her saying "no worries".

Katherine pulled out a fresh tea loaf from the oven and Tamara leant over the tin, closed her eyes, and breathed in the aroma of dried fruits and a hint of nutmeg.

"It'll take a while to cool," Katherine warned, "but I've got some genuine Yorkshire tea if you're interested?"

"You must spend a fortune in that treats-from-home section at the supermarket."

"Tamara, there are some things I can't do without." She pulled out two mugs and dropped a teabag into each. "It would be uncivilised."

"Excuse me," Tamara apologised as her phone belted out its ringtone of Beyonce's *Single Ladies*.

She moved into the hallway to take the call, and when she reappeared in the kitchen she couldn't stop smiling. "I've got an interview, at Carter Brown in the city. They want a contract Account Manager until the end of the year."

"That's brilliant news." Katherine rushed forward to hug her daughter. "See, I told you it was only a matter of time."

"I guess so."

Katherine took off her oven glove. "What's wrong?"

Tamara leant back in her chair, fiddling with the corner of the newspaper. Her smile had faded. "I don't feel quite as passionate about it as I thought I would."

"You've just been out of it for a while. You'll go in there and feel like nothing has changed. When's the interview?"

"Not until the day after tomorrow."

"Well that's good. It gives you a day to prepare, but not too long that you start getting nervous. Come on," said Katherine, grabbing the oven glove. "I can't wait any longer either." She turned the tin upside down onto a board and pulled the bread knife through the steaming loaf.

"I'd better not eat too much or I won't fit into the suits that I brought over with me," said Tamara.

"We're having a barbecue this evening, too, so leave room for some of Bobby's signature steaks."

The warm loaf was already melting on her tongue, but Tamara stopped at one slice before heading out to the annexe to pull out a work suit from the wardrobe. Like so many other things, it had been put to the back of her mind since she left the UK.

***

Two days later, Tamara took the two hour train journey to the city and her feet finally touched Sydney soil. Her cut-offs and Blundstones were gone, and in their place was a crisply ironed ivory shirt, with a tapered navy jacket and a pencil skirt that showed off her slim calves. Her toes had protested when she squeezed them into the points of her stilettos for the first time in months, but with her hair swished stylishly into a top knot she once again felt the part.

Catapulted back into city life with her interview at the offices of Carter Brown, it was as though Tamara had never tunnelled her way out of that world. Following the interview she strolled along the harbour enjoying the buzz, the sun soaking into her skin. She looked across the water at the magnificent Opera House and marvelled at the coat-hanger Sydney Harbour Bridge, happy to be in one of the most amazing cities in the world. She made her way along Circular Quay, licking at a Baskin Robbins Chocolate Cookie Crackle ice-cream. Leaning on the railings beside the water, she watched ferries take people back home or off on jaunts, and the returning vessels chugging to deposit the next lot of visitors and commuters to the big smoke.

Today felt like more than a step in the right direction; it was a gargantuan leap towards a new life. Before Christmas, Tamara wouldn't have dared to believe that this much change could come her way. But here she was, living the dream. She had been purposefully absent from Facebook, unconcerned with checking up on Bradley. In doing so, she felt a sense of freedom that she wished she could convey to others. With Facebook the world seemed a much smaller place, and it certainly had its merits, but it also fuelled desires and jealousies that impinged upon the normalities of life.

Tamara felt sure that she smiled all the way home to Brewer Creek. When she arrived at the town's small station and passed under the brick archway, a wolf-whistle made her spin around on the points of her heels.

"You're a bit dressed up for life in a small town, aren't you?" Jake leant his tanned forearm on the top of his open car window. "Do you need a ride home?"

"I think I'll be okay to walk."

"Don't be daft, it's on my way." He tilted his head to indicate the spare seat beside him, then leant over and pulled the catch of the door so that it fell open. "And it'll be a hard walk in those shoes."

Her skirt was almost too tight to climb up into the pick-up, and she had to reveal a lot of leg to get in. She hadn't missed Jake sneaking a glance either.

"I need to swing by Mrs Morris's place and drop off some medication for her cat," he said, indicating the bag at her feet as they drove away from the station. "She forgot to take it with her this afternoon."

"That's fine." Tamara pulled self-consciously at her skirt.

"How did it go?" When Tamara didn't reply, he said, "I assume you went for an interview for a job?"

"It went well, I think." She was conscious that she hadn't seen Jake for a while, but he seemed relaxed enough with her.

"Does this mean you're staying in Australia for a while longer?"

Tamara gave him a sideways look and watched the crease in his left cheek as he smiled and turned the corner into a narrow dirt road. He pulled into one of the driveways, switched off the

85

engine, and turned to face her. Surprisingly he added, "You know you've got friends here now, don't you?"

Hiding behind her sunglasses, she nodded. "I know." What else could she say? Living here had become much more than a means to an end until she was over Bradley, and the friendships she'd made over the last six months were part of that. Little by little she was starting to feel connected to the new life that she was forming in Australia.

Saved by the bell from getting any deeper into that conversation, Jake's phone rang. "I can't talk right now, April." He rolled his eyes at Tamara, a gesture that she wasn't sure he should be making to another woman. "Listen, have a chat with Tamara, she's here in the car." And with that he tossed Tamara the phone before he turned to walk up to the driveway to Mrs Morris's house.

Tamara enjoyed every moment of watching his bum in those familiar Levis until she remembered who was waiting on the phone that sat in her palm, burning a hole of guilt. How could she explain how she had come to be here in Jake's car, alone with him?

She needn't have worried. April obviously wasn't at all concerned as she launched into a spiel about the pub and how much fun it was meeting more people of her own age. She asked Tamara to go to the movies sometime soon.

"That'd be great," Tamara agreed, "but nothing too gory."

"It's a deal. And can you please do me a favour?"

"What's that?"

"Don't let Jake forget to pick up something for dinner on his way home."

When Tamara hung up the call, she couldn't help picturing a cosy dinner for two – wine and candles, the works. The thoughts twisted in her stomach more than she had expected; jealousy and guilt were two powerful emotions.

Jake's phone pinged with an incoming text message, and before Tamara had a chance to drop the device onto his seat she saw the words emblazoned across the screen:

I think Marty is finally out of our lives for good. Love Deb xxx

Tamara threw the phone onto Jake's seat like a hot potato just as he came out of the house and sauntered back over to the pick-up. Her mouth went dry. His flirting with her had been one thing, but this was damning evidence that he was cheating on April.

She stiffened as he climbed in beside her. So much for the gentle, approachable side she had seen with Mr Wilson. It had all been an act, and she couldn't believe that she had fallen for it. He was no better than Bradley. In fact, he was worse; he was devious and a liar.

Tamara held her breath as they set off, and stared out of the window. Reading someone else's text messages was such an intrusion, but then again, it was Jake's fault that she'd had the phone in the first place.

When they pulled up at the Harding property, she barely waited for the pick-up to come to a halt before flinging open the door. "Thanks," she mumbled.

She heard Jake's voice as she stalked into the house but she couldn't make out the words. She simply put a smile on her face and headed through to the kitchen to tell her parents all about her interview.

Chapter Ten

"We should be having something stronger to celebrate," said April, as Jake sat down opposite her at the pub. He passed her an apple juice.

"I'm working," he answered flatly.

"Jake, this is great. Marty has gone. I still can't quite believe it."

"I don't think we can relax yet."

"Come on, Jake, he's never done a disappearing act before. It's a good sign."

Jake was the one who had seen through Marty all along, even before that smack across his head and even before he realised that Marty was a criminal. He knew how cunning the guy was, and his mum's insistence that she had a feeling they wouldn't see him again didn't sit right with him; not yet anyway. Marty wasn't one to give up. He was a man used to getting his own way and to having the upper hand.

"Drink up," said Jake, doing his best to make April feel safe even if he wasn't quite there yet himself.

***

"I don't know what to do," Tamara told Beth. "If it was you then I would absolutely tell you, but I don't feel that I'm good enough friends with April."

"Look, Tamara. I can't tell you what to do," said Beth from her flat in London, "especially not at nearly midnight when I need to be asleep."

"Sorry."

"Don't be silly. You know I'm happy to talk any time."

"I wish I'd never seen the damn message."

"Well it doesn't sound as though he was thinking much when he gave you the phone in the first place."

"I'm pretty sure the only thinking Jake does is with an organ very much south of his brain," said Tamara, although it wasn't quite as black and white as that. One minute he seemed like a decent person and then something like this happened and made her question him.

"I guess you could look on it as a female solidarity thing." Beth paused and Tamara could hear the cogs in her mind churning from the other side of the world. "The question is, if the situation were reversed, would you want her to tell you?"

When Tamara hung up, she had her answer. She pulled the duvet back over herself; with nothing to get up for, she didn't intend to crawl out of bed until at least midday.

***

Beyonce's *Single Ladies* blared out. Dazed, Tamara sat up in bed and fumbled around in the Narnia-like duvet for her phone. She found it before the call disappeared into the voicemail abyss, and it was enough to propel her from her warm bed in the annexe to the kitchen.

"I got the job!" she squealed with all the enthusiasm of a cheerleader.

Katherine leapt across the room to hug her daughter and Bobby followed close behind, anxious for his turn, too.

"I knew you could do it!" Katherine had that same look of pride and joy she had worn when Tamara got her A-level results, and later, her degree.

"As soon as I get my first pay check, I'll be upping my rent here." Tamara held up a hand to silence them both. If they had money worries, it would be good to help out some more. "It's only right, and I've decided, so no arguments."

Bobby pulled her into a tight hug. "That's my girl. We've raised an independent, beautiful young woman, and we couldn't be more proud." He took a seat so that she could tell them all about the contract which would keep her in the country at least until the end of the year.

"What are you up to?" Tamara watched as her mum rummaged through her collection of cookbooks.

"I've invited Jake and April over for dinner."

Tamara froze. "Why?"

"Oh come on, Tamara. I thought you were all friends," said Bobby.

"We are," she shrugged, pouring a glass of apple juice from the fridge.

"Well I thought it was about time, seeing as we're the two vets in Brewer Creek now," said Bobby. "Jake has shown that he's a real part of this community and I want to make him feel welcome. I mean, look how he jumped in and helped Mr Wilson, and–"

"Of course he did, Mr Wilson paid him, didn't he?" Since she'd seen that text on his phone, she had gone back to thinking the worst of Jake in all facets of his life.

"Well, he seems like a decent, honest bloke to me," argued Bobby.

Katherine stood between the two of them. "Okay. It's time for you to help me work my magic."

She handed Tamara a set of ivory napkins. Tamara rolled each one into a cigar shape and threaded them into silver-plated napkin rings. It irked her that her mum continued to extol Jake's virtues when they didn't know the half of it: there were more juicy lies in that relationship than there were flavours in a jellybean jar.

She watched as her mum started to carry out a well-practised drill: The drill that would include hours in the kitchen preparing food to the nth degree, before retiring upstairs an hour or so before their guests arrived so that it looked as though entertaining was simply effortless.

Tamara pulled out the box of cutlery which they saved for special occasions, eager to discuss anyone or anything besides Jake Manning. As Katherine pulled tins from cupboards and lined up ingredients on the bench top, Tamara set the table and gazed out at a clear pale blue sky. Things were falling into place in so many ways, and the only storm cloud that she could see on the horizon right now was Jake.

***

That evening Tamara put her own opinions aside, and dressed in a rust-coloured shift dress with strappy silver sandals showcasing ruby-polished toenails. She hadn't worn the toe ring in a long time; it almost felt part of the old Tamara now.

Two silver bangles jingled as she walked down the stairs, and the diamond studs her mum had given her for her birthday shone happily in each earlobe. As she caught sight of herself in the oval mirror in the hallway, she felt a tingle swirl its way through her body at the thought of Jake seeing her tonight. She froze. It was happening again. She was falling for a man who wasn't right for her, who had too many faults to ignore, and she felt powerless to stop it.

When the doorbell rang, she took a deep breath and opened the door. "Come in." She attempted nonchalance but instead wavered on nervousness and excitement.

"G'day, Tamara." Jake stood behind an arrangement of gerberas and lilies in shades of pinks and purples, with lush foliage draped throughout. "These are to say thank you for inviting me over this evening. April sends her apologies but she's feeling a bit crook so she's tucked up in bed. Just a bit of a cold, nothing serious."

Tamara inclined her head for him to follow her down the hallway, guilty that her gut reaction to April's non-appearance was one of relief.

Before they reached the end of the corridor, Jake's arm wrapped around Tamara's and the same heady sensation she'd felt in the pub that day beneath his touch made her whole body stiffen. She turned to look at him and held his gaze until his hand fell back to his side.

"You jumped out my car in a bit of a rush the other day," he said.

That's because I know your secret, she thought. She forced a smile for the man who looked much more her usual type – dressed in smart jeans, an ironed, button-down, pale blue checked shirt, and a pair of chocolate brown leather boots without so much as a hint of mud on them.

"Welcome, Jake." Bobby appeared from the kitchen in time to save her from a sudden inability to think of something intelligent to say. He shook hands with their guest, placing his other hand on top in a truly welcoming gesture.

When Katherine saw the flowers, she said, "They're beautiful," and kissed Jake on the cheek. "Welcome to our home."

Tamara could tell that her mum was charmed by Jake, and she didn't blame her for being sucked in; she had only seen the nice bits. Jake sank into the welcoming, deep leather sofa, his legs still long enough to touch the floor. Tamara's never could; she could only ever curl them up beneath her.

"Can I interest you in a beer, Jake, or a glass of wine?" Bobby asked.

"A beer would be great, thanks."

Tamara tried not to watch Jake's mouth as he spoke, but it was like a magnet that refused to repel her eyes as she sat in the armchair opposite.

Beers were clinked together as Katherine arranged the flowers and the foliage in the crystal vase which Tamara had ordered online for Christmas. "It's such a pity that April couldn't make it," she said.

"We'll have to invite her over another time," Bobby agreed.

Tamara wondered if Jake was as uncomfortable as he looked, but he cleared his throat and said, "I'm glad you invited me. I really wanted to clear the air." He leant forwards so that his forearms rested along the length of his thighs, and he looked self-consciously into the top of his beer. "And for the record, I want to say that it wasn't my intention to come here to Brewer Creek and upset anyone."

"Nonsense, lad. A bit of healthy competition never hurts," said Bobby, and patted him on the back as good mates would do, but not without giving Tamara a look that told her he'd been right about Jake's intentions.

Being typical men, neither Bobby nor Jake laboured the point. The air was clear as far as they were concerned, but for Tamara it had just got a whole lot foggier. She looked away as Jake spotted her staring at his legs and the denim that hugged them all the way up to his chocolate brown leather belt.

"Can I do anything to help in the kitchen?" she called to her mum, seizing an opportunity to escape. She left the men talking business but found that Katherine had everything prepared already, from the gravy powder measured out in a jug to the crockery laid out in place settings on the table. She peeked through the glass oven door at the leg of lamb roasting away, its fat sizzling and sprigs of rosemary starting to crisp in the heat.

Katherine pulled out a jar of English Colman's mint sauce and waved it in Tamara's line of vision.

"Where did you find it?" Tamara gasped. It took her a couple of tries to open the stubborn jar before she could breathe in the mint and vinegar mixture, her all-time favourite accompaniment to a lamb roast. Her tastebuds had already begun a welcome dance as she set the sauce down on the table.

"I thought you'd appreciate it." Katherine turned the gas and flicked the ignition until the flames illuminated beneath a saucepan of multi-coloured vegetables. "My friend Margaret got it from one of the bigger supermarkets towards the city."

When Tamara peered inside the fridge, she found the dessert – a Pavlova topped with whipped fresh cream, raspberries, blueberries, and strawberries. "Very Australian," she smiled, shutting the fridge and turning to join the others. But she didn't get far; Jake was right behind her.

"Sorry." He leaned past her to put his empty bottle on the bench top. "You do scare easy, don't you?"

Tamara's heart rate was right up there as though Fergus was charging after them both again. Flustered, she asked, "Can I get you another drink?"

"I'll have a small glass of red, please; I'm driving tonight." He passed her a fresh glass from the table and she tried to stop her hands from shaking as he watched her pull out the stopper and pour.

"So did you hear about that job in the city?" He took a breadstick and dipped it into the creamy red pepper dip.

Tamara sucked in her tummy to prevent an embarrassing hunger growl from escaping. "I got the job, starting Monday."

"Ah. Back to civilisation, eh?"

"I guess so." She curled her legs beneath her on the armchair once again, away from Jake physically but not escaping his gaze.

"She's a clever girl, this one," Bobby said from the opposite end of the sofa.

"I expect she is." Jake's eyes never left her own. "Congratulations."

"Thanks."

Bobby and Jake were soon back to shop talk, this time it was a documentary about goats. The banter continued until the aroma of lamb glided through the air as Katherine took the meat on its journey from oven to table.

Bobby rubbed his hands together. "Looks like it's time. I hope you're hungry, Jake. Katherine tends to cook for twice as many guests as she has."

Everything from the food to the table setting was perfect. A long runner in ivory ran down the centre, and glossy white crockery was framed with elegant silver cutlery. In the centre of the table sat the lamb, and at one end sat the vase of flowers that Jake had brought. A bowl of Hasselback potatoes released steam into the air, and Katherine slotted a silver serving spoon into a large bowl of roasted zucchini, carrots, peas, shallots, and pumpkin.

Bobby carved and served the lamb while Katherine passed the china dish of vegetables around the table.

"So where did you study, Jake?" Bobby poured a generous serve of gravy over his dinner.

"At the University of Sydney; great place."

"Well, you must be clever." Katherine ground fresh pepper over her dinner. "I've heard it said that it's more difficult these days to get into vet school than it is to be a doctor."

Bobby's chest expanded with pride. "We're a clever breed, no doubt about that."

"Modest, too," Tamara teased her stepdad, tucking her legs underneath her chair so that they had no chance of meeting Jake's under the table. She was anxious to relax into the conversation in the same way that her parents were. Putting her doubts aside, she asked, "So Jake, did you work in the city before coming to Brewer Creek?"

"I worked in Neutral Bay, not too far from the big smoke."

"What made you move out here if you're used to the more domestic side of things?"

"I needed a change, I guess," he said, almost too quickly.

"I think we all need one of those sometimes," Bobby agreed. "That's why we chose to emigrate over here."

"How can you eat so much of that?" Katherine chuckled as Tamara smeared mint sauce generously across the juicy slices of lamb.

"Because I love it," she smirked.

The conversation turned to London and the foods and places that Tamara and Katherine missed the most. Jake seemed entertained by the criticisms of Australian chocolate and their dislike for Vegemite. He got full points for charming the parents, and bonus marks for insisting that he help to clear up the dishes before dessert.

"He's lovely, isn't he?" Katherine whispered to Tamara when

the men left them at the table. "It's a pity he's already spoken for. And don't you roll your eyes at me, Tamara Harding."

Tamara frowned. "I don't trust him. And you shouldn't either."

"Now what's brought this on? Bobby isn't worried about the competition, so you shouldn't be either."

Tamara deliberately changed tack. "Is everything fine with Bobby now?"

"He says he's fine, so what can I do? I guess he'll come to me eventually, if he needs to."

The men returned, and Katherine delivered the Pavlova to the table before easing out the slices of gooey-centred meringue.

"How are you getting on with the admin side of the veterinary practice?" Bobby asked Jake as he tucked into his dessert.

Jake waited until he had finished his mouthful, although Tamara smirked at the bit of cream sitting on his lip. His tongue flicked out to remove the offending white stuff but not without him shooting her a knowing grin first; he knew she had been watching him, and not for the first time that night.

"It's not as bad as I thought it would be," said Jake. "It helps that April has some common sense in that area, doing the business course. So she helps me out."

The talk turned to April's course and what it entailed before Bobby asked, "How many years have you been a vet, Jake?"

Jake's hand stroked his unusually-smooth shaven jaw. "Almost seven. Sometimes it feels like only yesterday that I finished my training."

By Tamara's reckoning – and she had never been the quickest at maths – that made Jake about four years older than her, so thirty-five.

"I always enjoyed the equine studies." Jake graciously accepted a second helping of Pavlova. "Even the dissecting was interesting."

Tamara was glad they had finished the lamb.

"I remember some gruesome dissection tales," Bobby began, but was interrupted before he got to tell his story.

"You men will have to save that kind of talk for later."

Katherine pulled a face. "I don't think Tamara wants to hear about it, and I certainly don't."

"Okay." Bobby planted a kiss on his wife's cheek.

"At least you wouldn't have to worry about snakes in the city or the suburbs." Tamara shuddered. "Mum says she's seen plenty of brown snakes out here. I've yet to have that pleasure." She placed her hand on the dining table. "Touch wood."

There was that sparkle in Jake's eyes again, as though he held all the secrets and wasn't going to let her in on any of them. "Sorry to disappoint you, but you still get snakes in the suburbs. Anyway, I thought you were getting used to the wildlife in Australia?"

She felt her cheeks warm at the subtle reference to their conversation on the little white bridge that night.

"Don't worry," he continued. "It isn't as common to get snakes in more built-up areas." He scraped up the last of his Pavlova, along with two stray raspberries covered in cream.

Tamara had visions of snakes joining her next week at work, or slithering after her around the harbour, and she shifted uncomfortably in her seat as Bobby recalled the huntsman incident from her first few weeks in the country. She hoped that Jake wouldn't recall her very first brush with the Aussie specimen, or talk about their encounter with Fergus.

"I'm glad you both find it so funny," she said, as the men fell about laughing. "And your impression is such an exaggeration, Bobby."

She felt something run up her leg and then Bobby's hand reached diagonally and pounced on her outstretched hand.

"Watch it! You nearly knocked my drink over." She realised that it was Bobby's foot beneath the table. He loved to wind her up; always had done.

Bobby helped himself to another slice of Pavlova, the only person who had any room left to do so. "Don't worry, love, for all the stories that the Australians love to tell, you know that they're probably embellished to scare innocent Brits like us."

"I do remember one little old lady in particular," said Jake, "who lived in the suburbs not far from the city centre. Mrs Slocombe–"

"What, as in *Are You Being Served*?" Katherine asked.

"What's that?"

"It's some dodgy British sit-com that I always hated," said Tamara, relieved that they had moved on from talking about her. "But Mum and Bobby used to love it. Mrs Slocombe was one of the main characters."

"Mrs Slocombe was Head of the Ladies Department," explained Katherine, "and I'll have you know, Tamara, it was a very popular show. It ran for thirteen years so I doubt we were the only ones who liked it."

Katherine ushered everyone into the lounge and onto the comfy sofa and armchairs.

"Mr Humphries! Leave my pussy alone!" Bobby's quiet chuckle crescendoed until it became a full-bellied laugh, and Katherine doubled over alongside him.

"You two are way too tipsy for parents," Tamara scolded, as she eyed the empty bottles lined up beside the sink. "And very embarrassing. Jake was in the middle of telling us a story."

"Jake, I do apologise." Katherine wiped beneath her eyes, careful not to smudge her mascara. "Please go on. Tamara's right, it's the wine."

"No, please continue." He smiled before he looked at Tamara, the corners of his mouth full of mischief. Her insides sparked as he leaned in closer. "Are you sure it was a sit-com and not some kind of porn flick?" he asked.

More sniggers erupted from Bobby and Katherine until Tamara shot them a look.

Jake continued. "Mrs S – I'll shorten her name if it makes it any easier – called the surgery because her dog was having difficulty breathing. It was a stinking hot day, and when I got there the dog had come in from the garden and collapsed on the floor. He could barely move. Thankfully, I'd seen snake bite cases before and we had some antivenom back at the surgery."

"That was lucky," said Bobby. "A lot of city vets don't carry it."

"Why not?" asked Tamara.

"It's expensive," Jake explained, "and it has a short shelf-life. And, as you pointed out, snakes are less common in the city. Anyway, we got the dog to the surgery in time to administer the antivenom, and he was fine."

Tamara shuddered, suddenly even more wary of the great outdoors, and felt a sudden longing for the concrete safety of London.

"I've got no idea how the snake got there," Jake continued. "I do remember how hot it had been that summer, though, and generally snakes scarper if you go anywhere near them. The hot weather can bring them into gardens to look for water."

"I'd rather leave a bowl of water at the foot of the garden and tell the snake not to bother coming any closer," said Tamara, "unless it wanted its head chopped off."

"City chick," Jake quipped, sending her stomach on a familiar loop-the-loop.

The conversation turned to fascinating vet tales, and Bobby had a few, including one about the dog that couldn't keep its food down.

"We took an x-ray and removed a mass. Turned out it was a hot pink G-string that the dog had swallowed!" Bobby wiped his eyes and that belly laugh warmed the lounge room all over again.

"I don't believe you!" cried Tamara.

"Cross my heart. But the worst thing was that the owner was sixty-four." He could barely speak now, he was laughing so hard. "I'm not sure who was more embarrassed, me or her."

Tamara rolled her eyes at Jake. "The wine," she explained again.

Katherine pulled out the box of filter coffee and four mugs. "Does everyone want coffee?"

"Not for me, thanks," said Tamara.

Jake checked his watch as though he had suddenly realised how relaxed he had been for the last few hours. "I'd better get going," he said. "Thanks for a lovely evening."

After he'd said his goodbyes, Tamara showed Jake out of the house. For a while tonight she had let herself forget his faults. She had allowed herself to relax and absorb his company, which she couldn't deny had been faultless. But now with an evening that had fallen silent, she longed for him to stop and tell her everything – good or bad.

"Give my best to April and I hope she's better soon," she said, hovering on the front doorstep.

He gave her the briefest of smiles and, without letting his guard slip even slightly, he started up the pick-up and left.

She leaned against the brick wall beside the front door and pulled away the strands of hair blowing across her face in the breeze. No matter how charming Jake had been tonight, and how much this could hurt him, Tamara knew that she had no choice but to tell April what she knew; she had to tell her about that text.

Chapter Eleven

When she'd lived in the UK, Tamara had taken on all of Bradley's problems and allowed feelings of loyalty to interfere with her better judgement. She didn't want to make that mistake again. She chewed nervously on her bottom lip as she lifted her hand to ring the doorbell at April's place. Part of her felt as though she was betraying Jake, but the rest of her knew this was the right thing to do.

April finally emerged, firmly pulling the ties of her dressing gown. She looked oddly relieved when she peeked out the frosted glass to the side of the front door.

"Are you okay?" Tamara asked when April had finally unlatched a number of security locks and bolts. "You've got this place done up like Fort Knox. Were you expecting someone else?"

"Of course not, come on in," she said, then repeated the same security procedure.

"I'll need to go home tonight, you know," Tamara giggled.

April ignored the sarcasm. "I was trying to do some study, but the bloody lecture notes may as well be written in Swahili today." She indicated for Tamara to follow her into the kitchen.

"It must be hard to motivate yourself some days." Tamara sat at the table and nodded at the offer of a cup of tea.

"Some days it's easier than others. I gave up about five minutes before you arrived and was about to run myself a bath."

"Lots of bubbles and a glass of wine usually do the trick. Is Jake around?" Tamara had checked that the pick-up was already gone, but she wanted to be sure.

"No, he's gone to work."

Good. "I actually came to see you."

April poured the boiling water over the teabags, and brought two steaming mugs over to the pine table along with a teabag tray and a small, china black and white cow filled with milk.

"I like the cow stuff." Tamara smiled as April poured milk from the spout, which doubled as the cow's mouth.

"I'm a bit of a freak," April laughed, "but I used to collect it, once upon a time." She pulled off the top of the sugar jar, which was in the same black and white pattern.

April took a slurp of her tea. "Ouch, that's still hot." She added a little more milk and then opened a cow biscuit tin. "Don't say it. I'm sad, aren't I?"

"Not at all," said Tamara, admiring the next piece of the collection. She pulled out a Tim-Tam biscuit. "Only one of these for me. I seem to have developed a bit of a taste for them."

"It happens." April shrugged and took a bite of the milky chocolate biscuit. But before she could dunk it in her tea a second time, she clapped a hand to her mouth and shot out of the room, leaving Tamara wondering what on earth was going on.

When April finally returned, she looked ghastly. "Throwing up has never been my thing," she said. "Have you finished that tea already?" She nodded towards Tamara's empty cup.

"It's a Harding trait. We all have mouths made of asbestos and only drink our tea and coffee while it's scalding hot."

April dropped the rest of her biscuit into the bin.

"I thought Jake said that you had a bit of a cold," said Tamara. "I didn't realise it was a nasty stomach bug."

"I don't have a cold. I'm pregnant."

Tamara wondered how April had managed to miss the thud when her jaw smacked onto the ground.

"It was a surprise to me, too," April continued.

"How many, I mean how far—"

"I'm only eight weeks along. I'm due end of December." She rubbed her tummy protectively even though it was barely rounded on her slender figure.

"Well, congratulations. And Jake must be really pleased, too." Tamara wasn't sure how she had managed to put that sentence together given the reason she had come to see April in the first place. And now, any guilt about seeing that private text on his phone was replaced by concern for this girl; April deserved to know the truth.

"If you don't mind, Tamara, I'd like to hop in the bath now. I think it'll make me feel better."

Tamara didn't move. "I can't believe I have to tell you this. I really wish I didn't have to. I mean, I could be wrong, but–"

"Tell me what?"

"I mean, we barely know each other. It's just that if it were me, then I would want to know…"

"Tamara, get to the point."

Taking a deep breath, she blurted it all out. "When I was in the car with Jake the other day, after I'd spoken to you on his phone, a text came in and I read it." She looked at the floor. "It had kisses at the bottom and it didn't seem like a platonic text. It talked about someone called Marty and that he was out of their lives. I'm so sorry."

April held up a hand as though she were a traffic warden stopping the cars and trucks zooming out of Tamara's mouth that wanted to say more. "Thank you for telling me." She moved to the door and started to take off the security devices: bolts, top and bottom; a chain; the key-operated lock.

Tamara had intended to tell April about Jake flirting with her, too, but the revelation about the text was quite enough for now as she tried to decipher the look on April's face. It wasn't one of surprise or shock, but there was something there – a fear even. Perhaps he had done this sort of thing before; perhaps April already knew what he was like, and telling her about the flirting wasn't going to help. Hopefully, when April confronted him, it would well and truly bring his behaviour to an end. It had to, surely. He was going to be a father.

"If you want to talk about it," Tamara began, "or if you need anything…"

"Thanks, Tamara."

When April shut the door, Tamara listened to the same security routine as before, and she hoped that April wouldn't shut out the people who cared about her in the same way. The girl had friends in Brewer Creek, including herself; only a friend would go through the pain of telling someone that the father of her baby was a two-timing rat.

***

"Come on April, it's me. Let me in!" Jake thumped harder on the door and swore loudly when his key failed to gain him entry. Eventually he heard the security gradually diminish.

"About time, what the hell were you playing at? It's three o'clock in the afternoon, for goodness sake, and we live in the middle of nowhere."

April ignored him and went through the same ritual with the front door once he stepped inside.

His voice softened at the sight of her drawn-out complexion and the dark circles under her eyes. "Rough morning throwing up?" he asked, as she drew across the top bolt. "You do know it would be much easier for him to prise open a window," he joked, instantly regretting it.

"Have you spoken to Mum?"

"Not yet." He put his hat and keys on the side table in the hall. "She says he's gone, but I won't be happy until he's under lock and key."

"And that's exactly why I'm so paranoid, Jake. I know you think I'm being neurotic with all those locks and bolts, but you didn't see the look on his face when he shoved me down those stairs." Her bottom lip quivered as she blinked when the tears welled up and one of them dared to make its way down her cheek.

Jake slumped onto the ottoman in the lounge and looked at

his sister as she stared into the brown-shaded psychedelic swirls on the badly worn carpet. He stretched his hand out to meet hers and gave it a reassuring squeeze.

"I see his face all the time, Jake."

He joined her on the sofa and put his arm across her shoulders. "I know you do. But I won't ever let him hurt you again, you hear me?"

She didn't try to hold the tears in any longer as she pulled another tissue from the box. "I'm sorry, it's probably all these pregnancy hormones zipping around my body. I guess I could do with Mum around, that's all."

Jake moved to the floor and crouched in front of her. "Come on, pull yourself together, Sis, we're fine. You know Mum had to stay behind. If she'd come here, Marty would be all the more determined to find us."

April blew her nose and reached for another tissue. "I know you're angry that she ever stayed with Marty and put us in harm's way, but people make mistakes, Jake. And she's our mum."

"I know, and I'm not angry with her any more, I promise." He had been furious with his mum at first, for allowing that man into their lives. But when she sent them away and stayed behind to face Marty, he had been proud of her. Worried sick about her children, and knowing Marty so well, she hadn't argued with Jake's reasoning for keeping the police out of it for now.

"I want to be a family again, Jake. Like we used to be, before Dad died and Marty came along."

"Me, too," he said. He had that same impossible dream.

"I'm sick of the pretence, of lying to people around here."

In the kitchen he poured a large measure of Jack Daniels. The secrecy was doing his head in, too, but what April said next made his glass pause mid-air.

"Tamara was here before," she said.

He hesitated a moment and then downed the liquid in one.

"She saw a text on your phone, Jake, with kisses at the bottom. She thinks you're having an affair."

It dawned on him then why Tamara had leapt from the car so quickly that day after going over to the Morris's place. His hand scraped on the stubble of his chin. "Well, that's just great. She'll think I'm a complete bastard now, won't she?"

In the twenty-eight years since his father had died, Jake had never questioned his role once – until now. He was the man in the family, he looked out for his sister and his mum. But right now he wished that for a change he could get something *he* wanted.

He winked at his sister. "It'll all work out, you'll see." And then he headed off to the shower to erase the doubt that was permanently etched on his own mind.

Chapter Twelve

Tamara had an easy return to working life. She spent her first day at Carter Brown in Sydney dealing with systems security and familiarising herself with the company brochures, mission statement, and background on some of their existing clients. By the end of her first week she had started working on a campaign to launch a gym in the city centre; in many ways she felt as though she had never been away from the rat race.

Danielle's suggestion of the local pub that Friday night to celebrate the end of a successful first week at work won over the lure of end-of-week drinks at The Ivy with one of her colleagues. Already Tamara felt the bonds of friendship in Brewer Creek, and it was a nice feeling.

She boarded the train at Circular Quay, changed at Central, and bagged the seat next to the window for the journey home; the best seat to stare vacantly at nothing in particular. Her thoughts turned, yet again, to what must have gone on in the cottage when Jake had arrived home that day she had spoken to April. She tried to accept that April was having a baby; Jake's baby, which meant that the attraction between them had to stop. It should never have started in the first place.

Once she had changed into a navy silk shirt and a pair of dark skinny jeans that complemented her curves, Tamara walked the short distance to town. She was glad of the comfort of a soft, leather pair of ballet flats rather than the heels she had been wearing all day. When she pushed open the door of the pub, Danielle was already lying in wait. Tamara smiled at the sight of the same two elderly men on the sofa in front of the fire, as though they were part of the furniture. She ordered a Diet Coke and planted herself on the stool next to Danielle.

"Tough first week?" her friend asked.

Tamara sipped the fizzy black stuff through a straw. "I'm a bit out of practice, that's all. But it was nice to be back; there's only so much corporate buzz I can get out of being in charge of the friendship tree."

Danielle giggled. "You're doing a good job at that, though, and it'll be easy to change now that it's all on your computer. Did you get very far organising the mobile library?"

Daphne was calling her regularly with new ideas for Brewer Creek, and the latest was to start a mobile library with unwanted books donated by residents. It was a great idea, and even though Tamara had no idea whether it would work, she had produced an eye-catching flyer and distributed it to every property listed on the friendship tree.

"There'll be three collection days where people leave boxes of books next to their mailbox," said Tamara, "and I'll drive around and collect them."

"I'm happy to help, too. Dad won't mind if I borrow the car."

"Thanks, that'd be great. I'm hoping people have lots of books and get really into swapping them. It's the next best thing if there's no library for miles around. Some residents are too old to get out to the bigger towns or cities, and others are too busy."

"It'll be a bit of a laugh to see other people's book collections, won't it?" Danielle giggled. "I wonder how many dog-eared copies of *Fifty Shades of Grey* there'll be amongst the elderly residents."

Tamara sniggered. "That doesn't bear thinking about."

Hugo wiped along the rich, walnut-coloured bar and chuckled.

"Are you eavesdropping?" Tamara asked.

"Guilty," he said. "My mum has a load of books for you, Tamara, but sweet romance is more her style."

Tamara looked over at Hugo's mum, Sally, cuddling up to Len at the end of the bar.

"I hope I find that one day." Danielle watched them, too. "I want to find someone to have a laugh with; someone who makes my heart flutter."

"You've been reading too many Mills & Boon novels," said Tamara.

"Are you telling me that you don't believe you'll ever be able to have both?"

Tamara shrugged. With her track record she hardly believed anything about love any more. She was as confused as ever.

Danielle tore the corner from a packet of peanuts and offered them to Tamara. "Did you walk here again tonight?" she asked.

Tamara nodded. "I love to walk, but you need a few more street lamps around here."

"Take a torch; that's what I do."

"That's a great idea. I suppose I'm too much of a city chick." The words caught as she remembered Jake saying them the previous week at dinner.

"We should go one day," said Danielle. "To the city, I mean; make a day of it."

"I'd like that."

Before she could say anything else, Danielle raised an arm and waved. "Here come the others."

April was first to join them, while Jake went dutifully to the bar. She definitely looked tired, but how much of that was pregnancy related, and how much was two-timing-bastard related?

Tamara sipped the rest of her drink, hoping that by preoccupying herself she would obliterate the fact that Jake kept looking over at her as though he hadn't done anything wrong. She wanted to stop obsessing about him full stop. He was like a blob of chewing gum stuck to her shoe, and no matter how hard she pulled in every direction she couldn't get rid of him.

"So what's it like being back in the real world?" April sat down on the stool next to Tamara. "Was your first week back at work as exciting as you thought it'd be?"

"It's been really great, actually. I was worried about being out of it for three months but it's like I've never been away." Good, at least April seemed fine with her.

"Glad to hear it."

"How are you feeling?"

"Better." April smiled.

When Jake sat down, an uneasy silence arrived with him.

"How long is your job for, Tamara?" Danielle asked.

"Until early December."

"So then it'll be make-or-break time?" Jake probed.

"Something like that," said Tamara, without looking at him.

April excused herself and went off in the direction of the ladies.

"How's your work?" Tamara decided to give Jake a turn in the spotlight, and this time she looked at him. What was going on between him and April was nothing to do with her, and she didn't want to alienate him. This was a good circle of friends and she didn't want to lose that.

"It's good."

"Oh, come on," said Danielle, knocking back a generous swig of beer. "You need to share more than that – you're like the *Bondi Vet* around here! Oh, no offence to Bobby–"

"I don't think Bobby would be too disappointed to hear that the role of *Bondi Vet* goes to Jake." Tamara giggled.

The corners of his mouth formed a smile and she noticed the rough stubble of his chin poking out a little. "You girls don't know the half of it. It's not all about bright, blond specimens showing off their muscles."

"Come on then," Tamara teased. "Enlighten us. What does it involve really? Bobby seems to lead a pretty relaxed life." She was enjoying winding him up.

"Well, I was up at five this morning at Bernard Walker's place to help his golden retriever, Bella, deliver a litter of six puppies. Then it was straight over to Mr Kelly's farm where I had to confirm whether his mare was actually pregnant–"

"Hmm, you've put me off ordering any food now." Danielle screwed up her nose.

"You'll have to get used to a damn sight more than that if you're going to hack it as a nurse," said Jake. "You'll be vomited on, have to clear up faeces, sort out severed limbs–"

"Okay, okay, enough!"

"Are you sure you can hack it, Nurse Danielle?" he teased.

"Hang on," said Tamara, "what has Jake checking whether a horse is pregnant got to do with gruesome nursing tasks?" She had been distracted from the conversation by April and Hugo chatting at the end of the bar, not unlike two people who were very interested in each other. The only difference was that April looked as wary as a customer in one of those shops with signs that read: "Do not touch; all breakages must be paid for." Maybe it didn't work both ways in her relationship with Jake; perhaps he could do whatever he pleased and flirt with whomever he liked, but she had to toe the line.

"Okay, city chick," said Jake, bringing her back to the conversation. "To check whether a horse is pregnant, you have to–"

"Put on a glove," April sniggered, as she returned with another mineral water and joined in the conversation as though she had only been gone a few seconds.

"Thank you, April," he said. "So you put on the glove, and then…"

His actions showed the rest.

"Euwww…" Tamara put up her hand in an urge to make him stop. "You know, I don't think I could ever get used to sticking my hand up an animal's arse. Not for any money!"

"Enough of the dirty talk," said Jake, getting to his feet. "It's time to assert my male dominance again and ask if anyone is willing to have their butt whipped at darts. Hugo's working, so it looks like I'm stuck with you girls."

"I'll play." Tamara was anxious to take her frustration out on the dartboard to distract her from watching him tonight and thinking about what his motives could possibly be.

Danielle and April stayed at the bar to order some more snacks while Tamara followed Jake to the dartboard, squeezing past the small crowd surrounding the pinball machine. She tried to drag her eyes away from his bum, which rivalled any she had seen before.

Jake used the board rubber to erase the previous game's scores and Tamara pulled the darts from the board, claiming first turn. As she stood and lined up her first shot, she felt two hands settle around her hips. With them came a surge of adrenalin that made her heart thump almost loudly enough for Jake to hear.

"Just to make sure you're not cheating," he said, guiding her hips so that she moved back until her feet were positioned behind the very faint, faded, solid line on the floor.

"No need to cheat, my friend." She felt confident and, with the memory of his touch still setting her insides aflame and fuelling her anger that he was still flirting with her, Tamara threw three darts, one after the other, scoring a respectable forty-five.

"Not bad... for a girl."

When it was his turn, Tamara watched the determination on his face, the power in his arm as he threw a twenty, then a five. His third and final dart missed the scoreboard completely and landed outside the outer wire above the one.

"Twenty-five," Tamara remarked, "not a bad effort." She tried not to grin; it was obvious that Jake had surprised himself by scoring less than her.

"Who's winning?" April bagged the table beside the bar so that she had a clear view of the game.

"Me." Tamara tried not to be too complacent as she took aim. Bang, bang, bang: twenty, one, and one.

"I knew your first go was beginner's luck," said Jake. He winked at Tamara before he pummelled all three darts neatly into the board.

The game continued in much the same way, alternating who was winning. Tamara felt a flutter of excitement as they circled each other like two animals contemplating going in for the kill.

Towards the end of the game, Tamara stood behind the line

with the dart poised between her fingers.

"Good luck," Jake whispered. She felt his lips graze against the top of her earlobe and the dart left her fingers, shot through the air, and promptly rebounded off the black faced circle and onto the floor. She turned to glare at him before she took her other two shots.

When it was his turn, Tamara waited until the third dart and when he lifted his arm she stood on tiptoe, leaned in, and returned the favour. "Bullseye," she breathed into his ear.

The strength of his throw and the focus of his eyes prevented him from missing the board altogether, but he got a measly score of fifty-five.

"Nice tactics." He nodded approvingly, his pupils dilating as he held her stare.

She stood behind the line and prayed for a miracle.

"Bullseye!" she thrust her balled-up fists into the air as her dart stuck firmly in the centre of the board. "Did you see that, girls? I think that's the first time I've ever scored one!"

"Good shot," said Jake, while the girls whooped and cheered in female solidarity. "But you haven't won yet; still got a hundred and thirty-nine on the board. Think you can do it?"

"Maybe," she said, "but no psyching me out this time. Play fair."

"Where's the fun in that?"

God, why was flirting so addictive?

She felt him walk around the back of her, and waited until he wasn't near enough to try anything before she aimed her final two darts of the round.

"Come on, Tamara!" Danielle hollered from the sidelines.

Her total was down to ninety-nine, but it wasn't meant to be. Jake stood up and it wasn't long before he took the final victory.

"Nice try with the distraction," said Jake, as they took a seat at a small, round table. "I could've completely thrashed you if you hadn't put me off."

"I don't know what you mean." Tamara tried to switch on the

platonic side of her brain.

April pulled on a chunky navy cardigan, which hung on her slender frame as though she were a child trying on a grown-up's clothes. "I'm not feeling too great," she explained. "Would you mind taking me home, Jake?"

"I'm ready to go." Tamara waved to Danielle, who in return made a gesture asking her to stay. She shook her head. "Another time," she called over.

"I'll drop April home first," said Jake, as they climbed into the pick-up. It made sense as their place was closest, and April looked like she wasn't far away from either vomiting or keeling over. But it meant that Tamara would be alone with Jake in a confined space, and she wasn't sure that that was such a good idea.

When they pulled up at the house, he waited for a few minutes, presumably for April to do her locking-up ritual. Tamara watched the lights in the house flick on before the gravel crunched beneath the tyres and they were on their way again.

Jake flicked his headlights to full-beam as the properties became more spread-out with acres separating them. Tamara gazed up at the moon hanging in the sky like a gigantic white bauble against a rich, inky backdrop.

"Danielle seems to be coming out of her shell a bit more these days," said Jake, obviously as awkward as Tamara was right now with no dartboard or drink to hide behind. "She's pretty excited about her change of career."

Tamara nodded. "She'll make a good nurse."

Jake adjusted the radio from the monotone of a late night newsreader to some mellow music. Tamara opened the window and let the breeze whirl her hair around her face, hoping that it would clear her head of the constant confusion she felt around this man. She had flirted shamelessly tonight, as much as she had flirted with Bradley when they first met, and she felt incredibly guilty.

They pulled slowly into the driveway of the Harding property. "Thanks," she said, and swung her legs from the pick-up.

When Jake's hand wrapped around her arm, she froze. "Wait, please, Tamara. I need to talk to you. I–"

"No need." A couple of days ago she would've melted at those words, but with all the lies that surrounded Jake, she knew that she had to keep her distance. They were friends and would never be anything else.

"I'll see you soon," she said with a smile.

***

Jake's hand smashed down on the steering wheel as he drove back to his place and swore loudly enough for the sheep in the surrounding fields to hear his every word. He hated knowing what Tamara thought of him; he hated that he was helpless to do anything about it.

When he arrived home, April was already asleep and he watched her, glad that fear hadn't kept his sister awake tonight. Out in the kitchen he poured himself a glass of fruit juice and took it out to the veranda at the back of the house. He looked up at the moon and the stars winking back at him, unsure how much more he could take of this whole mess. It had taken all his inner strength not to wrap his arms around Tamara tonight and shower her with the truth. He wanted to breathe in her silky-smooth hair, touch his lips to her skin that he knew would be velvet to the touch. He wanted to shout from the rooftops that he wasn't the person she thought he was. But what would happen when he did? Would she forgive him for keeping the truth from her for so long?

Chapter Thirteen

Vivid dreams about Jake prevented the deep sleep that Tamara needed that night. At times she had felt as though he was right there beside her, but as she sat on the edge of her bed looking out at the morning sun lifting Brewer Creek out of its misty haze, she knew that it was just that, a dream.

She pulled on a pair of grey tracksuit pants and her favourite sparkly silver slipper socks before flicking on the kettle in the kitchenette of the annexe. She usually made her morning cuppa in the main kitchen of the house, but this morning she needed to be alone with her thoughts.

She tucked herself back beneath the duvet to drink the cup of steaming coffee, and watched the silver clock on the wall, its rhythmic second hand ticking its way round the circle until it reached the top again. Almost halfway through her coffee, she grabbed the laptop from the floor beside her bed and pulled it onto her lap. She still had an hour to go before she had to be at Bobby's surgery – as brilliant as he was at looking after animals, his abilities weren't so great when it came to paperwork – and she double clicked on the icon to open up the internet. She clicked on Facebook, one hand clasping the coffee mug and the other scrolling down the News Feed. She smiled at a photograph of a former school friend on the London Eye; she read Beth's updates saying that she had too much work and how it interfered with her social life.

But it was the next post that made her hand shoot across her mouth to stifle her gasp. She didn't even notice that her coffee had ended up all over the bedclothes.

Bradley Cox's name was there, on the screen, on her News Feed. Her entire body froze as she tried to take in the words on his status update: *Down Under.*

Heat rose through her chest and shivers of shock cascaded down her body. It was then that she noticed the brown liquid seeping further and further into the bedding. She pulled some tissues from the box beside the bed and did her best to mop up the excess liquid before it did any more damage. She balled up the soiled linen ready for the laundry, all the while her heart pumping, trying to grasp what was happening.

Down Under could only mean one thing, couldn't it?

She dragged the laptop back onto her knees and scrolled down Bradley's profile details and through several photos: The first had to be at a work function, as she could see two of his colleagues messing about in the background; the second was a picture of him skydiving with one of his mates last year; and the third was the most disturbing of all, because it felt oddly familiar. The scene depicted a cafe, and even though there were bound to be thousands just like it littering the country, Tamara was sure she recognised it.

Out in the laundry she poured blue liquid over the linen in the washing machine and listened as the water whooshed into action when she pressed the start button. Back in the annexe she pored over every pixel of that picture, trying to dissect it. It wasn't one of the classic backdrops of Sydney: the Opera House or Circular Quay. But deep down she was sure that she had seen that exact same set of tables and chairs; that exact café frontage.

When Tamara finally stepped outside, she met ominous dark grey masses looming above, determined not to let the sun win the fight to dominate the sky. A rainbow looped over the barns at the far end of the paddock as she collected her gumboots from inside the back door and grabbed the freshly baked teacake to take to Mr Wilson on her way to the surgery.

The shock of the photograph had caused Tamara to skip

breakfast, and her stomach didn't like it one bit. The smell of her mum's baking seeped through the sides of the plastic box, taunting her as she drove along, her mind elsewhere. Usually she smiled at the sight of orchards draped in colourful fruit, lifting a hand in greeting as she passed neighbours or residents out for a daily walk. But not today.

She indicated right into Reed Lane and towards Mr Wilson's place. What was Bradley even doing in Australia? He'd never shown any desire to come here over the years she had known him. What was he playing at? And if he was still here, in Sydney, then why hadn't he tried to get in touch? The name Brewer Creek had probably gone in one ear and out the other with him, but she was surprised he hadn't messaged her again.

Befriending Bradley on Facebook had been the right thing to do. At least now she had a big fat warning that he may not have given up on her just yet.

Tamara dropped the teacake at Mr Wilson's but didn't stop for a chat, using the excuse that she had to help Bobby out. At the surgery, with Bobby out on a call, she tackled the box marked "for shredding". There was a certain satisfaction listening to paper being sliced thinly and passed out the other side; she wished that it was that easy to obliterate her love life.

***

At home that evening, it was Tamara's turn to cook the family meal. She stirred the prawn paella and guarded the pan to stop Bobby sampling it before it was ready. When the toasted crust formed sufficiently on the base, she transferred it to the three bowls.

Bobby rubbed his hands together as they sat at the table. "This looks amazing, Tamara."

"I'm pulling my weight, that's all. While I'm staying here I don't expect to be cooked for, cleaned up after, or anything else."

"I can't help mothering you," said Katherine, pouring water

into the three awaiting glasses. "Sometimes I forget that you're all grown up."

"And I'm grateful, but don't make me too comfortable," Tamara warned. "I opened up the concertina doors in the annexe this morning and I know it'll be glorious when you put the pool in. You may never get rid of me!"

"You'd better get digging that hole then, Bobby," Katherine teased.

"Mr Wilson said to pass on his thanks for the teacake," said Tamara, loading her next forkful. "Did you know his name is Joseph?"

"You know, I think I did know that," said Bobby, "but everyone always calls him Mr Wilson. It's been that way ever since we moved here."

"I wouldn't even have known that was his name if I hadn't seen it on a letter when I grabbed his post from his mailbox."

"I suppose when you get used to calling people by a name, it sticks," said Katherine. "Look at how you like to call Bobby, *Bobby.*"

"Does it bother you?" Tamara asked him.

"Not at all. You called me Dad for years, remember?"

"It didn't make you feel redundant when I stopped?"

"Not at all, love."

Tamara watched him tucking into the paella with all the enthusiasm of the same man she had known and loved for years. She had called him Dad right up until she was thirteen and battling puberty and braces simultaneously. But as she got older, Tamara wanted to appreciate both Bobby and the dad who had left her through no fault of his own. Bobby hadn't been offended; he'd told her that he was simply proud to be a part of her life.

Tamara had no real memories of the father who had been in her life so briefly. He'd been killed in a car crash when she was only four, and now her photographs were treasured reminders of what her dad had looked like on the outside, with skin many shades darker than hers. It still pained her that she would never know the sound of his voice or the feel of his arms around her, but she couldn't have asked for a better stepfather than Bobby.

Tamara looked at him now. "I want you to know that just because I call you *Bobby*, that doesn't mean that I think any less of you." She stretched a hand across the table and covered his.

Affected by her sudden openness, Bobby sniffed. "How much paprika did you put in this?"

She laughed, flicked a tissue from the box at the edge of the table, and passed it to him.

"You're a big softie," said Katherine, before she looked at Tamara. "Promise me you'll keep calling me Mum. It was bad enough when you stopped calling me Mummy; it felt like you had grown up too fast."

Bobby shook his head. "Watch out. *She'll* start crying in a minute."

Tamara recorded the touching family moment in the album of her mind, and after a while she said, "I worry about Mr Wilson, all on his own."

"Come on now, Tamara." Katherine placed her fork in her empty bowl. "He's been on his own for a long time, many people are. Residents keep an eye on him; we're like that around here. And when I bumped into Jake earlier, he said that he's going round to fix up the back fence for him later this evening."

At the mention of Jake's name, Tamara's stomach flipped over like one of those pancakes she had tossed as a young girl. Her ringing phone rescued her.

Katherine piled her plate on top of Tamara's. "You cooked, we'll clean up." She shooed her daughter out of the kitchen to answer the call.

Tamara often used the phone while lying on the sofa in the lounge, sprawled out on the rug in the den or moving around the kitchen making a snack, but this time she went into the annexe and closed the door.

"So what's news?" Beth was already at work and making her call before her first meeting of the day.

"Well, I do have some. Are you ready for this?"

"Ooh, does this mean you're getting some action from the Aussie men? So how's Jake… should I be calling him McDreamy or McSteamy?"

With *Grey's Anatomy* a firm favourite for both girls, either description would probably do. But Tamara had to focus.

"What about Russell Crowe?" Beth went on. "Have you bumped into him yet, or any lookalikes?"

"I think Bradley is in Australia. Well, I don't *think*, I *know* he is."

Silence from the other end.

"Hello, are you still there?"

"That was the last thing I expected you to say." The sounds of multitasking had vanished. "What the hell is he playing at?" Beth hissed. "Has he tried to get in contact? Does he want to meet up with you?"

Tamara told Beth all about the status update and the photograph. "The funny thing is, since I accepted his friend request, he hasn't tried anything, which is completely unlike him. Maybe I'm being paranoid. I mean, being in Australia doesn't mean he's here for me, does it?"

"Yes!"

Tamara took the phone away from her ear. "Ouch, that hurt."

"Sorry, didn't mean to yell. But Tamara, why would he go to Australia for any other reason than you? He's barely left the comfort of his flat in over two years, unless it's to come to your place for sex, to go to work, or make it to the pub."

"Don't be so dramatic. I doubt he'll come anywhere near here, I'm two hours away from the city."

"Does he know where your mum lives?"

Tamara involuntarily shivered. "I probably mentioned Brewer Creek over the course of two years, yes. But I'd say it's pretty unlikely that he would've remembered, don't you?"

"Don't bank on it. Just watch your back. And if he turns up, make sure you send him packing."

"I will, don't you worry."

Beth finished the phone call with the suggestion that if Bradley should find the Sydney Harbour Bridge, he ought to take a big leap off of it. To Beth the situation was black and white and simple to fix, but to Tamara it was anything but.

Chapter Fourteen

Jake parked outside Brewer Creek station, but the puppy he was looking after temporarily wasn't yet at the stage where she knew that she had to obey *every* command, not only the commands that she chose. She had already taken off towards the archway to greet passengers from the train.

Tamara was one of the first to emerge and Jake watched her for a moment. He hadn't seen her for a couple of weeks but it definitely hadn't been a case of "out of sight out of mind". When Waffles reached her and jumped up at her legs, he made his way over, too. "Watch it or she'll ruin your stockings," he said.

Tamara crouched down so that she could make a real fuss of the puppy. "And what's your name?"

"This is Waffles," said Jake, realising that he was jealous of a dog nuzzling at her wrists and getting all her best attention. His eyes couldn't help but follow her legs all the way up from her ankles as he realised that she wasn't wearing any stockings. She didn't need to; she had great legs.

"What brings you here?" she asked. It looked as though Waffles was as enamoured with her as Jake was himself.

"Bobby asked if I could swing by and pick you up. Your mum knocked off early and he had an emergency call out at the Nielsen's farm." He scraped Waffles up into his arms to make the transition to his pick-up easier.

"I thought you'd nabbed Mr Nielsen as your client?" Tamara followed him over to the pick-up.

With Waffles safely tucked in the back of the truck, Jake tried to ignore the effect of Tamara's perfume when she climbed in next to him. Unlike smelling salts, the perfume didn't make him more alert; it made him giddy and tongue-tied.

"Mr Nielsen requested Bobby, and it's more than fine by me."

He apologised when his hand briefly brushed Tamara's bare knee as he pushed the truck into drive from reverse. He wished he had some control over how his body kept responding when she was anywhere near him, but he was helpless. He hooked an arm around the back of Tamara's headrest and reversed out of the parking space.

"How's April?" Tamara asked.

"She's fine. She had a check-up and everything seems to be going as it should be. The morning sickness seems to be easing off, too."

"Do you know if you're having a boy or a girl?"

God, he hated lying.

"I've got no idea."

"Didn't you ask?"

The corners of his mouth turned into a grin. "I'd love to know but April didn't want to find out." He was only the uncle but Jake was surprised at how excited he was with that role. He wondered how much that would be magnified when, one day, he had kids of his own.

All too soon they were at the Harding property.

"Are you coming to the pub tonight for the darts competition?" he asked.

"I can't. Danielle and April are coming over for a movie night; strictly chick flicks, I'm afraid."

"Ah well, all the more practice for me so that I can beat you again soon." He watched her swing her legs out of the pick-up, but not before she leaned closer to him as she made a fuss over Waffles. Jake's body responded in its usual way, and he drove home wondering how much longer he could keep up this pretence.

"I've got *How to Lose a Guy in Ten Days*, *The Holiday*, and *Bridesmaids*." Danielle shrugged off her cardigan and slung it onto the bed in Tamara's annexe. She upended her shoulder bag on the small, round table and out tumbled the DVDs, a block of Cadburys, and an enormous bag of Doritos. "They're all great films and every single one includes a leading man to die for," she grinned mischievously.

Tamara pulled out a jar of salsa from the food cupboard. "Great minds think alike," she grinned, revealing another packet of Doritos that would do for later if they ran out. She emptied the crisps into a large ceramic bowl, then twisted open the salsa jar with a satisfying pop. She set them both on the low-lying coffee table in front of the couch opposite the small plasma TV that Bobby insisted she have for her stay. She suspected he had an ulterior motive: when the annexe was free once again, he could use it as a sanctuary and watch as many veterinary programs as he liked.

"Wow, what's in that?" Danielle asked when Tamara pulled out a jug of fruit punch from the fridge.

Tamara cast her mind back to when she had concocted the recipe half an hour ago. "It's banana, apples, pears… oh, and a bit of orange, some mango juice, then sliced lemons and strawberries on top and a bit of sugar." She pulled out two coupé champagne glasses. "I thought we'd have the fancy glasses."

"They're awesome. I've only ever seen them in old movies."

"They're sophisticated, aren't they? I feel like I'm back in the 1950s with Marilyn Monroe when I drink out of them."

Danielle relaxed into the leather recliner. "Ah, this is the life."

"I'd get used to it if I were you. Wait till you're a fully-fledged nurse in the city, going to all those big parties with hot doctors and gorgeous surgeons. It'll be *Dom Perignon* in these glasses rather than naff fruit punch."

"Hey, there's nothing naff about this. But the champagne

sounds good," giggled Danielle.

Tamara sifted through the choice of DVDs. "You know what? We should have a girls' weekend in Sydney before you get underway with the study."

"That sounds awesome, when?"

"Well, I'd say as soon as we can arrange it. We could get onto that website that has late deals for hotels and get ourselves a bargain."

Danielle snapped off a row of chocolate squares and offered some to Tamara. "Let's ask April, too. The poor girl looks done in; more so than my sister ever did when she was pregnant."

"It's a shame she couldn't make tonight, it'd do her good to relax for a while." Tamara pulled out a DVD. "What about *How to Lose a Guy in Ten Days*?" She slotted the disc into the DVD player when Danielle nodded.

"He's gorgeous," Danielle swooned when Matthew McConaughey came into view. "I've never had a serious boyfriend, you know."

Unable to hide her surprise, Tamara asked, "Really?"

"You can't be that shocked when you've seen the lack of choice in town. Brewer Creek is no London."

"It's different, I'll give you that."

"Brewer Creek has been my home all my life, and it's not that I hate it and want to escape, but I've always wanted to do nursing and I can't wait to get out there and see different places, try a different life. I want to see the bigger picture."

"You're doing the right thing, Danielle. Nobody would say that the city is better; it's all about personal choice. But how can you know you're making the right choice when you've only seen one side of it? And besides," Tamara continued after sipping her punch, "there's nothing to stop you coming back here at a later date. Nursing is a great career for that; you'll never be tied to one particular place."

Tamara felt satisfied at the new direction Danielle was heading in, but as she turned to watch the movie she wondered exactly what direction her own life was about to take.

***

When Monday morning came around, Tamara felt sure that if Bradley had wanted to find her he would have done so by now. He was probably well away from Sydney, and certainly nowhere near Brewer Creek.

"Good morning, Tamara. You missed a great night on Friday." Sadie, one of the younger members of the office crew with all the enthusiasm of a graduate public relations assistant, breezed past on her way to a meeting.

"Maybe next time," Tamara called after her. She trawled through her emails, wondering how there could be so many when it was before nine o'clock on the first day of a new week.

"I need you this morning." Tate passed by Tamara's desk with the essential corporate fashion accessory of the moment – a takeaway coffee – as though what was contained in that flimsy cup with the plastic lid would unleash special powers to make you work like a demon and impress those around you.

"We need to go back to Simpkins in Lane Cove as soon as possible," he continued, sipping from his little cup of power. "We need to show them the mock-ups for the regional magazines we'll be targeting."

Maybe getting out and about today was a good thing. It would stop her from brooding about Bradley and obsessing about where he was, or whether he was going to pop up around any corner when she least expected it. Her past was in the UK, and when she grabbed her bag to go with Tate, she decided that was where it was going to stay.

At the offices in Lane Cove Tamara guided Simpkins through the text of the article which was to appear in half a dozen regional newspapers to advertise the expansion of the health club. She tantalised them with ideas for the future and the international scope that they could achieve.

127

"You did great in there!" Tate followed her out of the building, and they simultaneously pulled their sunglasses down from the tops of their heads before they made their way towards the shopping strip in search of some lunch.

Tamara was relieved. She felt under enormous pressure being on a contract, but giving this client her all had paid off.

They chose a café with tables and chairs spilling out onto the pavement.

"The best part is that this all goes on expenses," said Tate, flashing a card at her once they had decided what they wanted to eat.

As Tate recited their order over at the bar, Tamara took a deep breath and relaxed. It was great to be back in the corporate world in so many ways, but she was glad that this was a relatively short contract. She wasn't sure she would be quite so content if this was a permanent position. Something had changed in her since she had arrived in Brewer Creek, as though its laid-back, non-city-like attitude had rubbed off on her and this move was now about more than just her love life.

Tamara watched two young girls take their places on the bandstand which sat in the walkway framed with shops on either side. She watched them dance as freely as the sequins sparkling madly on their dresses, and giggled as they chased a lorikeet. The bird flapped its bright green wings away from danger and over to the much safer old lady who was sitting on a bench distributing the remains of a coffee scroll.

"You okay there?" Tate must have seen her face plummet in a matter of seconds.

Tamara's insides began to curdle and all she could manage was a nod, because here she was, laughing away in the sunshine, sitting in the exact same spot where that photograph had been taken. Bradley was in Australia and had been far too close for comfort.

Her insides felt the same as they had five years ago, sitting at the top of The Big Drop in Dreamworld on the Gold Coast, as she had plummeted down the tallest, vertical free-fall ride in the world. Her heart had been in her mouth then, just as it was now.

The only question that remained was whether Bradley would dare to show his face – and, more importantly, when?

Chapter Fifteen

Tamara and Bradley had met two years before, at a work function, where they bonded over their mutual hatred for fancy dress. A new client of Tamara's had been in the process of opening a chain of Mexican restaurants, starting in London, and in the spirit of the launch – or rather, in the spirit of showing her employer, Wellington Smart, that she could make anything possible – Tamara had chosen the best from a bad choice of costumes.

Dressed in her tequila outfit, she leaned against the bar drinking a mocktail, satisfied that the party was a success.

"You can't drink that, Tequila girl." A voice came from behind. "Not while you're wearing that."

"I can do whatever I like," she said, deliberately defying this cliché tall, dark and handsome stranger. "I've mingled, I've organised giveaways and the entertainment for tonight." She indicated the sombrero-clad singer beside the far wall, strumming away on a guitar and prattling on in fake Mexican.

She watched this man take in the sight of her tight black dress teamed with an apple green, shiny Tequila apron, and the glittery gold top hat that perched on top of her head. She saw his eyes linger a moment too long on her black, patent heels before they slowly took in every inch of her.

"So what are you dressed as?" she asked, scrutinising his outfit. He wore tight black trousers that hid nothing of his taut physique, and a black polo neck which hugged muscular biceps and a defined chest.

He shrugged and pulled down some seriously dark shades. "I

would say *Men in Black*, but seeing as there's only one of me, I suppose you'd better make that *Man* in Black."

"Ah, easy," she said, wishing she could've got away with something like that.

"I hate fancy dress," he said. "I did my best to find something and was offered an enticing hot-dog outfit that looked as though it had ear wax smoothed down the front to create the effect of mustard. Oh, and I was offered a smelly sombrero costume that required the wearing of a mangy, itchy moustache."

She laughed as she sucked the remains of her cocktail through the straw and fidgeted under his gaze.

"You've got really striking eyes," he said, locking them with his own.

She moved to turn away but his arm stopped her.

"Sorry, that sounded like a cheesy chat-up line. But you have. They're exotic next to your skin, and kind of cat-like."

Was he for real?

"Come on. Give a guy a break."

Something in his voice made her stop. His confidence was borderline arrogance but there was something about him that made her yearn to know more. And besides, he was the best looking and most interesting person she had met the entire night.

"So tell me." She faced him again, grinning. "Do you have a cat, with my eyes?"

He swigged his beer and leant against the bar. "You're playing with me now." Something in his voice tugged at her belly. "I did have a cat, years ago, when I was little."

She lifted her glass towards her lips to stop him gazing at her mouth.

"My arsehole of a father had her put down rather than pay the hundred and fifty quid to treat her cancer."

Clearly it wasn't a joke, and this suave, sexy man with kind toffee-coloured eyes had a certain vulnerability that made him all the more appealing to Tamara, as though the complex layers of his personality gave him an air of mystery which at once she wanted

131

to solve.

The coolness of the mocktail slipping down to her tummy took away the heat of the hustle and bustle inside the restaurant as the owners and promotion staff began to party hard.

"I'm Bradley, by the way." He held out his hand.

Hmm, nice firm handshake, unlike the wet fish she had met on the other side of the bar earlier.

"Tamara," she said, and returned his smile as he waved the barman over and whispered something in his ear.

She watched as four or five people did what looked like the conga in the distance. She was pretty sure that wasn't even loosely related to anything Mexican.

Bradley grinned as the barman returned. "Here you go." His chiselled, smoothly shaven jawline spelled danger as he passed a shot glass Tamara's way, along with a board which he placed on the bar between them. On top sat a small pile of salt and a collection of chunky green lime wedges. "That is unless you're driving?" he asked.

She shook her head as Bradley, not wasting any time, licked the salt, downed his shot, and grabbed a wedge of lime to suck on. "Your turn," he said.

Tamara gulped at the prospect of doing the same now: licking, drinking and sucking, all in front of this man she had just met. She went through the motions of the tequila slammer, grimacing as she sucked on the lime wedge whilst her insides felt alight from the liquid.

Bradley's head tipped back as he laughed, showing a to-be-expected, dentist-cared-for set of pearly straight whites. "Would you like another one?"

She nodded. Why not? She had circulated enough; time to let her hair down. "Are you trying to get me drunk?"

His smooth voice fell over her like velvet as he stood closer and said, "Not at all." He waved the barman over and she surreptitiously watched him pay for the drinks; he was by far the sexiest man she had ever laid eyes on.

"So how are you involved with this launch?" She pulled a face as she finished her second tequila shot.

"I'm a journalist. I've got to write a story about the opening. I'm a bit of an all-rounder really, but I'd like to get into sport; I didn't really want this gig." He regarded the crowds in the restaurant and the Mexican music coming from the relentless band. "No offence intended. It's turning out to be a great party since I've met you."

The word "likewise" was on the tip of her tongue, but Tamara just smiled and broke Bradley's stare by looking round into the crowd. They talked for a while about work, and Tamara loved the passion Bradley had for sports journalism. But most of all he made her laugh in a way that took her by surprise. On the one hand he had this air of mystery, and then all of a sudden his sarcasm and wit would take centre stage.

"What do you think of the three amigos over there?" Bradley gestured to three men behind Tamara.

She gulped as she felt his body up so close that it was almost touching her, and tried to focus on the three men. They exchanged jokey remarks about the first man's cummerbund, which looked so tight that it would double as a form of gastric band surgery; Tamara dabbed at her eyes when Bradley pointed out the second man, who was sweating profusely beneath the itchy-looking moustache stuck over his top lip the wrong way up; and they giggled as all three men nearly took the other guests' eyes out when they underestimated the circumference of those hats.

Discreetly wiping beneath her eyes for telltale signs of mascara mixed with tears of laughter, Tamara turned round. But the second she did, she drew a sharp intake of breath as Bradley's body closed in on hers.

"So…" He sat on the tall bar stool and, with his hands on her waist, he pulled her into him.

She felt giddy, as though her legs wouldn't be able to hold her for much longer, and she froze beneath his touch. She could feel his breath on her face, light and tempting, and then his hands were across the back of her neck, sending a shiver all the way down her spine.

"Do you want to come back to my place for a coffee?" he whispered, his breath against her ear.

She swallowed hard as her body fizzed at the suggestion, knowing that he was unlikely to be her barista for the evening.

Right from the start the heat between Tamara and Bradley had been like their own fiery Mexican chilli pepper. Their romp back at his place that first night had signalled the start of a serious relationship which was unfamiliar territory to both of them. Bradley was tender, yet passionate and sexy all rolled into one remarkable parcel. And as the weeks went by, they shared their time between her flat and his, barely sleeping each night, the passion overcoming any tiredness as they explored one another's bodies.

They laughed for hours on end, giggling at private jokes; daft things mostly, like his insistence that he would get rid of the Christmas tree from her flat because she would make a mess of it. He had ended up pulling it through the door top first rather than root first, and the branches had given a hefty ping in protest and scattered pine needles across the entire lounge. Tamara's sarcasm at the "job well done" had made them roll around on the floor in stitches – Tamara inside, and Bradley lying in the hallway with neighbours passing by looking at them like they had lost their marbles.

To the whole world Tamara and Bradley looked like a couple who were unequivocally in love. She felt invincible, permanently surfing the crest of a wave when it came to Bradley Cox, and she couldn't believe her luck.

***

"Can you make the pub tonight?" Tamara asked Bradley one morning as she pushed her hairdryer into her overnight bag. "I'm meeting Beth after work, so you can come and say hello. I think she wants to get to know this guy who is taking up all my time," she teased.

Bradley held his skin taut and pulled a razor across his chin. He swished the metal blade in the sink before emptying it, and waited for the water to gurgle down the plughole before he gave her a peck on the cheek. "That sounds good," he said.

Tamara wrapped her arms around his bare waist, his towel covering the bottom half of his body. "Thanks, it would mean a lot to me."

When he kissed her his face held a lingering hint of shaving foam freshness.

"Anything for you," he said.

Tamara pulled away from the cuddle and the hardness beneath his bath towel. "I don't have time," she giggled, pulling on her jacket. She smiled at the tulips in the tall, glass vase by the door: yellow, pink and white – "just because" he had said.

***

"Has he texted you?" Beth asked Tamara, as they made their way to the tube station when Bradley failed to show up at the pub.

Tamara shook her head. "I hope he's okay." She tried to ignore the look that Beth gave her. She had tried to get Bradley and Beth to meet on several occasions, but somehow he had always come up with a plausible excuse.

The sound of a tin can being kicked across the street made both girls jump.

"Hey, it's my little tequila!" a voice slurred.

Tamara's heart leapt at the voice she had wanted to hear all night. Still in his pinstripe suit but with his shirt buttons undone and his tie hanging loose, Bradley stumbled backwards but caught himself on a railing before he could tumble down the steps leading to the Underground. "That was close," he laughed. "Hey, how's my little tequila?"

Tamara rarely saw Bradley with any mates. When they were

happily ensconced in their own little world, everything was perfect, but now she was seeing a side to him that she hadn't realised existed before. Reeking of alcohol, he draped his arm possessively across Tamara's shoulders.

"Nice to meet you, Bradley," said Beth. Tamara silently thanked her friend for making an effort.

"Hey, boys!" Bradley gestured over to his mates, ignoring Beth.

One of them was zipping up his fly after urinating against a shop window, and Tamara turned away in disgust. She began to feel Bradley's weight as he leaned on her more.

"Boys, I'm going to be busy, if you know what I mean," Bradley slurred. "I'll catch you tomorrow."

"I'm going back to Beth's tonight, for a sleepover." Tamara said quickly. It wasn't that he was drunk tonight; it was the way his mouth wasn't creased in its usual smile but rather a sneer. His eyes had an emptiness that she hoped she could blame on the alcohol.

"What the fuck? What are you, like six-years-old?" He shoved her away.

"Bradley!" she cried in disbelief.

"Oh go then, go! I'll see you another time; when you're not having a 'sleepover'." He attempted air quotes but couldn't coordinate his fingers.

"Leave it, Tamara." Beth pulled her back before she could follow him to reason with him. "Arsehole," she said, loud enough for him to hear.

He sauntered off in the distance with his friends. They sounded like drunken hooligans and he was far from the tender man who always dressed immaculately, never so much as a chest hair out of place. The man Tamara could see swaying and kicking an empty can of Coke to his mates wasn't the same Bradley who had bought her flowers and cooked dinners for her, or the Bradley who brought her breakfast in bed on a Sunday morning. It certainly wasn't the same man who made her giggle helplessly if she was feeling down.

The first in a long line of apologies, which spanned the next two years, arrived on her doorstep the following day in the form of a dozen, long-stemmed red roses.

"I'm so sorry, Tamara." Bradley delivered them in person.

"You'd better come in."

He followed her into the kitchen, put down the box of roses, and pulled her into his arms before kissing her hard and whispering his regrets into her hair.

"Why were you like that last night?" she asked.

"It was the drink talking."

"I don't think so. We've been drinking together enough times for me to know that it's more than that."

He fiddled with his watch. "There's things about me that you don't know, Tamara; things that I haven't shared with anyone."

Gradually the Bradley she knew with the kind eyes and the soft voice dropped his façade and shared his past with her; shared the story of his father's temper.

"I get so angry sometimes," he said, letting Tamara hug him close. "It's crazy to think that Mum stayed with him, but he didn't do it all the time. There would sometimes be months and months between his outbursts and in that time they rarely even fought, except for the trivial bickering about whose turn it would be to put the rubbish out, or who'd used up the last of the milk and didn't think to get more."

From that moment on, Tamara vowed to be there for Bradley, to help him. But the verbal abuse continued and in between every torrent and every accusation, he weaved a plethora of romantic gestures: thoughtful and touching actions designed to melt her heart. Somehow, every time, he knew what to say and do. He spoiled her, treating her to posh dinners in London, surprise weekends away. They had an unforgettable holiday to Florida where they spent ten nights taking in sun-drenched vistas, relaxing in Tiki bars, and tucked away in their very own romantic cocoon. It was there on the beach on their very last day, with the water glistening from head to toe as the droplets ran from his body like sparkling jewels, Bradley had taken her in his arms and she'd thought she would be with him for ever.

***

The catalyst in Tamara's decision to finally leave Bradley had come on a spring evening which had otherwise been perfect. They had left hand-in-hand to walk to Tamara's flat, where she promised she had a good supply of ice cream and a selection of toppings. As they walked, she dropped his hand and instead snuggled neatly into his chest, smiling at his warmth and familiar woody aftershave.

When they passed a man of a similar age, Bradley pulled away. "What's he looking at?" Bradley snapped so loudly that Tamara could've sworn she saw the curtains of an end-of-terrace twitch in curiosity.

"Bradley," she hissed. She didn't want to risk riling the man; you never knew who you were picking a fight with these days.

"You were eyeing him up, weren't you?" Bradley accused.

She rolled her eyes. "I was not, and please be quiet." She carried on walking in the direction of her flat and heard his sulky plod behind her. For the next twelve minutes – she used her watch to time the uncomfortable silence – he said nothing. This behaviour had been happening more and more lately, and Tamara was almost at the end of the line wondering what had happened to the fun and the romance in their relationship. The previous week she had apparently been giving some man the come-on in the pub, when in fact she had been looking at the girl he was with, as it was someone she'd known at University; the week before that she had been accused of flirting with the guy who battered her cod in the local chippy.

When they finally reached the front entrance of her block of flats, the door was wrenched open from the other side. She said a friendly hello to the man who lived in the flat next to hers as he passed them by, but it wasn't until they were inside Tamara's flat and she had pulled out a carton of Bailey's *Haagen-Dazs* from the freezer that Bradley spoke.

"Are you sleeping with him?" he hollered across the room.

"Who? Eric?" she asked, reaching for a spoon instead of the scoop. Bradley was being ridiculous. She started eating the ice-cream straight from the carton.

"Well, are you?"

"You're being paranoid, Bradley. He lives in this building; he was just being friendly, as many people are." She knew her tone was condescending and she could see that it wound him up. Usually she did everything she could to avoid that, but not tonight.

"I don't see why you're so insecure," she added, goading him to the point of no return. She carried on eating ice-cream straight from the tub as he sulked by the front door like a small child who needed constant reassurance.

She couldn't face a night of sulking followed by the inevitable verbal torrent that would take them into the early hours of the morning and give the other residents in her block of flats their entertainment for the evening. So she said, "I think you'd better leave." She left the ice-cream carton open and walked towards the door.

He stood his ground, folding his arms. "You can't tell me off like some naughty schoolkid."

"Well, if the cap fits!" she yelled.

The next thing she knew she had fallen backwards from the force of a shove from the hands of the man she loved. She lay still on the carpet for a moment, looking up at him in confusion. The same snarl sat on his face and his eyes didn't flicker a change of emotion. She felt her forehead on the area just above her temple and checked her fingers, but no blood. Still, it throbbed like hell.

She waited for him to crouch down beside her and beg her forgiveness or mutter apologies.

Instead, all she heard was "Slag!" And he slammed the door behind him.

Chapter Sixteen

As June rolled into July, the clouds in Brewer Creek brought rainfall like nothing before. Since Tamara had identified the exact spot where Bradley's photograph had been taken, she had been on tenterhooks waiting for him to appear on a city street corner, or for her phone to ring and to hear his voice. She avoided Facebook as much as possible, her heart in her mouth every time she checked her messages. So far, nothing.

Tamara settled into a routine at work, and the team she worked with had done so well recently that their boss had taken them out to celebrate. When she emerged from the annexe the morning after, Tamara winced at the sound of oranges begging for mercy as they were rammed down into the juicer. Moments later Katherine produced a jug of fresh juice and three glasses, and gave her daughter a wink. "How are you feeling?"

"Rough," she growled, her eyes still half shut. "Who's the third glass for?"

Katherine stepped back, grinning, and there was Jake.

Oh God, he was the last person she needed to see right now.

"Good morning," he chirped. "It looks as though it was a good night."

"You could say that." She slumped at the kitchen table and gulped the juice down in one.

"I've got some books for the mobile library," he said, tapping the pile on the side of the table as he drank his juice.

Was he tapping them or pounding on them? Tamara gratefully took the headache tablets from her mum and the tall glass of iced water.

"How many books do you have now?" Jake asked.

"Over four hundred, all stashed in Danielle's parents' garage."

"What happened to the classic car?"

Tamara swallowed the tablets with the help of a gulp of water. "They sold it to a collector."

When she saw the time on Jake's watch, Tamara groaned.

"I'm sorry, love," said Katherine. "Bobby said not to worry if you can't make it in this morning."

"No, I promised. I'm supposed to help out at the surgery," she explained to Jake. "I'd better get dressed." At least she was wearing thick, winter pyjamas this time, although she tried not to cringe at the fluffy rabbit slippers on her feet as she shuffled into the annexe.

"You're probably still over the limit." His voice followed her. "I'll take you."

She was too hungover to argue.

***

The pyjamas were rather different to the last pair that he'd seen Tamara wearing, but she still looked sexy; a sweet kind of sexy, rather than sophisticated, was probably the best way to describe her, especially with those hairy slippers.

"I'll drive slowly," he teased.

"I'm not that bad."

"But your face is green."

"It is not; I'm fine. Just drive."

He caught her smirk as she turned away to look out of the window.

"So where did you go?"

"We went to *The Slip Inn,*" she replied, "but stayed there an insane amount of time, hence the headache today."

"And the thirst, the cravings for fried eggs and bacon–"

"Enough," she begged, opening the window.

Okay, so he didn't want to make the poor girl vomit, especially not in his pick-up. "April's looking forward to the weekend away," he said instead, wishing he could watch her rather than the road as she sat back against the seat, eyes closed.

"I can't wait either."

"But you go to Sydney every day for work." He indicated then pulled up at the front of Bobby's surgery.

Her eyes flipped open as the pick-up crunched across the gravel and came to a standstill. "It's not the same. This will be about relaxing, shopping, dinners–"

"Getting drunk? Okay, cheap shot, I can see that you're delicate."

Lucky for him, she laughed. "I'll be fine by the weekend. Thanks for the lift."

"Hey, any time." And he meant that.

Back at the cottage, he watched April out in the garden, hanging up washing, something she wouldn't dared to have done a couple of months ago. The thought of Marty showing up usually kept her inside or plastered to Jake's side, but the friendship with Tamara and Danielle was working wonders. April was finally beginning to realise that she had a life to live and that looking over her shoulder every five minutes wasn't letting her do that. He knew they couldn't let their guard down yet – and he certainly wasn't – but Jake was happy to do the worrying for both of them. Besides, it gave him something else to do other than think of Tamara and how much he wanted to put his arms around her every time he saw her.

He chuckled when he thought of Tamara's face that morning, hungover and horrified to find him waiting in the kitchen. It made him wonder whether she cared for him, even a little; he dared to hope so.

***

At the surgery, Tamara made herself a cup of coffee. The lack of sleep and the alcohol refusing to leave her system demanded it, never mind the shock of facing Jake first thing this morning when she knew she looked pretty rough. Out in the annexe she had showered and tied her hair away from her face, without the help of a mirror. Ignorance was bliss and all that.

As the kettle came to the boil, she thought about Bradley. The fact that he had followed her to the other side of the world was the least of her worries. What unnerved her was that he didn't appear to have tried to make any contact. It reminded her of the Wellington Smart corporate bonding day three years ago on the old Air Force base in Buckinghamshire.

There, dressed in old black tracksuit pants and a khaki top with extra camouflage gear donated by the organisers, her heart had pounded somewhere outside of her chest during the paintballing event which had lasted an entire day. She had been pummelled by her colleagues and only managed one successful shot herself, which had been a total fluke: She had tripped over Ellie Rogers, who was hiding out ready to get the boss, and as a result her paintball gun went off and hit Gavin May square on the arse. By the end of the day Tamara was more exhausted from being scared out of her wits than anything else.

This feeling she had now about Bradley – waiting for him to jump out and reveal himself – wasn't too far from the fear she had experienced that day, waiting for those bright-coloured splodges to come at her from out of nowhere.

"Hello?" A voice came from the front door of the office, as Tamara took her first sip of coffee. She pulled the cord to open up the venetian blind covering the glass.

"Hi, Mr Wilson," she smiled. "What can I do for you?"

"Firstly, you can take these," he said, handing her a couple of battered books: two Thomas Hardy classics that looked well-read.

"Thank you." She put them beside her bag. "I'll add them to the collection."

"I'm looking forward to the mobile library," he chuckled. "I don't do much reading and I should do. It's a wonderful escape."

"You're not wrong there. It's wonderful that everyone is so supportive," said Tamara.

"Well, that's Brewer Creek for you," he said. "Anyway, I didn't just come to give you those. I wondered if we could take one of the dogs out for a walk." His hands pushed into his fawn, cotton trousers, Mr Wilson smiled like a lost child who wanted a friend.

"That sounds like a lovely idea." She set her empty cup down beside the desk. "We have a couple of dogs out the back and I'm sure their owners would appreciate us exercising them."

She diverted the office phone to call her mobile so that she could take any calls for Bobby. He had a mobile himself but deemed it "unprofessional" to have it switched on when he was with a client, which Tamara had to admit she admired. There was nothing worse than being given someone's undivided attention only to have it rudely snapped away.

She waved her phone in the air. "I'll have to answer this, I'm afraid, if anyone calls," she said, to excuse herself of the same anti-social behaviour, and then checked the notes on the cage of a black and white border collie. "Come on, Lucky, it's your lucky day!" she joked, and looped a lead over the dog's neck.

"What's she in for?" Mr Wilson pulled on his navy cap when they stepped outside.

"She had a growth removed from her back, but it wasn't cancer so she's in the clear." Tamara gave a thumbs-up before she told Lucky to sit. Then they crossed the road to the fields and took the track that had already been carved out by the many people who had trampled that way in the past.

"You're a natural." Mr Wilson smiled as he watched Tamara instructing the dog who seemed only too happy to obey her every command.

She laughed. "Years of practice, Mr Wilson. Not recently, of course. I think Bobby gets enough of an animal fix at work these days, but once upon a time we had a couple of dogs, two cats, guinea pigs and goldfish."

They crossed over a small fence and walked along the edge of a paddock, stopping to pat the horses as they hung their noses over the fence to stake their claim on the grassed area.

"Lucky's owners are out of town for another couple of days, according to Bobby's notes," said Tamara. "They're buying livestock for their farm, so she has a little while longer with us. I think he finds it hard to let the animals go sometimes." She saw a shadow of sadness pass over Mr Wilson's face. "Sorry, I didn't think."

"Ah, don't be daft, pet. Ada was old; it's the circle of life."

They walked on until they reached a quiet lane. Once a tractor had trundled past, they crossed over and into an enormous field where Tamara loosened the lead from around Lucky's neck and let her run free.

"I found another of Ada's old toys squashed down the side of the sofa." Mr Wilson produced a chewed, purple ball from his pocket and threw it gently underarm to the grass that sat far back from the road. Lucky happily retrieved it and he repeated the pattern.

"I'm sorry I haven't been able to come round as much lately," said Tamara.

"Oh, don't worry your pretty little head about that." Mr Wilson ruffled Lucky's fur and carried on the relentless game. "Who wants to spend all their time with an old bloke like me?"

"Rubbish! I really enjoy my time with you. There's no rule that says you and I can't be friends."

"You should spend more time with people your own age. What about young Danielle? She always says 'G'day' when we pass, stops for a bit of a yarn, too. I've known her and her family for years."

Tamara had only met Danielle's parents a handful of times; they were always so busy, whether it was rounding up animals, feeding them, or fixing up something on the farm. She admired their work ethic and knew that Danielle would carry the same values into the world of nursing when the time came.

Mr Wilson shuffled along beside Tamara. While some friendships were full of banter and analysing the world as it was or as it should be, others were about enjoying precious moments, being along for the ride, and appreciating life just the way it was. Theirs was a friendship unlike any other that Tamara had experienced, particularly with the absence of any surviving grandparents; she valued it a great deal.

The local church bell chimed ten o'clock and Mr Wilson waited for the air to quieten before he asked, "So how about that young bloke Jake?"

"What about him?" She picked up the toy and slung it as far as she could, hoping her exertion would hide any awkwardness.

"Do you think I haven't seen the way you two look at each other?"

"Mr Wilson!" She nudged him as though he were a boy in her class at school rather than a man old enough to remember life before the invention of credit cards. "He's a friend," she said matter-of-factly.

Lucky skidded to a halt, drooling at the mouth and panting as she dropped the ball at their feet.

"Last one, my girl." Mr Wilson threw the toy past the cherry blossom and into the thick wispy grass at the edge of the field. "You mark my words, Tamara, Jake's taken with you. The way you two look at each other is the same way me and my Margaret used to look at each other."

When they came to a large rock – smooth to the touch – they sat down. Lucky settled at their feet with the chew toy, and Mr Wilson leaned down to tickle the dog's tummy as she basked in the winter sun.

"My Margaret used to drive me round the bend at the start. What is it you call it these days? Playing hard to get?"

Tamara giggled. "That's right."

"Well you see, I kept asking her to dance at parties; I asked if she wanted to go for a walk; I asked her to go to the circus with me; she always turned me down. Then she was a bridesmaid at her brother's wedding – wearing the most garish thing I've ever seen, might I add – but when I asked her to dance, she actually said yes."

He began to laugh. "I think she only said yes that night because the dress had one of those enormous hoop things and was buttoned up so tight that she knew I couldn't get up to any funny business. Dancing with that felt like I had coat hangers wrapped around my shins the whole time."

Tamara matched his warm smile. "You must miss her."

"I do. When you spend that long with someone they become a part of you, and when they go there's an emptiness that's hard to describe. It took me a long time before I could even wake up without expecting her to be lying next to me in the bed."

Tamara watched Lucky wrestle with the toy as though it had a life of its own. Mr Wilson was right to pick up on the spark between her and Jake, but she had already pushed Jake into the too-complicated box months ago.

"I hope that one day I find someone who makes me as happy as your wife made you," said Tamara, looking at the old man's wrinkly hand, still sporting his treasured gold wedding band.

Mr Wilson patted Lucky as her chin rested on his knees and she looked up at him, panting from her antics. "Is there someone else, back in England?" he asked.

Inexplicably, Tamara found herself wanting to tell her new friend everything, but she didn't.

"You're not over him, are you?" Mr Wilson said when she didn't reply. "I may look old, but I watch people in this town. And from the moment you arrived, I knew you hadn't just come over to see the family. You know, sometimes I'd walk past you when you were on that white bridge over the creek and you wouldn't even see me, your mind was a million miles away."

Tamara wondered how many other people had seen her doing the same thing: first Jake, now Mr Wilson.

"There was someone, in the UK," she began, "and you're right, coming here was partly to leave him behind and work out what I wanted from my life."

"And do you think you've found what you're looking for?"

147

"I'm getting there."

When they carried on walking, Mr Wilson asked, "Did he hurt you, Tamara?" He kept his gaze straight ahead.

"Yes, he did. I became his only real friend and he had a lot of problems; he depended on me."

He nodded as though he understood. "It must've been hard to walk away."

How could Mr Wilson see what Beth never could?

Tamara's breath caught in her throat and she stopped to loop the lead over Lucky's head, ready to cross the road. The black clouds above were distant enough to tell her that they should be safe to get back before the heavens opened.

"You're going to think I'm an old softie," said Mr Wilson, "or perhaps you'll think I'm a daft old coot, but love like I had doesn't come our way more than once in a lifetime, Tamara. You've got to grab it. And when you get it?" He looked right at her, his eyes twinkling and his cold hand grabbing hers as firm as he could. "Don't you ever let it go."

He bent down towards Lucky and she wagged her tail in farewell. "Thanks for the walk, girl," he said. "Bye, Tamara."

"Bye," Tamara called back. She walked briskly on in an attempt to escape the storm clouds that had started their drum roll, and were getting ready to belt out their final tune. She marvelled at the way older people saw the world so differently to the younger generation, with a depth that wouldn't exist without the experience of life and all its obscurities. She wondered if Mr Wilson had been talking about Jake when he handed out his last piece of advice, and hoped that nobody else in this town had noticed the same connection.

***

Back at the surgery, Tamara filled a water bowl for Lucky and watched the dog lap it up before wolfing down the biscuit she offered. She read the notes on the cages and fed the other animals, before settling down at the computer with a second cup of coffee and opening up Facebook.

She lifted the cup to slurp the hot liquid before it had a chance to cool, but froze at the message lurking in her Inbox.

It was from Bradley.

Short and to the point, he said that he had been backpacking for the last six weeks and was heading back to the UK in less than a month. He wanted to see her and, in his words, he wanted to "clear the air and make amends".

Slouched in Bobby's enormous chair, Tamara swivelled around and around, her head tilted back staring at the ceiling and her eyes following the familiar cracks in the plaster. From an early age she had known how lucky she had been with her own family. Her friend Natalie's parents had got divorced, and their custody battle had been regular entertainment outside the school gates; a classmate, Billy Hunter, had had to cope with the death of his mum at aged seven, then his dad had turned into a drunk, a role which had also been played out way too close to the school's perimeter. Tamara knew she had won part of life's lottery on happiness in the wake of her own family tragedy, and the compassion that flowed through her veins forced her to feel that people like Bradley, who hadn't been quite as lucky, deserved the chance to put right their mistakes.

When she left the surgery an hour later, Tamara had made a decision. The rain began its light pitter-patter dance on her umbrella and, as she put one foot in front of the other, her determination grew. She had come this far, so she made a promise to herself that Bradley wasn't going to be invited into this new life she was forming without him. It was time for him to face the world on his own.

Chapter Seventeen

After Bradley's email, Tamara wanted nothing more than some time with friends to put him to the back of her mind. Huddled in the lift of a luxury hotel in Sydney's CBD with April and Danielle, she waited as they were whisked up to the seventh floor. With the whoosh of the lift, she let out a breath of relief.

They'd nabbed a last minute deal on the internet and found three rooms in a hotel with a rooftop swimming pool, a sauna, steam room, and a spa. Danielle was so excited she was on the verge of hyperventilating, and it was great to see April looking so relaxed for once.

Tamara's room was decked out in neutral tones: furnishings in hues of brown and gold, the bed covered in classic white, with a gold runner along the end. A small balcony overlooked the depths of the CBD, and if Tamara stood in the corner she could see the Harbour Bridge with a row of climbers making their way to the top like ants trudging up an ant hill. Smiling, she took a photo on her iPhone and fired it off to Beth, attaching a message saying: "Wish you were here xx."

A rap on the door and Danielle's excited voice dragged Tamara back inside and away from the view.

"Already in my swimmers," said Danielle, pulling out a navy and white polka dot shoulder strap from beneath her t-shirt to prove it.

April was waiting for them beside the rooftop pool, its bright blue waters merging with a paler blue sky. Clad in a green bikini that matched her emerald eyes, Tamara took a leisurely pace through the water while Danielle powered through it more fish-like than human. They finished the afternoon with a steam before heading back to their rooms to glam up for the evening out.

Outside the hotel, April linked Tamara's arm. "I feel frumpy next to you two," she moaned.

"Rubbish," Tamara retorted. "You're not frumpy. You're having a baby, and that's the most beautiful thing in the world." She pushed the thought of whom April was having the baby *with* out of her mind.

"Yeah well, seeing you two in your swimmers didn't exactly help."

"You're glowing," Tamara argued. April looked stunning in black trousers, patent heels, and a silver silk maternity top that crossed over at the front. "And you're all bump and nothing else, you'll soon spring back again."

Since Tamara had told April about that text, neither of them had mentioned it again. Like dirty leaves in a gutter, it was as though the topic had been swept away. She wondered whether April's insecurity with her appearance was heightened by the concerns she surely must have in her relationship.

"This is a-ma-zing!" Danielle pronounced every syllable slowly as they reached Circular Quay and the lights of the Opera House. "I'd forgotten how beautiful Sydney is." She breathed the air in deeply. "You mustn't let me drink too much tonight," she warned, as they walked on.

"I think you're already drunk on happiness, aren't you?" said April.

April was right, of course. Tamara looked over at Danielle and knew she was looking at a different girl. Instead of the customary plait, her hair hung loosely around her shoulders and the dungarees she favoured on the farm had been replaced by a figure-hugging black dress which did Danielle's womanly figure justice.

"I thought we'd start at *The Argyle* for drinks," said Tamara. "Then we'll move on to the *Waterfront* for dinner." It felt so good to be out with the girls for the night, and although Tamara missed

151

Beth, her friends here were special now, too.

"That's right," grinned Danielle. "No steak, lamb or beef for me; I've had enough of farm animals to last me a lifetime. It's seafood all the way tonight. I don't want to see anything on my plate that I would ordinarily see skipping around at home. This weekend is about getting away from the familiar and exploring new territory."

Tamara grabbed Danielle when she stumbled on the uneven stony pavement as they passed under the entrance to *The Argyle*. "Heels are tricky, they're not like wellies."

"Gumboots," the others chorused, meeting a roll of the eyes from Tamara.

They grabbed a spare table outside as soon as it became available, ordering gin and tonics for Danielle and Tamara, pineapple juice for the mother-to-be.

"It's lovely to get away from it all, isn't it?" April rubbed her tummy protectively.

Tamara was desperate to ask what "it all" was exactly, but April had quickly leapt into question time with Danielle, asking her about nursing, whether she would specialise, whether she would settle back in Brewer Creek one day.

"I'm a bit nervous about it all, to be honest." Danielle moved the slices of lemon and half-melted ice-cubes around her glass with a straw. "I wish I was more like you, Tamara."

"Whatever makes you say that?"

"Because you've got guts, that's why."

Tamara wondered if Danielle would still say that if she knew how often she had let Bradley back into her life, that she had feelings for April's boyfriend, and that really she had no idea what path her life was going to take next. She felt like the least gutsy person she knew.

"I think sometimes you have to live in the moment." It was the best piece of advice Tamara could offer, and the only advice that felt genuine right now.

"I'll try to remember that." Danielle stood up, grabbing her purse. "I'm getting another round."

Tamara grabbed Danielle's arm to stop her from moving away. "You stay here, I'll get the drinks. And when I go, discreetly look behind you at the guy standing near the wall in the checked shirt. He hasn't stopped watching you since we arrived."

She left Danielle and April, but in record time she was back distributing the drinks. "So?"

Danielle smirked. "He's so cute! But I don't think he was looking at me."

A husky "G-day" behind Danielle made her turn around in slow motion.

"I'm Will," said the very guy they had noticed.

Danielle introduced herself and the pair soon moved over to the wall, leaving Tamara and April at the table.

"He's cute," April smiled. "She looks happy."

Tamara didn't miss the melancholic edge to April's voice, and decided to brighten the conversation. "Do you think you'll try to find work in the city when you finish your course?"

April shifted on her stool, and took a few lingering gulps of her pineapple juice. "I don't know yet. I'd like to, but we're starting to settle in Brewer Creek." She was as guarded as ever, but this time she looked as though she was making herself stop talking rather than feeling as though she should.

Tamara used her straw to stir the ice in her glass. "But why come to Brewer Creek if you're intent on seeing the big city?"

April shrugged, her eyes fixed on her drink.

"Did you ever find out who that text was from?" Somehow the words were out before Tamara remembered her promise to herself not to mention it again.

April trailed her fingers through the condensation of her glass. "There are things that are complicated, with me and Jake, I mean. I – I want to tell you, but I can't, not now. Can you trust me, Tamara?"

Right then Danielle bounded up, and the moment was over. She waved over to Will, who was leaving the courtyard with his mates. She stayed cool and calm, right up until he was out of sight, then she turned to her friends, her eyes wide, and squealed, "He asked for my number!"

Tamara hugged her. "He was gorgeous, but then again, so are you. And Will – that's a sexy name."

"He probably won't call," Danielle shrugged.

"Right, that's it." Tamara stood with her hands on her hips. "I want to say one word to you and it's a word I want you to remember and recite every day – no, multiple times a day."

"Okay. What?"

"Positivity," she said firmly. "You need to stop trying to find some excuse for things not to work out. You wanted some of my so-called guts? Well, that's my first word of advice."

"Consider myself told!" Danielle giggled.

As they made their way down the hill towards the harbour, Danielle nattered on about Will, his job, his life, his friends. Her smile was almost a match for the arc of the bridge that dominated the harbour, but Tamara was distracted. She desperately wanted to get back that conversation with April before Danielle had interrupted. April had been about to open up, she was sure of it.

She turned around, expecting to see April walking behind her. But the other girl was standing on the pavement some eight metres back, stuck against a wall, clutching her chest as though her heart had stopped.

"What's the matter?" Tamara ran to her.

She didn't move.

Tamara followed April's gaze to the opposite side of the street, but all she saw was another brick wall. "Is it the baby?"

April's face had paled, and her breathing came in gasps. "I'm fine," she managed to say, then kept on walking as though nothing had happened.

Tamara and Danielle exchanged bewildered glances and followed her in silence. What followed was a strained conversation at the restaurant overlooking the water, and somehow the night wasn't quite as relaxing or amazing as it could have been.

When they left the harbour to make their way back to the hotel, darkness fell around them and the stars above winked knowingly. By the time Tamara climbed into bed that night, she was left wondering just how many secrets the residents of Brewer Creek actually had.

Chapter Eighteen

The girls made the most of a lie-in the next morning, and after Tamara and Danielle raced each other doing laps in the pool, they made their way along Cockle Bay Wharf. They sipped on fizzy drinks and looked out over Darling Harbour, and Tamara tilted her face to the warmth of the sun as it peeped out from behind the handful of clouds passing idly overhead.

Whoops of joy resonated from children splashing one another from head to toe in the fountains which were surrounded by dancing bird statues. The second Danielle disappeared to get them all ice cream, Tamara turned to April. "What happened last night?" She might as well be blunt.

"I don't know what you're talking about."

"April, I don't know how it works in Australia, but back in the UK friends help each other out; they tell each other things because it can actually help."

April's shoulders visibly drooped. "Please don't worry about me, there's no need."

Danielle handed out the ice creams and Tamara went over to dip her toes in the water from the fountains. It was no use. She had tried to distance herself from April, from Jake. But they were both friends and whatever was going on with them, she had a nasty feeling that it was more serious than either of them made out.

***

On Sunday morning all three girls were anxious to make the most of their last morning in the city, and headed to The Strand Arcade for coffee and to peruse the mixture of quaint, traditional shops. They visited the designer outlets manned by menacing security guards in black suits and shades who made them too nervous to even go in, and they finished with lunch at *Jamie's Italian* on Pitt Street, where they tucked into seafood pasta and drank ginger mojitos.

"This weekend really took it out of you, didn't it?" Tamara watched April wilt into her seat when they boarded the train on Sunday afternoon.

"This human growing inside of me is taking every last ounce of energy that I have."

"Maybe you and Jake need a night in a hotel," Danielle suggested. "A romantic night for the two of you, away from work, away from study; it could be what you need before the baby comes."

April smiled politely but said nothing. She was retreating into her shell like a nervous snail, and nothing seemed to be coaxing her out. Tamara stared out the window and thought of Jake. Every time she heard his name she felt as though she was stepping in quicksand, falling for him more and more despite knowing that being with him was impossible.

A rattling noise whisked Tamara's mind away from Jake as Danielle shook a plastic container of strawberry Tic Tacs in front of her.

"Thanks." The confectionery in a mixture of pinks landed in the palm of her hand. "Hey, I wonder when Will's going to call."

"He probably won't," she shrugged.

With a roll of her eyes, Tamara rummaged in her handbag, found her purse and pulled out a twenty dollar note. "I'll say he'll play it cool and won't want to seem too keen. So I bet he'll call you on Tuesday. Tonight is too early; Wednesday is too far away."

"Twenty bucks says he calls tonight." April slapped a twenty dollar bill into Tamara's hand, and she smiled back, glad that she was joining in.

Danielle held a twenty to her chest for a second before adding it to the other two. "I say he'll call on Friday."

"He won't leave it a week," Tamara insisted. "The sixty bucks is as good as mine!"

***

Jake slung April's suitcase into the back of his pick-up, disappointed that Tamara already had a ride home with Danielle. He couldn't tell Tamara how he felt, and he knew she thought he was a two-timer who didn't deserve April, but that didn't stop him from wanting to spend time with her, even if that time had to be platonic.

As they pulled away from the station, April looked far from relaxed. "You forgot your mobile," he said jokingly. It had probably done her good to get away from everything and be incommunicado for the weekend.

Her hand shot out and clamped around his arm, making him jump. "Marty's here, Jake. He's here!"

He screeched to a halt at the side of the road. The look of terror on her face was unmistakable.

"I saw him in the city," she babbled, and as Jake's fists clutched the steering wheel, her explanation tumbled out bit by bit.

"I didn't have my phone and I knew that you'd fly into a panic about me," she explained, "so I figured I'd wait to get back here before I told you. God, it was awful. We were on our way to the restaurant. We were walking down a hill and there he was, standing across the other side of the road trying to light a cigarette. I felt for sure that he'd look up at any second. God, I'd recognise those tattoos anywhere."

Jake didn't doubt it. On one forearm sat a familiar red rose with loopy red writing surrounding it, saying Deborah, and on one set of knuckles sat the word "Don't" and on the other, "Care".

"I hardly slept a wink, Jake. I was either jumping up to double

158

check the door was locked or looking out the window because that was easier than going to sleep. I very nearly told Tamara everything this weekend. I think we were stupid to keep this to ourselves, it's too much."

Jake pulled down the visor to block the winter sun as he fought to stay calm.

"He looked awful, Jake. His clothes were filthy, his hair was longer than I remembered, greasy-looking, and I could even see his fingers as black as though he'd scraped them through tar." Her voice shook. "I think it's time to go to the police. I can't live in fear like this, I can't."

Jake pulled her to him and held her tight. The man had turned up in the very State where they had been convinced they would be safe. But telling the police would mean that Marty would implicate them both, and it was their word against his. Jake had no idea how far the man would go. Would he plant incriminating evidence? Would he have some other lowlife back up his claims? When they had decided to leave Perth and hide out for a while, even Jake had assumed that eventually Marty would either lose interest or slip up somewhere along the way. Then he would've gone to jail and left them free to get on with their lives.

"He may be in Sydney, but he hasn't found us." Jake spoke with conviction. "He could be here to carry out more robberies. Maybe he assumes that by moving around he's less likely to get caught."

"I hope you're right, Jake, I really do."

Marty was sly, and their whole undercover story that had felt too far-fetched at first was probably the only way he hadn't found them sooner. But had the extra time been worth it? Perhaps hiding out had made the situation a whole lot worse.

Jake hated that they had lied to everyone in Brewer Creek, but he didn't want to underestimate how far Marty would go to get revenge. This had become a terrifying game of cat and mouse, and even though he didn't say it to April, he had the unsettling feeling that Marty was getting one step closer.

Chapter Nineteen

Tamara pulled her suitcase up the front steps and into the hallway, but instead of being happy to be home, her face fell when she heard raised voices coming from the kitchen.

"What's going on?" she asked.

Bobby was pacing up and down. He threw his hands in the air. "And to think we had him here for dinner. In this house! Well, he can shove that where the sun don't shine!"

She stood aside as Bobby stormed out.

"Bobby, come back." Katherine followed him. "Don't do anything silly."

"Is anyone going to tell me what's going on?" Tamara asked again when Bobby drove away.

Katherine slumped down on a chair at the kitchen table. "Jake signed a contract with Dogtails Kennels. That's always been Bobby's contract."

"So why did they ask Jake?"

"I don't know. But Bobby is fuming. I thought the competition in town was harmless, until now. I don't think I've ever seen him this angry." She buried her head in her hands, and only looked up when Tamara passed her a steaming cup of coffee.

"Why won't he let me in, Tamara?" Katherine wrapped her hands around her mug.

Being secretive wasn't Bobby's style; he usually liked to get things out in the open. Even when Tamara had faced a change of schools after they moved house when she was nine, Bobby had sat them all down at the kitchen table as though he was chairing a meeting and they had discussed the pros and cons. So why couldn't they talk about things now?

Tamara picked up the car keys.

"Where are you going?" Katherine asked.

"I'm going to talk to Bobby."

"Please tell him to come home."

Tamara tried to go easy on the accelerator as she pulled out of the driveway. She neared the turnoff for the surgery but when she thought of the overflowing madness on Bobby's face, she snapped and found herself turning in completely the opposite direction – to Jake's place.

His pick-up stood out front and she came to a dramatic halt behind it, blocking him from getting out. She jumped over a dip of squelchy mud and came face-to-face with him as he stepped out of the front door.

"Tamara?" He looked startled.

She folded her arms and prepared for the onslaught to come out of her mouth.

"What's up?"

"What the hell do you think you're doing?" she bellowed.

He backed away and started to rummage through the equipment in the back of his pick-up, looking for something. "What are you talking about?"

His indifference added fuel to the fire, and Tamara yanked his arm away from the vehicle. "You know exactly what I'm talking about. I'm talking about you, snatching away the contract with Dogtails Kennels. I don't know how you have the nerve to do something like that."

"Look, Tamara," he held up his hands, "I don't know what you're talking about. I didn't take anything away from Bobby. Dogtails approached *me* and they didn't mention anything about Bobby. Did they promise him the contract?"

She hesitated. Bobby wasn't exactly on the ball these days, and it wouldn't surprise her if the renewal had slipped his mind. Dogtails wasn't run by a resident of the town, so loyalties were less likely to have been an issue. But there was no way she was going to let Jake off the hook that easily.

She stood up straighter, ready for a fight. "No, they didn't promise it to him," she conceded, "but he's had that contract for years." She turned and went back to her own car. "Why are you so determined to ruin everything, Jake?" She knew that her words were about more than her family's livelihood.

"Now wait a minute." He stormed after her and snatched the keys from her hand before they reached the ignition. "You must live in a strange little world of your own where no problems exist. It's all so bloody black and white to you, isn't it?"

"Hey! Give them back."

"Not until you hear me out." He held the keys up in the air, way out of her reach.

She tried to grab them, but even on tiptoes it was impossible so she went for the verbal onslaught instead. "And you're one to talk about me living in 'my own little world'. I'd say that you live in a pretty warped one of your own. I mean, does the word 'honesty' mean *anything* to you? Now give me back my keys, or so help me God I'll kick you where it hurts!"

Jake took a step back to protect whatever he could, and reluctantly dropped the keys. "Thanks for hearing me out." He shook his head, got into his pick-up and honked the horn until she moved her car.

Her legs, her arms, and her whole body shook from the confrontation as she drove on towards Bobby's surgery. How had Jake managed to turn it around so that it felt as though she was in the wrong?

"Bobby?" She called out as she opened the front door to the office. She didn't know whether she would find the angry man or the gentle giant who had been so familiar to her since she was a little girl.

"In here, Tamara." The voice told her that it was the latter.

In the back room, where a whiff of disinfectant still hung in the air from that morning's clean, she found Bobby pushing carrots through the cage of a rabbit that had a bandage on one of its hind legs. He didn't look up when she turned a bucket upside down, brushed the dried mud from the bottom, and sat down next to him.

"Do you know that this rabbit was where it all started?" Bobby wiggled his finger in the cage to stroke the fawn-coloured creature with deep-set brown eyes and a nose that twitched as fast as a disco light. He opened the end of the cage and pulled the rabbit out to eat its carrots on the floor between his outstretched legs.

"Not this rabbit, of course," Bobby continued. "When I was little my dad bought me my very first pet, a rabbit called George. From the moment I laid eyes on George I knew that all I wanted to do was look after animals like him for the rest of my days."

Tamara watched as this rabbit, Nesbit, did a few hops to Bobby's other leg and the piece of carrot that lingered beneath it. He ran his hand along the animal's soft fur as Tamara said, "Mum told me what happened with Dogtails."

Bobby's hand momentarily stopped, then he returned Nesbit to his cage, stood up, and went into the office. Tamara followed and, from behind the books on the shelf, he pulled out a bottle of Glenfiddich. "Purely for medicinal purposes," he smiled, tilting the bottle towards Tamara.

She shook her head. "It's way too early for me. And I had a few drinks last night anyway."

"That's right. Sorry, love. I haven't even asked about your weekend away."

She dismissed his concern with a wave of her hand as he poured himself a small measure of whisky, took a sip, and sat on the leather chair behind his desk. He swirled the whisky in his glass as Tamara took the seat opposite.

"Mum's worried that there's something you're keeping from her." There, she'd said it; she should've said it months ago, before it came to this.

Bobby looked out the window towards the empty car park and Tamara wasn't sure whether he had heard her question, until he said, "I haven't been as on top of things as I usually am. I was angry about Dogtails at first, but…" He pinched the bridge of his nose and exhaled long through his mouth. "To be honest, I don't think that it's Jake I'm angry with. It was my own stupid fault. I knew the contract was coming up for renewal but I didn't do anything about it. I should have been on the ball and called them months ago. If I had really wanted it," he added.

"So you didn't even want the contract?" Now she was confused.

"Your mother is pushing me to retire," he went on, as Tamara watched him.

"Mum doesn't understand why you won't retire," she probed. "She has no idea what's holding you back. Is it money? Or are you worried that you'll be bored and end up going senile and in a loony bin for geriatrics?"

He let out a soft chuckle at her flippancy. "You put it so delicately, Tamara."

She moved to the other side of the desk to hug him. She listened to the quietness of Brewer Creek all around them, and for a while they stayed there, Tamara wanting to protect the man who had done the same for her all her life. She watched the passion in his eyes as he talked about his life as a veterinarian for more than thirty years; she saw the sparkle in his entire face when he recalled animals by their names, and owners who had entrusted him.

"You know," Tamara began, "it's a wonder you've made any profit; you're too kind for your own good."

Bobby pulled open his desk drawer. He took out a small photo album which he gripped on his lap.

"What's that?"

He didn't answer her question, but instead said, "I studied to be a vet as soon as I could. For years I worked in surgeries before establishing my own practice. You won't know this, but another part of my dream was to keep it in the family."

"Oops, sorry," she said.

"Don't worry, I knew when I met your mother that she would

never go for it, and as the years went on it became obvious that you were a corporate girl through and through. And, might I add, I'm tremendously proud of that."

He finished his drink and slid the photo album across the desk to Tamara, motioning for her to go ahead and open it. He watched her as her eyes took in the first picture.

"This isn't Mum," she said, as she looked at a picture of Bobby standing next to a bride.

"That was Nancy, my first wife."

Her voice shook when she spoke. "You were married before?"

"Yes."

She flipped to the next page of the album and looked at another photo pushed into the four old-fashioned adhesive corners which had yellowed over time.

Bobby's eyes glazed over but didn't leave Tamara's. "The little boy was my son, Archie."

She stared at him in disbelief.

"Archie and Nancy died in a house fire when Archie was six years old." His words caught in his throat, like razor blades gently slicing away at his insides.

"Does Mum—"

"She doesn't know anything." He studied his hands, unable to meet her gaze. "I'm so embarrassed at how dishonest I've been with you both."

"But I don't understand. Why didn't you say something before?"

After a while, he said, "I couldn't tell her. I couldn't tell you." He looked down at his hands. "You see, I was supposed to be there that night but I'd gone drinking at the local pub and… "

Tamara wanted to stretch a hand across the table and hold his, but she was too stunned to move.

"I heard the fire engines." He looked heavenward, tears pricking his eyes as he remembered details. "I can still remember them, their blaring sirens into the quiet of the night. Sometimes it's as though I can taste and smell the smoke that wrapped around me as I ran towards the house. God, you hear the sirens, but you never think it has anything to do with you."

Tamara tried to process what he was telling her.

"I used to wish I'd died that night."

His words shocked her deeper than she thought possible. "Don't ever say that!" This time her hand moved across the table and took hold of his. She felt his fingers clench hers as though she were a lifeline to pull him to dry land.

"It's true." His eyes closed. "I thought I'd failed as a father and a husband; failed to protect them." He broke off and pushed his balled-up fists into the sockets of his eyes. "And now I've failed both you and your mum by telling lies all these years."

"I don't understand why you couldn't trust us, Bobby?"

"I never said anything before, because I blame myself. If I'd been there, then maybe I could've done something. If I'd left the pub earlier, I might have been home when the fire started and got everyone out. If only I'd—"

Tamara's heart lurched at his pain as he clammed up again, his voice scared away by the tears in his eyes. He had lied to them for years but there was a strange relief that washed over Tamara; a relief that came with knowing the truth, whether it was what you wanted to hear or not. She could see the torture in his eyes, the guilt that had eaten away at him for so long. He was the most selfless man she knew and she wouldn't wish this kind of secret on anyone.

"You've got to stop blaming yourself, Bobby."

Their hands interlocked across the table until Bobby pulled the photograph album closer. It was as though he knew it was time to acknowledge the existence of this family he had kept under wraps for so long. He flipped through the pages and settled on a picture of his son, Archie, in old-fashioned shorts. He turned to the next page which showed Archie cuddling a German shepherd.

"You were exactly the same," he said.

"What do you mean?"

"You were always affectionate with animals, dogs in particular;

it used to terrify your mother."

"I remember." She smiled, relieved that he was talking to her calmly. "She'd tell me over and over again that I had to ask the owner's permission first, in case the dog was dangerous."

"And you ignored her every time." When he smiled, he kept his eyes on the photograph, his fingers tracing the past. Tamara felt like a thief, waiting to steal away his precious memories.

"Is the practice in trouble?" She needed to know the whole truth now.

He shook his head. "I don't ever want to disappoint her."

"Mum?" When he nodded, she said, "You're not a disappointment, Bobby. But Mum deserves the truth."

"I know she does."

Tamara had gone full circle in a matter of minutes, from loving the only dad she had ever known to feeling anger and hurt that he hadn't told her about Nancy and Archie. And now, here she was back at the start again, feeling for this man who held onto an unimaginable sorrow.

"When the unthinkable happens, Tamara, it stays with you always. It affects every minute of every day of your life, always there at the back of your mind. I dreamt of a family-run practice, and Nancy and Archie... well that's what they were." He broke off and his hands covered his face until he said, "It feels like I'd be giving up the final piece of them if I retire. But I couldn't explain that to your mum, because then I'd have to admit the truth; that I'd failed them."

Tamara grabbed his hand. "You didn't fail them, and you haven't failed us, not by a long shot, you hear me?"

"Then why can't I put the past in the past, where it belongs?"

"Because you're you, Bobby, and you don't switch your emotions on and off like that. It's the reason why I love you so much. But don't underestimate me. I'm old enough to realise that whatever love you still have for Nancy and Archie doesn't detract from the way you feel about us now. We will never replace them; they were a part of you. And they still are, through your memories."

The strong man that Tamara had always known kept his poise and said, "You know I *never, ever* regretted marrying your mother for one single day of my life, and I *never* regretted having you as my daughter."

"I've always known that," she said with a smile. "I've never once doubted you."

"I…" His voice wobbled when he tried to speak, and he looked down at the open page with the photograph of his son holding a vet's bag. "That's Archie at work. He was always playing alongside me, and liked to feel as though he was doing his bit for the animals in my care."

Tamara leaned in closer to see the picture. "Where did you get the vet's overalls to fit him?" She felt an instant connection to this child whom she would never get to know.

"They're from a dress-up shop," he chuckled.

She let him savour the sight of his son some more before she said, "If only you'd said something before, it could've helped you see what a tragic accident it was; that it wasn't your fault."

The wind had picked up outside, and Bobby watched the branches of the gum trees as they bowed in the breeze along one side of the car park. "It happened a fair few years before I met Katherine and I'd dealt with grief, guilt, anger, the whole gamut of emotions. I'd moved away from the area, and for the first time nobody knew anything about me. Nobody looked at me with those sad eyes, those looks of pity. I could get on with my life and be that-happy-Bobby-from-the-surgery. I took great comfort every day I worked, and eventually I stopped thinking about it at every waking moment and having nightmares night after night.

"Knowing your mother as I do now, then yes, she would've understood. But at the time I suppose I was naïve enough to think that she would look at me differently, not trust me with her daughter. I hadn't been there to save my son and he died along with my wife. I didn't want Katherine looking at me with pity or with fear; I didn't want her *ever* thinking that I would let something happen to either one of you."

When Tamara's eyes begged the question, he said, "I know I need to tell her." She watched him take in the four walls of the office, the certificates that graced the walls, the books neatly standing up like soldiers. "I know I can't hide behind this place any more," he said. "I kept your mum away from the books because I knew that she'd want me to retire straight away. We are *very* financially stable – hell, I could take her on a world cruise if I wanted to; maybe have a house here and one in the UK near you."

The chair creaked beneath him as though it was as tired of all this as he was. "I think that Jake taking the Dogtails contract gave me someone to lash out at, and the financial concern seemed the only way I could hang on to the practice for a bit longer." Bobby chuckled and that familiar belly laugh almost rose to the surface. "Did you know that Archie used to call us the A-team?" He turned another page of the album to reveal a photo of Archie helping to bandage a kitten's paw. "Not the A-team from the telly, but the *Animal Team*."

Tamara moved to give her stepfather an enormous hug. "Bobby?"

"Yes, love?"

"Can I ask whether your secret was what drove you to come to Australia in the first place? Was it a way to escape what happened?"

He hesitated. "I suppose part of me wondered whether I could really leave my past behind, but deep down I knew that distance wouldn't matter. So no, love. Emigrating was my and Katherine's plan for years, instigated by the miserable winters in the UK and the attraction of an outdoor lifestyle." He looked at her now. "We thought you'd join us eventually, and not just for a holiday."

"Who knows, maybe one day I will," she grinned.

"Are you angry with me?" He dropped his gaze. "For not telling you, I mean?"

"You know, I think the only time I've ever been really angry with you is when you wouldn't let me go to the school disco with

Alan Grey, because you'd seen him driving some souped-up banger and racing another car down the high street. I don't think I could ever be that angry with you again."

This time the full belly laugh echoed through the surgery; the sound of Bobby Harding. "Boy, do I remember that?" He whistled. "You slammed your door – took a good dose of Polyfilla and a few coats of paint to patch that up – you called me all the names under the sun."

She giggled, relieved to have the old Bobby surface again. But then she grimaced. "Oh no," she shut her eyes, remembering. "I stopped off at Jake's before I drove here."

"And?" he asked.

"And I really let him have it about Dogtails. I was really awful to him. Do you think I need to apologise?"

Bobby leant forward in his chair. "I don't know much about that boy, Tamara. But I think I'm a good enough judge of character to say that he isn't out to sabotage anyone's business. There'll be more to him than meets the eye, you mark my words. And another thing…"

"What?"

"That boy likes you." He winked.

"Yes, well that boy is going to be a father, remember?" She picked up her car keys. "Come on, I promised Mum I'd bring you home." She linked Bobby's arm as he got to his feet. "And Bobby?"

"Yes, love?"

"Don't book her a cruise. Mum couldn't think of anything worse."

His laugh rumbled around the surgery as they left together, father and daughter, starting a new chapter in their lives.

Chapter Twenty

When Tamara and Bobby returned to the house, Katherine was in the kitchen progressing through a recipe for Beef Wellington, Bobby's favourite. The radio played in the background and Tamara knew that her mum was in her own world, contemplating what was happening within her marriage as she folded in the ends of the pastry.

When she heard a noise behind her, Katherine turned and pressed her face into the safety of Bobby's chest. "I was so worried about you."

Tamara took control of the lunch and brushed the sides of the pastry with egg before slotting the beef into the oven. She peeled the vegetables already laid out on the chopping board as her parents hugged one another in silence.

"Thank you," said Katherine, turning her head to the side.

Tamara couldn't speak. She knew what was coming and had promised Bobby that she would be with him every step of the way. And with the photo album in his hand, the meat safely in the oven, and the vegetables waiting, he found his moment.

The truth came out more coherent than she had expected it to and Katherine let him hold on to her hand throughout, as though the energy and feel from her skin kept his momentum going.

A stunned silence engulfed the room. Katherine stared at the embroidered edge of the maroon tablecloth, her eyes unblinking. And then she pulled her hand away.

Tamara's eyes darted between both of her parents, feeling each and every stab of pain. There were no tears, no raised voices. The only sound came from the whirring of the fan oven.

"I'd better get the vegetables on." Katherine moved to stand but Bobby stopped her.

"Please sit down, Katherine." He gave Tamara a look that begged her to stay. This secret that he had kept for years was out now and Tamara knew he was afraid that if she left, he wouldn't be able to find the words to explain everything to his wife, to look for a way to move past this.

Katherine rubbed her clean hands against her apron. "I don't understand. I don't understand how you could've kept this from me. In all the years of our marriage, in every facet of our lives, you have always been so honest."

Distraught, Bobby didn't look up.

Almost afraid to touch her husband, Katherine's hands moved to the safety of her lap. "I thought we shared everything."

Tamara put a hand on her mum's arm and felt her body retract. Katherine sat as still as the salt shaker in the centre of the table, her back rigid as though one nudge could topple her over and cause her to smash into tiny little pieces all over the floor.

Bobby pulled the photo album from its place on his lap and laid it on the table. He pushed it slowly towards his wife.

"What's that?" she asked.

"It's my past."

"Is it photos of them?"

When he nodded, Katherine shook her head. "I'm not ready."

Bobby looked as though he had aged twenty years in the last twenty minutes.

"I hardly know you, Bobby," said Katherine.

His shoulders slumped further. "Don't say that. Please, don't say that."

Katherine stood and walked away from the table. Tamara sat and took Bobby's hand and they waited in silence for her mum to come back. But all they heard was a click of the front door. With a gulp Tamara realised that there was nothing she could do or say to take away that pain in Bobby's eyes. This rock-solid couple, the epitome of a great marriage and the one constant in her life, was broken and she didn't know whether it could ever be fixed.

Chapter Twenty-One

Tamara found her mum leaning up against the fence of the Jackson property, watching a calf finding its feet.

"How did you know where to find me?" Katherine asked.

"Just a feeling I had." Tamara leant up against the fence, too, glad that Fergus wasn't around today – not that she went into strange fields any more after their last encounter.

It was obvious that her mum had been crying. Her cheeks were still flushed, her eyes bloodshot.

"I watched that calf being delivered," said Katherine, her gaze fixed ahead. "We were on our way home from the Blue Mountains when Bobby was called out to help."

When they had returned to the house that day, Tamara knew that she had never seen a couple more in love. Throughout her adolescence and her adulthood, if ever there was any doubt that a man and a woman could find true love, then all Tamara had to do was look at her parents – until now.

"Bobby was amazing that day," Katherine continued. "He convinced Matthew Jackson that his son, Kenny, was quite capable of taking charge of the delivery. The calf was as it should be – front feet first, followed by its nose against its knees – and with the aid of some calf ropes and a puller, and Bobby guiding him every step of the way, Kenny helped to deliver the calf safe and sound."

Tamara smiled at how much her mum knew about animals after so many wonderful years with Bobby.

"Calves are physically mobile from the moment of birth," said

Katherine, "not like human babies." She nodded towards the calf. "You didn't walk like that until you were almost nineteen months old."

"That's late, isn't it?"

"I suppose so, but I wasn't worried. I think that you could worry yourself silly at every stage of a child's development if you let yourself." When the wind lifted her hair, Katherine moved it away from her face. "You were later than most to read, too."

"I didn't know that."

"Oh you'd never know it now. Bobby and I spent hours working with you to get you to the same level as the rest of your classmates. Do you remember those books he made for you?"

"Yes!" She'd forgotten all about them until now. Bobby had hand-drawn four books with stories about them as a family. "Hang on, let me think: *Tamara takes Bo to the vet*; a story about a trip on a ferry, from what I remember; and my favourite, the story about shoe shopping."

The look of joy on Katherine's face as she remembered those books was priceless. "He spent hours illustrating those simple stories, and then cutting out letters on squares so that you could make the words yourself and put together your own sentences."

"Do you still have the books?" Tamara asked.

Katherine laughed. "Bobby will never throw them away. He's secretly hoping that you'll pass them onto our grandchildren one day."

Tamara smiled. "One day I will."

"He was so proud of you when you caught up to your friends in reading, and I still remember the day you got your University degree."

Tamara winced. "I seem to remember he cried, in front of my friends."

"He's a big softie," Katherine gushed. "When you landed your job at Wellington Smart, he told everyone he knew about his clever daughter and how proud he was." Her laugh echoed across the fields. "I had to tell him to stop telling all the clients or they

175

would start complaining and go elsewhere."

Tamara suspected that all this happy reminiscing was about to come to an end.

"Don't you see?" Katherine turned to face her. "The lies that he's told over all these years makes my past feel like a sham."

"It wasn't a sham, Mum."

"But nothing was real. What he's told me now makes everything else feel like a lie." She sniffed. "I don't think I've been in this much pain since your father died."

Tears sprung to Tamara's eyes. She hadn't shed many tears over the father she barely knew, but was well aware that it would have been easy for her mum to have fallen apart back then.

"The pain was quick, severe, and raw when Anayo died," said Katherine. "But this pain, knowing that Bobby has lied intentionally for so long; this pain is like someone slowly turning a knife, and I keep wondering when it'll stop or whether it will keep on getting worse. How can I trust a man whom I've always thought was so honest, so genuine?"

After a while, Tamara said, "I don't have all the answers, Mum. I can see this from your point of view, but I can see it from his as well."

Katherine looked crestfallen.

"Please don't look at it as me being disloyal, because that's not true. And I'm not trying to simplify the situation, either. Fundamentally, lying is wrong, but I don't think that Bobby did it out of spite. You need to listen to him now that you've had the initial shock, you need to see the man you love and give him a chance."

One of the heifers came over to investigate who these two people were leaning on the fence, then after a quick sniff turned her back.

"Bobby raised me to be open and honest," said Tamara. "Perhaps part of that upbringing stemmed from him knowing how horrid it is to keep secrets from the people you love, and maybe he didn't want me to repeat his mistakes. But whatever his reasoning, I won't ever regret having him in our lives. I feel blessed, Mum."

"But to keep a wife and a child from me – from us…"

"It's huge, I agree, and I'm not so naïve that I think you should gloss over it and carry on as normal. I know that that won't happen. But please give him a chance to try and explain."

"I don't think that I can."

"But how do you know until you try?"

***

Back at the Harding property, Bobby was standing at the kitchen sink looking out over the rear of the property. Mesmerised by the gum trees, he didn't hear them until they were already in the kitchen.

Katherine sat down at the table as Tamara made the tea.

"I need you to tell me again, Bobby," said Katherine. "I need you to tell me everything from the start, and please, don't leave anything out."

He started from the beginning, right from the moment he married Nancy, then when Archie was born, all the way up until the moment he lost the life he once had.

"I wanted and needed to start afresh," he said. "The pain was overwhelming. Everyone knew. I would pass people in the street and I could see the pity in their eyes, and I knew that to have any hope of ever moving past losing my family I had to start again."

"When you met us, were we…" Katherine couldn't get the words out.

"Were you what?"

"I need to know. Were we replacements for the family you'd lost? Or did you want us for who we were?"

His face fell. He shook his head over and over. "I guess I deserve that question." He reached a hand out, and this time Katherine gripped it.

Tamara set the tea quietly down on the table and pulled out a chair as Bobby continued.

"You girls came to me when I least expected. I thought I'd never get over the family that I'd lost. All I wanted to do was get away and start over, on my own, throw myself into work and try to make sense of it all. And then one day, there you were, both of you in the park right beside the practice."

Tamara couldn't remember – she was too young – but they had walked in that park, he had taught her to ride her very first bike there, and she had heard the story a thousand times. Apparently it had been Tamara who had struck up a conversation with him first, about the mist hanging in the air and exactly how it came to be there.

"That first time you let me buy you coffee, Katherine, I knew that I'd found a friend. But you were sophisticated, well-dressed, and there I was in my tatty jeans probably smelling of animals or disinfectant. I thought that you'd never look at me twice."

"Why would you think that?" Memories of those first days seemed to work like medicine, soothing her, chasing away the fear that she wasn't the love in his life that he had always claimed.

"Because you're you: you're beautiful, funny, elegant, and I'm me, plain old Bobby. I promise you that I never once used you and Tamara to put together a family to replace the one I lost. I regret now that I didn't tell you everything, but I couldn't bear the thought of you being with me because you felt pity for me. I wanted your love, the unique love between a man and a woman, and I wanted nothing less."

Katherine slid the album to where she was sitting, but it remained unopened.

"It's still me, Katherine. I'm still me."

"I need to know, Bobby, what made you suddenly tell us now?" Her hands sat firmly on top of the album and Tamara held her breath.

Guiltily, he said, "I was angry about Jake and Dogtails, but I was more mad at myself that I'd put off retirement because of some silly notion about keeping Nancy and Archie's memory alive. That's why I pretended that we were struggling, refused to let you see the accounts."

Her grip strengthened around his. "Bobby, your memories are all in your head, safe and secure, under lock and key for good. Nobody can take those away from you. Retiring wouldn't change anything."

"She's right," said Tamara. "I think that if Archie was here, he'd be telling you the same thing."

"Do you know, he'd be almost forty by now," Bobby smiled, running a hand across his chin. "He'd probably be telling me I was too old." He let his own memories unlock and release him into the present, then he turned to Katherine. "I'm so sorry, so very, very sorry."

As Tamara crept away, she watched them lean into each other, their heads touching. Her eyes filled with tears as she heard Bobby weep more than she had ever heard any man weep before.

***

Tamara pulled the Beef Wellington from the oven. It had dried out a little in the time that she'd taken sanctuary in the annexe, but it was still edible. She threw the vegetables into the awaiting pans and set the table as Katherine and Bobby reappeared from their walk up to the orchards.

Katherine dropped some fresh lemons into the bowl beside the sink and Tamara wrapped her arms around her mum. When she looked up into red-rimmed eyes, she didn't see the fear and shock that had been there before, but rather a look of contentment, a look that said that this wouldn't destroy a marriage which had the sturdiest of foundations.

"I'll get that," said Tamara, at the sound of the doorbell. It was only when she opened it that she remembered how she owed someone a big apology for jumping to conclusions. Jake stood on the doorstep, and for a moment her vocal chords forgot how to work.

His hat hung from his fingertips and his hand edged nervously along the tiny indented pattern around the brim. "Can I come in?"

"Sure."

He followed her silently through to the kitchen, and if Jake noticed anything out of the ordinary, then he was too polite to say.

"I've come to talk to you about the Dogtails contract," he began without preamble when he saw Bobby. "It's yours if you want it. I don't want anyone thinking that I've come to Brewer Creek to cause trouble." His voice quavered and the deep blond strands of his hair shone under the kitchen lights.

"The contract's yours, Jake."

Tamara wasn't surprised at Bobby's reaction. He had other things on his mind now.

Jake stumbled with his words. "I don't know what to say. I—"

"No need to say anything." Bobby shook his hand to show that there were no hard feelings, and Jake must have picked up on the atmosphere in the room because he nodded his goodbyes, picked up his hat, and walked back to the front door.

Tamara followed him out to his pick-up. "I owe you an apology, Jake," she said, before he managed to sit down in the driver's seat. "I'm sorry I lost it at you. Bobby said that he hadn't answered Dogtails' emails about the renewal, and he'd forgotten about it until the last minute."

She softened at the watery glint to his eyes that she had never seen before. His hand rubbed across his chin making scratchy noises against the stubble. "We all want to protect the people we love, Tamara."

His eyes held hers for long enough to make her insides bubble up like a thick, melting pot of chocolate fondue. The wind churned up around her as she stood glued to the spot, and she could feel a stone underfoot, digging into her skin.

"Have you seen Mr Wilson?" she asked, anxious to salvage something from the stilted atmosphere. "He asks after you."

"I'm off to see him again later," he said, the anxiety on his face replaced by a contented smile.

He pulled the door of the pick-up shut and stretched his arm out through the open window, and Tamara froze as his hand moved towards her face. She held her breath and then, like a crafty magician, he pulled a thin twig from her hair that must've caught as she passed by the bare bush near the front door.

"He challenged me to a game of poker last time," said Jake, unaware of the effect his touch had had on her.

When she regained composure, she said, "He's got me playing sevens and gin rummy." She bent down to remove the stone from underfoot. "You should take Waffles to see him, he'd love that."

Their eyes locked before he said, "I'd better go."

And away he went with his secrets still intact.

Tamara ate her lunch quietly and nobody spoke of Jake or much else. Afterwards she went to the bathroom and used a pumice stone to attack her feet. She slathered on some peppermint moisturiser and, feeling restless, pulled on a pair of trainers, left her parents to have some quality time alone together, and plucked the car keys from the hook in the hallway.

***

Jake opened the tin of dog food and scraped half of it into a bowl. Already he had become too attached – it was one of the perils of being a vet. He had offered to take Waffles when the owner, in ill-health and eager to re-house the dog before he went into hospital, couldn't find anyone to take her off his hands. In the short time that he'd had the dog, Waffles had gone from bounding around like a frenzied psychotic canine to a more controlled, yet still playful dog who now understood "heel", "sit", "walkies", and all the other dog language that they had jointly deciphered in their time together.

Having a dog around the place had helped settle April's nerves, too. Since that weekend in Sydney and her sighting of Marty, all her sense of safety had vanished. Instead of glowing and enjoying her second trimester, some days it was next to impossible to convince her to even leave the house.

Jake scribbled a note to April and propped it on the kitchen bench so that she would know he wouldn't be gone for long: he knew that the minute she realised she was alone, she would bolt that door and put the chain across, but it wasn't worth waking her now to put the fear of God into her again.

"Come on, girl." He tapped the floor of his pick-up and Waffles jumped obligingly into the back. He loaded up the dog basket with a bag of tricks that he had packed, along with a lead, some tins of food, a few toys, and a blanket that smelled of his place. Waffles sat wagging her tail and sniffing the air all the way to Mr Wilson's, as though she was taking in her altered surroundings already.

"Those training classes sure paid off, didn't they?" Jake fussed over Waffles when she sat at his command. He tapped lightly on the front door and tried not to look quite so taken aback when the door eventually opened. "Hey."

"Hey." The skin between Tamara's eyebrows creased in that cute little way they did when she wasn't sure what to say.

"We weren't expecting you, were we, Waffles?" He bent to stroke the tufts of fur at the ends of the dog's ears, a move that was sure to make her tail wag with fervour. Looking away from Tamara was the only way to put him at ease.

"Mr Wilson, Jake's here." Tamara held a hand of cards between her fingers and used her other hand to make a fuss of Waffles, who sniffed inquisitively at her ankles.

"Come in, lad." Mr Wilson appeared behind Tamara, who was giggling at Waffles' tongue tickling her legs. "I'll put a brew on. Make yourself at home."

"I was at a loose end," Tamara explained, as Jake followed her into the lounge room and Waffles became more interested in Mr Wilson.

Was it too ambitious to hope that Tamara was here because she knew that he was coming over this afternoon? When he and April had come up with the elaborate scheme to tell people they were a couple, his only concern had been avoiding Marty and keeping his sister safe. Back then he hadn't factored in falling for someone as special as Tamara, but life had a funny way of providing surprises.

"Here you go, Jake." Mr Wilson delivered a slightly too-full cup of tea and, careful not to trip over Waffles, set it safely on the side table next to the tatty green velvet winged chair.

"And what can we get for you, you beautiful thing?" He bent down the best he could to make a fuss over Waffles, and on cue Jake stood and went back outside.

He reappeared with the basket and set it in the lounge as Tamara shuffled the deck of cards.

"I've won every game so far, Jake." Mr Wilson smiled impishly.

Jake grinned as Mr Wilson rummaged in the basket and pulled out a chew toy for Waffles. "That's her favourite." He gestured at the bite marks in the toy that proved his claim. "Actually, Mr Wilson, I need to have a serious talk with you."

Mr Wilson lowered himself into the winged chair opposite Jake, one hand ruffling Waffles' fur. "Is everything okay, lad?"

Jake tried to drag his gaze away from Tamara, her soft shoulders beneath a white sleeveless t-shirt that showed off her silky skin. "Waffles is almost one," he managed, "and she needs a good home. I'm too busy with my work to give her the attention she deserves." He watched the dog settle at Mr Wilson's feet and gnaw on the chew toy, making it squeak in protest. "She likes you."

Mr Wilson understood. "But she's yours. I can't possibly–"

"I really need you to do this for me." He had known all along that Mr Wilson wouldn't accept Waffles if he thought Jake was being soft and feeling sorry for him. He was an old man, but he still had his pride, and Jake wanted to respect that.

"She doesn't deserve to be locked inside all day while I work," Jake continued. "She needs to be walked, fussed over; to be with someone who has time for her. And she's well-trained already." He had seen to that. Mr Wilson needed companionship but it had taken some time to get Waffles ready to do that rather than run the old man ragged.

Mr Wilson stood and held out his hand. "Jake, it would be an honour." He bent down to Waffles. "You hear that, my girl? This is going to be your new home, now what do you think about that?" Waffles' tail thwacked against the carpet. "Come on. Let's go outside in the sunshine. There's a patch out there where my dear old Ada is buried, and you can play there. I think she would've liked that."

Mr Wilson shuffled outside onto the grass, still wearing his slippers. Jake could tell that Tamara was watching him as he unloaded the basket and took the dog food out of the box and towards the kitchen. He hadn't intended to do this in front of anyone, and he suddenly felt self-conscious as though his motives would come into question.

"Let me take those," she said, holding out her hands for the paraphernalia that came with a pet. "I know where they go."

Jake looked out of the kitchen window as Tamara stacked the tins in the cupboard and found a home for the dog biscuits. When she was finished, she stood next to him and they watched man and dog bond in the fresh air beneath a sky that was so busy with clouds that afternoon, it was as though they were on fast forward.

"You've made his day, you know," she said.

On the patch of newly-grown grass that was still in its infancy, Waffles rolled onto her back for Mr Wilson to tickle her tummy. The old man's smile would match the vibrancy of the blue-mauve jacaranda tree behind when it came into full bloom in the spring.

"I needed to talk to *you* about something, too." Jake turned to Tamara as she turned the taps on full pelt, ready to wash the mugs from their tea. He could see no end to this pressure cooker existence, and he was torn between his desire to share everything with this girl and the need to protect the other women he loved.

When she squirted washing-up liquid into the water, he said, "It's about April." And before he lost his nerve, he added, "The baby isn't mine."

"What?"

He leapt forwards and turned the taps off just in time, before the kitchen turned into Niagara Falls; why there was no overflow outlet baffled him, but he pulled the plug out for long enough to take the level down a couple of inches.

"Thanks." Tamara didn't look up. She loaded the dirty crockery into the sink and kept her gaze on Waffles sniffing at the back fence outside. Without looking at Jake, she said, "But you two *are* a couple, right? I mean, who's the father? Why are you with April, I don't get it?" All the questions fired at him, one after the other.

He pushed his hands into the pockets of his faded jeans and watched her looking for another job to occupy her hands. "It's complicated."

She laughed, but now she looked at him, her eyes searching for answers. "That's a cop-out if ever I heard one. You know, April hinted to me in the city that there was something I didn't know. What are you two hiding?"

"That text you saw was from my mum," he said. He wanted to tell her that April was his sister, but it was too risky. Marty had connections all over Australia. Jake had been witness to interstate calls, emails that he should never have seen. He knew that just because they were on the other side of the country, they shouldn't assume Marty wouldn't be able to put out feelers and track down a vet and his sister, new arrivals in a small town. He had to wait a little while longer and then he would tell her everything.

"I don't understand," said Tamara. She was a different girl to the one who'd metaphorically had him by the balls that afternoon. "I feel as though you and April keep giving me pieces of a mega puzzle, but my head can't put them together. Why didn't April tell me who the text was from? I don't understand why she wanted me to think that you were cheating on her."

Because it was easier than the truth, he wanted to say.

He took Tamara's hands in his own as she slumped down onto a kitchen chair. He gripped her hands firmly, reassuring her;

reassuring himself. Then he gently tilted her chin so that she met his gaze, his face inches from hers.

When the back door opened, they sprung apart before he had a chance to say more. Mr Wilson wiped his slippers on the mat and Waffles bounded up to Jake and Tamara for a fuss. Tamara's eyes pleaded with Jake for a proper explanation as his heart thumped in his chest. All he wanted to do was take her in his arms and kiss her, never let her go.

A faint vibrating sound from her phone on the kitchen table took her attention away from the moment. "Sorry, I thought I'd switched that off."

Jake watched her answer the call. He watched her face change.

"Is everything okay?" he asked, desperate to talk with her some more, spend time with her; show her that he wasn't the arsehole she thought he was.

She patted her pockets for her car key, then found it on the table where her phone had been. She kissed Mr Wilson on the cheek and murmured goodbye to Jake.

"Everything's fine," she called, before heading out of the front door so quickly that Jake had the feeling that now *she* had something to hide.

Chapter Twenty-Two

"Can I get you a coffee, tea, coke, water?" The civil words flowed uncontrollably out of Tamara's mouth – a reaction to the shock as she closed the door of the lounge behind them. The main part of the house seemed a more sensible option than taking him into the annexe.

Bradley shook his head. "No thanks."

"What are you doing here?" She felt her chest constrict at the sight of him here in Australia, looking out of place in a pair of crumpled, khaki shorts and a plain navy t-shirt, instead of the familiar designer suit and tie.

"You never replied to any of my messages." He took his hands from his pockets and started towards her.

Tamara moved quickly to the other side of the room and gestured for him to sit down as she flopped into one of the other armchairs. She didn't trust herself under his touch; the touch that she knew would weaken her resolve through its tenderness and familiarity.

She stared at the caramel carpet. "I didn't ignore you," she said.

When he moved to kneel down in front of her, she was left with no choice but to look at him.

"I miss you, Tamara. Why didn't you say goodbye? Did it really mean so little to you?"

His body moved and collapsed like a concertina onto the armchair beside her in defeat. "Was I really that awful?"

Her top teeth bit into her lower lip. "You're right, I should've said goodbye. But when you pushed me, I–"

"I didn't mean to push you over, Tamara. I'd been drinking, and what I meant as a bit of a playful shove went too far."

"Well if you hadn't meant it, why didn't you contact me after it happened? Why didn't you apologise there and then?"

He shifted in his seat and clasped his hands together nervously. "I don't know. I think I was embarrassed, ashamed. I think I panicked because doing that to you reminded me of what my dad did to my mum over the years. I never want to be *that* person; I'm *not* that person."

His remorse tugged at her heart in a way that almost caused her physical pain. She had never been the sort of person to turn her back on anyone.

He leant across and took one of her hands in his; this time she didn't pull away. "I'm not here to go over old ground. I'm only in Sydney for a few more days and I thought we could hang out, as friends if that's what you want. I'd like to spend some time with you."

And there it was, as much as she didn't want them to, the butterflies in her tummy felt as though they had started to take part in an illegal rave. She knew she should do what was best for her, but at the same time she was drawn to Bradley, drawn to their history, and felt for this man who had no other genuine friendships to call upon.

There was a quiet knock at the door before Katherine came in with a tray bearing two cups of tea and some freshly baked scones, along with homemade raspberry jam and fresh cream.

"Thank you, Mrs Harding," said Bradley.

"You're welcome." She glanced over to Tamara, who gave her a look to reassure her that everything was fine, and left the room again leaving the door ajar.

Seeing Bradley sitting at the kitchen table when she arrived home had been a major shock to Tamara, but in a way perhaps it was what she had needed. The fact that she was in an entirely different environment, with her family close by for support, made her feel more empowered than ever to stay in control. She passed

Bradley a scone and set down a cup of tea beside him.

"How did you know where to find me?" she asked. She didn't touch her own tea.

"You told me the name of the village where your mum lived ages ago."

She couldn't believe that he remembered.

"From what you'd told me, I knew that Brewer Creek wasn't a big town so I figured somebody around here would know where I could find you. I asked in the shop and the lady in there pointed me in this direction." He grinned. "She showed me this friendship tree thing that you're responsible for. I didn't realise you'd changed career."

It riled her, the way he took the piss out of something that he knew nothing about, and she bristled at the thought of him coming in and belittling Brewer Creek and its sense of community.

"I haven't changed career," she snapped. "I'm working for a firm in the city."

Bradley quizzed her about her job and then regaled stories of his trip all the way up the East Coast of Australia. As he spoke, Tamara's mind drifted to Jake and what had happened in Mr Wilson's kitchen before they were interrupted. The way he made her feel was different to the effect Bradley had on her. Bradley had been mysterious right from the start, but most of the pull had been about the heat of their relationship and the grand gestures which had fooled her into thinking she was in love with someone different.

She came out of her reverie as Bradley described a peculiar jellyfish that he had encountered up the coast, and she pretended to be amazed, her eyes widening as though she was impressed when he indicated the size of the thing.

"You look different," he said, perhaps detecting her disinterest.

"What do you mean, different?"

He gestured to her shorts and flip-flops, her vest top. It was a far cry from her wardrobe back in London, full of seriously-cut suits and tailored dresses teamed with skyscraper heels. She also knew that her daily walks and fewer nights in front of the TV agreed with her figure, and her curves were now more toned. It didn't escape her notice that Bradley looked leaner, too, tauter from not sitting behind a desk all day, but she didn't mention it.

He looked out the window over the acres of fields beyond. "How can you stand being out here?" He lowered his voice. "What with that daft tree and everything, it seems so slow."

Tamara collected the plates and cups and stacked them on the tray. "It's not slow, Bradley. It's just different." He'd always had set ideas about the world, how places should be, how people should interact. She was surprised she hadn't noticed it quite so much before.

She moved to take the tray to the kitchen, but he grabbed her wrist before she could pass.

"I miss you," he said.

She felt his breath against her cheek and his lips grazed the skin beside her mouth. Her mind knew what she wanted to do but her body was responding in a totally different way. It had been so long since she had felt his touch that when he took the tray from her arms and wrapped his hands around her waist to pull her close, the feel of him left her defenceless. She let herself drown in his kiss: passionate, familiar, and just as wanting as it had always been.

As he pulled away, he breathed into her hair. "When are you coming home?" His body slouched so that his eyes were in line with hers. "When are you coming back to London, to where you belong?"

When his lips grazed her neck, it was enough to bring her to her senses. She pulled away. Already she had visions of him standing in the Arrivals hall at Heathrow ready to pick up where they left off.

"Are you telling me that this is what you really want?" he continued. "You don't miss your flat, your friends, your life?"

She folded her arms. "I'm not coming back to London yet; who knows when I will? I have a life *here* now. I have friends, I'm with my family, and I've got a whole new city… a whole new country to explore. You must get that, being a traveller, surely?"

He shrugged and she knew that he didn't. She realised he had never understood her and had never really bothered to try.

He looked out of the window at the unfamiliar landscape. "This isn't you," he said matter-of-factly. "It's not you at all."

He was like a boomerang, and every time she threw him as hard as she could he somehow came back and landed at her feet.

"Can I see more of you while I'm here?" he asked.

This time she picked up the tray and wedged it firmly in front of her as a barricade. "There's a pub in town. We'll go there for a drink and perhaps you can meet a few of the locals; my friends." Seeing that she had a social life would let him know she was moving on and not doing too bad a job of it. It would also grant him some time with her without having to be alone. She knew he wouldn't cope with having to share her for too long; he'd never wanted to share her with anyone.

"The last train back to the city is at ten o'clock," he said, as she took the tray into the kitchen.

Without looking back, she said, "I'll make sure you're on it."

***

"You owe me some money." Danielle stuck out her hand as she shuffled her bottom onto the stool next to Tamara.

Tamara frowned for a moment and then gasped. "Did he call?"

"Uh-huh! And it's Friday… so the money is all mine!"

Tamara threw her arms around her friend and gestured to Bradley at the other end of the bar to order another beer.

"I said I'd go to the city next weekend. He offered to come out here but I'd much rather go there for the first time."

"Don't blame you. So where are you meeting him?"

"Out front of the same bar where we met the first time. He lives in Manly, so he suggested we catch the ferry over there if we have time." She took a deep breath. "I'm going to get on that same website and book a room in the city again. And before you say anything, it'll just be me staying there. I won't be leaping into bed with him. Not yet anyway!"

"I'm so happy for you," Tamara said.

Bradley cradled the drinks and the girls manoeuvred them from his hands as Tamara made the introductions. She could feel a few locals glance their way but, casually dressed, Bradley almost blended in.

Tamara watched his mouth tug back at the corners as though tasting some type of petrol. "Don't you like it?" she asked.

"It's not the—"

"It's not the same as we get back home. I know, Bradley. But that doesn't mean it's no good; it's just different." She looked at Danielle, who was busy making well-aren't-you-going-to-explain type facial expressions.

"I know Bradley from my time in London," said Tamara. "He's in Australia travelling with some mates."

"Great. So how are you enjoying this awesome country so far?"

He swallowed his glug of beer a little easier this time, and then recounted some stories as Danielle listened intently and Tamara pretended to do the same.

"I've only got a couple of months left – I took four-and-a-half months' unpaid leave in all, but I'll have to get back to reality at some point. I was hoping I could persuade this one to come with me." He patted Tamara's knee, oblivious to the way she tensed up.

Tamara silently thanked Danielle for not carrying on that line of conversation, and instead asking him more about his exploits in Sydney and up the coast. For a while Tamara saw nothing but the *good* Bradley; the *kind* Bradley. But there was no escaping the possessive Bradley. His hand stayed in position on her knee.

"So what do you do, Danielle?" he asked.

Danielle explained her family situation and her goal over the next couple of years, and Bradley asked polite questions, sounding interested. But when talk turned to Brewer Creek, its residents and all its idiosyncrasies, Tamara noticed the tension in his jaw as he saw how effortlessly she had slotted into this town. No longer was she a puppet that he could put down and then pick up again when he wanted to, untangle its strings and start playing with it in the same way.

"Does anyone want another drink?" The need to escape his touch became intense, and Tamara headed up to the bar where she reeled off their order, hoping that Len wouldn't be too efficient this time.

"A Diet Coke please, and a light beer," came a voice from beside her, as Tamara counted out the money.

She daren't turn to see if April had brought Jake in tonight but she didn't need to. She could feel that he was here without glancing around. She could feel her throat constricting again, unsure how to handle the situation with the two very different men in her life.

"I know that Jake told you," April said, as they waited for their drinks. "About the baby, I mean."

When Tamara didn't speak, she added, "He likes you." She nodded to Len to drop a slice of lemon into her Diet Coke.

Tamara glanced over and saw the man from her past and the man whom she wished could hold her future, shake hands; the contrast of the city meeting the country as they exchanged pleasantries.

"Let's join the others." Tamara hooked her fingers around the drinks.

"Hang on." April pulled her back. "He really does, and I know him well, Tamara. He will tell you everything when he can but–"

"Who's the father?" Tamara hadn't meant it to sound so accusatory, but it was another part of the puzzle that she was growing increasingly frustrated with trying to put together.

April looked down, but her words came out fighting and firm. "The father is a married man, Tamara. What can I say? I picked a dud, that's for sure."

"I'm sorry."

"For what?" she asked.

193

"For the situation you're in. I assume the married man has no intention of leaving his wife?"

She shook her head. "It's fine. I'm better off without him; I see that now."

Tamara knew there was more, but she could tell that was all she was going to get for tonight, and she needed to get back to the others. The last thing she needed right now was for Bradley to go quiet and sulky if he picked up on any signs of attraction between her and Jake. New friends in her life were one thing but another man was quite different, and she didn't want a scene. She wanted Bradley to leave here knowing that she had moved on, but she didn't want to hurt him any more than she had to.

"April, this is Bradley," she said, as she took a seat on the stool beside him. "He's a friend from London."

Bradley leant across and shook April's hand. "It's nice to meet you. Tamara has told me a lot about you all."

She had done nothing of the sort, but it seemed the natural thing to say and anything that could make this moment less awkward was welcome right now.

"Well, we've heard nothing about you." Danielle sipped her drink. "Are you two, you know, together?"

Tamara recoiled, but the question shouldn't be surprising given how close Bradley had shifted towards her as soon as she sat back down.

"We used to go out, back in London." Tamara tried to keep her tone light and avoid Bradley's gaze – or Jake's, for that matter. She knew Jake was eyeing her with interest, and momentarily she was back there in Mr Wilson's kitchen with him telling her as much as he could, almost admitting that he had feelings for her.

"What do you do back in London, Bradley?" April asked.

"I'm a journalist."

"That's exciting. Do you work for the tabloids?"

"I work for a regional newspaper, but eventually I'd like to get into something more major; sports journalism, I hope."

"So where did you guys meet?" Danielle passed around a bag

of salty peanuts.

Tamara jumped in with a snapshot version of the story of the launch party and the tequila costumes before Bradley could beat her to it. As she told it, his arm snaked across her shoulders and she fidgeted beneath.

"So what do you do?" Bradley asked Jake, with an unnecessary brusqueness. Tamara knew what he was doing. He was trying to find out whether he was on a better standing than this other man; which of them had the better job and prospects.

Jake chatted happily about his work in Brewer Creek, but all the while Tamara was aware of Bradley's hand moving back to caress her knee. Jake watched the uninvited gesture and, as Bradley's hand inched a little higher up Tamara's thigh, she noticed Jake's bottle of beer pause mid-air. The whole time they had been dating in London, this possessive behaviour had been Bradley's way of letting the world know that Tamara was his.

The evening continued pleasantly enough. April talked about her course and her assignments, and Danielle showed sympathy, knowing that she would soon be doing the same. Jake told a few tales of assignment deadlines back when he was doing his training to be a vet, and Bradley sat quietly, not contributing to the conversation but being a part of the group nevertheless with his hand practically superglued in place. He was like a skittish feline marking out his territory. All that was missing was him standing up and peeing all around Tamara's stool.

"I've told this girl, that once we get back to London she'll have to smarten up her image." Bradley signalled Tamara's jeans with the small, yet obvious rip in the upper thigh.

"I think she fits in quite well." Jake took a confident swig of his beer and watched the hard line form on Bradley's lips. "Maybe she'll end up staying."

Tamara stood up abruptly; she couldn't take the tension any longer. "We'd better go." She pushed her empty glass onto the bar. "Bradley needs to catch the last train," she explained, unable to meet anyone's gaze.

When they left the pub and Bradley held the door open for her, she stole one last look at Jake sitting at the bar. She could barely breathe when her eyes locked with his.

Neither she nor Bradley spoke on the short drive to the station, and when Tamara pulled up in front of the brick archway, she kept the engine running.

"I was out of order tonight, wasn't I?" Bradley broke the silence. When Tamara looked at him, she thought how out of depth he was in this unfamiliar territory, as though his internal compass had gone off course.

"I guess it's my jealousy getting the better of me," he went on. "I forget that we're no longer together because that's not what I want."

When she still didn't speak, he said, "I've told you how I feel but all I really want is for you to be happy." He pulled the door open and stepped out into the night. "Goodbye, Tamara."

She drove away without a second glance, eyes fixed straight ahead and her mind ticking over the events of the day. And then, in the safety of the annexe at the Harding property, she turned on the radio to muffle the tears which flowed from the shock of seeing him, and the sadness in her heart that deep down he really did love her. Sometimes loving someone wasn't enough; sometimes it simply wasn't right, and seeing Bradley that afternoon hadn't brought the closure that Tamara had hoped for. Instead, she felt all the more vulnerable and as though the sense of self that she had tried to establish for so long, was rapidly spiralling out of control.

Chapter Twenty-Three

Jake's mind was on anything but the paperwork in front of him. April was feeling the tiredness more and more, and he'd told her to rest up while he waded through invoices and receipts and put together what he needed to complete this year's tax return.

He tapped his pen up and down between his teeth and thought about Tamara. He'd seen her that morning, running under the archway at Brewer Creek station so that she didn't miss the last train. She'd seen him, smiled and waved, and all the while he had wished she'd miss the damn thing so that he could swoop in and save the day. Driving her to the city would have finally given him the chance to talk to her.

Since that night in the pub Tamara seemed to be keeping a low profile, and any attempt on his behalf to bump into her *accidentally* hadn't gone according to plan. Jake had gone to the Harding place one week night under the pretence that he had a new email address to be included on the friendship tree, but Tamara had been at the movies that night and Bobby had taken the details to pass on to her. On Saturday he had dropped by unexpectedly with a query about Dogtails, but that time she was working extra hours in the city to finish a project.

As much as Jake needed to talk to Tamara, the Universe obviously had other ideas. He knew he hadn't imagined the way she had looked at him that day in Mr Wilson's kitchen, and that was why he was so surprised at how she had reacted with her ex. The Tamara he knew didn't take any crap from anyone – he'd been on the receiving end of her anger enough to know that – but the

Tamara he saw that night seemed brainwashed into behaving in a different way, convinced that she owed the guy something. The Tamara he knew would have pushed Bradley's hand away from her, told him to get lost. But she hadn't and Jake wondered why not. Was the London-Tamara so very different to the girl he knew from Brewer Creek? And if so, why did Bradley have such a hold over her?

***

Tamara walked along Cockle Bay Wharf as the sky changed from an orange haze, which hinted that the sun had had enough for another day, to a collection of clouds that looked ready to welcome the moon. The water had lost its sheen and the boats tired from their daily commute, and as she passed undercover to the station, she squeezed through a group of giggling girls out on a hen night. She pulled out her ticket ready to make the short trip to Central Station where she would connect to the train for Brewer Creek, but turned at the sound of her name.

The person behind her tutted at the hold up and moved along to use another barrier.

"I've been shouting to you for ages." Bradley bent over, out of breath. "I saw you down by the ferries."

He was dressed in a crisp, black dress shirt and jeans, and his breath reeked of beer.

"I thought you'd left." The harsh words were out of her mouth in a flash as his familiar crisp aftershave invaded her personal space. "I've got to go, Bradley." She moved to push the ticket into the barrier but his hand stopped her.

"Come on, Tamara. Please, have one last drink with me? I stayed away from you when you asked, didn't I?" His eyes pleaded, along with the hand that gripped hers, pulling it towards his chest. "We're still friends, aren't we?"

"I've got to go." Her head voiced its argument but at the same time, the opposition – her guilt and the knowledge that he needed a friend – shouted at her, too.

Sensing her hesitation, he snatched the ticket from her hand and pocketed it.

"The last train is in two hours and I need to be on it," she said.

They walked back along Circular Quay until they reached the Opera Bar, and took a free table beside the water with a view of the Opera House, the reflection of the lights cast across the water.

"I ordered you a mineral water, as requested," said Bradley, when he came back from the bar.

He was certainly going all out to not put a foot wrong.

"How's the job going?" he asked.

"Good, thanks."

"And what about the second job, as the friendship tree co-ordinator?"

She shrugged. "That's fine, too." She opened her mouth to tell him about the mobile library, but what was the point? He would only ridicule the small town and its people whom he had prejudged from the second he set foot in Brewer Creek.

A ferry honked its horn as it moved away from the quay, churning up the water in its wake, and Tamara waved a hand in front of her face to avoid the unpleasant cloud of smoke drifting from a passer-by.

"What are you doing back in Sydney, Bradley?"

He looked out over the water. "The other guys wanted a couple more days here – Dan got himself a girlfriend," he laughed, "so he's spending a bit of time with her before we leave. Jon's with them now in a bar on Cockle Bay Wharf, but when I saw you I had to talk to you again."

"You do realise that we're not going to get back together, don't you?" She needed to spell it out to him. It was the fairest thing for both of them.

"You mean when you come home?"

"Who knows when that'll be, Bradley? Maybe not for a long while; things are going really well here for me."

The waiter set down a glass of water and a beer, and removed the table number.

"I would never hurt you, Tamara."

She sipped her iced water. Over time, since she had got to know Bradley and he had confided in her more and more, she had started to wonder whether violence was something you could inherit, like a defective gene. It sounded crazy, but what if it were true? She didn't want to be one of those women who hadn't seen it coming, who were in so deep that they couldn't get out.

"I didn't want to let it get any worse between us," she said, "and that's why I had to get away."

"Worse?" His hand rested on top of the table, centimetres from her own.

"You know what I mean."

"I'm not my father," he said. "I told you that."

Her shoulders slumped because she knew that he believed what he was saying. She stretched her hand out until their fingertips touched. "I know you're not like your dad; I've never thought that." She said the words to placate him, but she knew that the verbal abuse and then the shove when she stumbled and hit her head all had a risk of spiralling out of control.

"How are your parents?" she asked.

He pulled away, leaving Tamara's hand outstretched across the table and empty.

"Come on, Bradley. You said it yourself, we're friends. I'm asking because I'm concerned."

Out of familiar surroundings, he seemed like a little boy playing in a man's playground, many times removed from the usual confidence he oozed.

"Mum never really talks about it. I've tried asking her how things are between them. As far as I know, the last time he went too far was last year at Christmas, when the firm were going through a major restructure and he thought he'd lose his job. She loves him, Tamara; she'll never leave."

His sorrow turned to anger. "Sometimes I get so annoyed with her. She should've stood up to him." He stared up to the top of the Opera House, its roof illuminated in a wintry white glow, and then to the stars beyond.

"Is that what you think I should've done? Should I have stood up to you more when you turned nasty?" Her question surprised him, but not as much as it surprised her when he took her hand and gently rubbed the skin on the underside of her wrist.

"I'm prepared to see a counsellor if that's what it takes to get you back." Tears welled in his eyes, and Tamara wondered whether he was telling her what he thought she wanted to hear.

"What I don't understand, Bradley, is why you were so possessive over me. We were okay when it was just us, we had fun, but then–"

"We can still have fun, Tamara." When she shook her head, he leaned across the table and tilted her chin so that she looked right at him. "I don't even understand myself. All I know is that when I met you I knew I'd met someone special, someone I wanted to spend every day and night with. I suppose I was so insecure that all I could see was the risk of that ending."

"But we could never live in our own private world without any outsiders butting in. There would always be other people, whether it was at work, as friends, or people we simply pass by and greet with a smile or a 'hello'."

"I've got my faults, Tamara. I'm the first to admit that. But I'd do anything for you. I love you."

The power of those words held an inexplicable force and she felt rooted to the spot.

"Tamara? Say something. Do you still love me, too? Please, I need to know."

In all the confusion, a chair scraping nearby alerted her to the path they were beginning to follow. It was happening again. He was appealing to her nicer side; the side that always gave him a second chance, and if she wasn't careful to avoid those first rumblings of the avalanche, before long she would be buried in its wake and unable to escape.

"I shouldn't have come." This time it was her chair that scraped violently across the concrete as she stood up. "I have to go." She left the Opera Bar, colliding with a waiter and muttering apologies to half of Sydney.

"Tamara, wait!" He was with her before she reached the barriers of the station at Circular Quay. "Stop, don't leave like this. Please." He gently kissed each tear that ran down her cheeks, the tears that were tumbling out now; tears she thought she had finished crying back in London. He found her lips and she collapsed against him as he hugged her tightly, their past a source of comfort in her muddled mind. She felt his hands in her hair, tempting her and making her tingle all over, and she wondered how this could feel so right when it was anything but.

"Stop fighting it, Tamara. Stop fighting," he urged, as his lips found hers and they became lost in each other.

She pulled away and they stood, staring, each of them fighting to grab the air around them that seemed so deprived of oxygen. She fell into his embrace yet again, except this time she was running her hands through his hair, down over his neck, his back. She could feel the familiarity of his entire body pressing against her as he pushed her up against a wall beside them.

They found their way back to his hotel room, and barely through the door she undid his shirt and he tore hers off before he hitched up her skirt until it was around her waist. In his face she saw a complete contrast to the insecure, lonely man she had sat opposite at the Opera Bar. His mask was back on and the sex was an escape for both of them. He knelt down in front of her and ran his hands slowly, tantalizingly all the way up her legs, showering them with hungry kisses. Images of Jake flashed faster and faster through her mind, but she blocked them out and dug her nails into Bradley's shoulders as he lifted her against the wall. She wanted him as much as she had every time back in the UK, and for now her heart overruled her head as she let him have her.

Chapter Twenty-Four

"Is there something going on, love?" Bobby asked, when Tamara emerged from the annexe.

She shook her head, and he went back to reading his morning paper at the kitchen table as she poured cereal into a bowl and splashed ice cold milk over the top. Over the last few days she had spent a lot of time dissecting what had happened in the city with Bradley. He had gone up to the Blue Mountains with his mates, giving her some valuable space to think. And despite a few text messages between them, now that she was away from him once again the moment of severe weakness had, in a weird way, helped to strengthen the way she felt.

"I noticed the photograph of Nancy and Archie in the office on one of the shelves," she said to Bobby.

"Your mum said that we should put it up."

She tilted her bowl to get a decent spoonful of cereal. "I'm glad."

"Me, too, and I put it somewhere that it wouldn't look over us like those photos in the lounge room or lining the walls beside the staircase–"

"Well, I'm happy for you to replace a lot of those, especially my hideous graduation picture."

The full belly laugh that erupted from Bobby told her all that she needed to know. If it was possible, the love between her parents had grown stronger since Bobby had revealed his past, and she knew she needn't worry about them any more. But she also knew she had to take control of her own life, in the same way that

Bobby had managed to do with his. The reality of sleeping with Bradley had really hit when she'd arrived back in Brewer Creek that night. She had made the last train – just – and emerged through the brick archway of Brewer Creek station, dishevelled and guilt-ridden, only to bump into Jake. They had barely exchanged pleasantries before she climbed into Bobby's car, but the way he looked at her, she knew he could tell where she'd been.

Tamara rinsed her bowl as Bobby disappeared to get ready for work, and then she sat looking out at the land from the back of her house; the landscape that was her new world, her fresh start away from Bradley and everything that had stopped her from being truly happy. She looked at the gum trees lining the horizon, their bark like oil paintings with lighter greys merged with darker shades. She watched a kangaroo in the distance, bounding up to the rickety wooden fence that sat on the curve of the hill at the rear of the Harding property.

"Is everything okay, Tamara?" It was Katherine's turn to ask this time. "You look miles away."

"I'm admiring the Aussie landscape," she smiled, a feeling of contentment washing over her for the first time.

"It's quite different, isn't it?" Katherine sat down beside her and they both took in the view. "Do you remember the first night you were here and you saw the possum?"

"He was hilarious." Tamara relaxed back in her chair now. "Every night, from that night onwards, he'd run across the top of the fence at exactly… when was it?"

"Nine o'clock," Katherine confirmed.

"That's right, and he'd scurry all the way to the end of the fence and then leap off to take a new adventure. Those wide eyes didn't miss a thing, least of all me, a strange British person lounging on the back veranda."

"I wonder if he'll come tonight," Katherine pondered.

"We should start keeping watch again," Tamara suggested.

They watched the kangaroo, its head darting left to right to check for danger before it bounded off down the other side of the hill.

"I met up with Bradley again." Feeling childlike with her sudden confession, Tamara looked down into her lap.

"I thought as much." Katherine sipped her cup of tea and then said, "I thought it was over between you two before you left the UK. Is that why he's here, to win you back?"

"You make it sound like I'm some grand prize."

"You are, Tamara," she smiled. "But I'm worried about you again, and why do I get the feeling that you haven't told me everything?"

She met her mum's gaze this time, and the whole story poured out, right from the day she met Bradley – minus the details of ending back at his place – until that evening in her flat when he had shown a side to him that she hadn't realised even existed.

"Tamara, why didn't you tell me?"

"Honestly? Because you were thousands of miles away and I didn't want you to have that burden. You were worried enough about Bobby and I couldn't land all that on you as well."

"Well you should've done. I would've coped." She shook her head. "Does Beth know everything?" When Tamara nodded and smiled, she said, "Well, that's something I suppose; she's always been there for you, hasn't she?"

"That was the doings of a friendship tree, if you remember?"

"Gosh, yes. I do!" Katherine laughed as they reminisced about the raven-haired headmistress, clearly proud of her school and the huge oak that stood as though looking out for unsuspecting pupils.

"I think that if it hadn't been for my history with another friendship tree, and my soft spot for the whole concept, I probably would've handed Daphne's co-ordinator job onto someone else by now," Tamara giggled.

"I thought you had it under control, now that it's on the computer."

"I do, but trying to organise this mobile library is a bit time consuming, and now Daphne's talking about a darts tournament to get some of the younger members of the community to interact." She couldn't help the eye roll that accompanied her remark. "I haven't got around to it yet. All it takes is a bit of imagination and some flyers popped through people's doors, but with everything else going on I haven't had a chance." She hesitated. "I'm meeting up with Bradley again tomorrow, in the city."

"Do you think that's wise?"

"I can see clearly now, Mum. I can see that I've got to end it once and for all. I should've done it back in London rather than run away. That wasn't fair on him, and I see now that it didn't help me all that much either. I'm not a robot that can switch off its feelings, and Bradley isn't all bad. I think we both deserve to end our relationship properly."

"Did I ever mention that I'm proud of you?" Katherine hugged her daughter.

"Once or twice," Tamara grinned.

Chapter Twenty-Five

When Tamara saw Bradley waiting for her on the grass area near Circular Quay, her heart sank at what had to be done.

He stood up, and when he leaned in to kiss her she turned her head so that his lips collided with her cheek.

"Can I get you an ice-cream?" He pulled some change from his wallet.

"No thanks."

"But you never say no to ice-cream." He lifted his sunglasses up so that she could see his eyes, and moved in closer.

She backed off. "We need to talk."

The smile that had pulled her in years before when she had revelled in his company over those tequilas, beamed back at her and she ushered him back to the grass area away from the crowds bustling towards anxiously awaiting ferries.

"Fire away," he said. "I'm all ears."

She wished he'd take her seriously. "I left the UK for a reason," she began.

"I know, you told me that already. But like I told you: I love you. And I'll do whatever it takes to show you that."

Tamara stared out at the green and yellow boat making its escape from Circular Quay. "It's not enough anymore, Bradley." When he tried to take her hand, she pulled it away. "Leaving the UK was incredibly hard," she said, "but it's by far the best thing I've ever done."

"So you're dumping the UK for the sun and the surf, eh? It's as simple as that?"

"Not at all, but I want to leave my old life behind. More than that; I *need* to leave it behind. And if I choose to go back to London, it will be to a different version of what my life was before."

Arms resting on his bent knees, Bradley looked out to the ferries chugging contentedly away from the quay. "I'm assuming that I don't quite slot into your idyllic picture of life with the white picket fence and the two-point-four kids."

"You make me sound like a complete bitch." Her stomach churned when she thought about severing contact with him after today, but the sun beat down on them and gave her the extra confidence that she needed. "I'm sorry it didn't work out, Bradley."

Bradley tugged at the blades of grass, scattering them to the wind when they came off in his fingers. "Well, I guess it was a long shot."

"What was?"

"Coming here; coming to Australia."

"But you said you were travelling."

"All true, yes, but there was an added incentive."

"Me?"

He nodded and looked away. Tamara resisted the urge to put her arm around him and said, "You need to figure out what makes you happy, Bradley. For a while I thought that I could help you work through what was going on with your family, in your life, but you need to do that on your own. It's not my fight." She took a deep breath. "You're a good person and I hope you'll be happy one day, I really do."

After a while, Bradley stood and held out a hand. "Come on, we've got all day and you can show me what it is that you've come to love about this city."

She hesitated.

"Come on, Tamara, as friends."

"Just as friends," she reiterated firmly.

They took the ferry over to Watson's Bay for lunch and were

soon filling themselves with fish and chips from a classy restaurant.

"Give me fish and chips from a market any day," said Bradley, when they couldn't fit another morsel in. "It's not that I'm saying lunch wasn't delicious–"

"Don't worry, I'm with you," she agreed. "The lunch was divine, but there's nothing like English fish and chips eaten out of a newspaper-wrapped cone."

"With your fingers numb from the cold making it painful to pick up the food," Bradley laughed, reminding her that there were more layers to him than most people knew.

Next they headed to the markets at The Rocks, meandering through the stalls as Bradley picked out souvenirs. As Tamara enjoyed his company, she realised that perhaps she wasn't such a lousy judge of character after all; there was a kind-hearted man buried beneath a great deal of hurt.

Bradley picked up a cuddly kangaroo with a joey in its pouch. "What about this?"

She screwed up her nose.

"Just for that, I'll buy it." He picked out a snow globe with a background of the Opera House and the Harbour Bridge, before handing over the cash to the lady manning the stall.

When they walked away, Tamara giggled. "Those are some of the tackiest souvenirs I've ever seen."

"Hmm… there's something wrong about snow falling across the green and yellow ferry sailing past the Harbour Bridge, isn't there?" He shook the snow globe to prove his point. "So, where are you taking me next?"

Tamara pulled out her phone again, the map function doing overtime as they navigated their way around Sydney.

They headed to the Queen Victoria Building, where Bradley dragged his heels around the shops until Tamara caved and they left. They visited the aquarium where Bradley did a questionable impression of a dugong and made Tamara pose on the seat with the concrete mermaid as he snapped a picture on his phone. From there they headed over to The Chinese Garden of Friendship and were surrounded by water features, beautiful lotus flowers, and architecture that transported them back in time.

Back at The Rocks, they ordered sinful iced chocolates at a Belgian chocolate café.

"Would you have dinner with me tonight?" Bradley asked.

Tamara used the long spoon to scrape the sides of the glass of the remaining chocolate mixture. "I really should be getting back home."

"Come on, for old time's sake."

On the way to the city, when she had been gearing herself up for what was to come, Tamara had assumed that she would say her piece and then leave.

"I've heard the three hundred and sixty degree views of the city are amazing from The Sky Tower Restaurant," he persisted. "And after that, you're free to go. I promise."

"Don't say it like that." Oh, what harm could it do? One dinner and that would be it, for good. "Do we need to book?"

When Bradley held up a fist to punch the air, his elbow knocked his iced chocolate into his lap, covering the bottom of his shirt and the crotch of his jeans.

Tamara laughed helplessly.

"I look like I've wet myself." He laughed, too, and Tamara realised that he looked happy. His grin spread to his eyes and reminded her of the good times, before he had become so controlling and allowed the past to dictate the present. She felt a pang of sadness, but there was no turning back.

Bradley mopped the front of his jeans and his shirt the best he could. "I'll have to change. Come on, I'm only a couple of blocks from here."

She hesitated briefly but then finished her drink and picked up her bag. She was still in control, wasn't she?

***

210

Jake stood at the window of the rental cottage looking out to the fields, which were barely visible beneath the storm clouds and the downpour that had hit Brewer Creek already that morning. His fists tightened against the draining board. Some days it got to him more than others, and last night he had tossed and turned amidst nightmares about Marty. After what that man had done to his family, he wondered whether he would be able to control himself if he ever set eyes on that scum again. Jake wasn't a violent man, but everyone had their limits.

The rain thundered on the roof of the veranda and gushed out of the drainpipes at ground level, but he relaxed when he opened the back door and breathed in some much-needed fresh air.

"Sorry, did I wake you?" he asked, when April appeared in the kitchen behind him.

"No, I sleep more soundly than a bear in hibernation these days."

At least one of them managed to. On the flip side, his fitful sleep sometimes included dreams about Tamara, and that he could cope with.

April filled a glass of water and joined him beside the back door. "It looks as though it's going to be a wild one." She pulled her dressing gown tighter at the neck as the breeze made for her. "What are you thinking about?"

"Nothing," he said, but he didn't fool her. He carried on looking out into the darkness. It felt fitting; he couldn't see a damn thing, much like he couldn't see a way forward out of this mess.

"Can I hazard a guess?" April stepped away from the cold now. "Were you thinking about Tamara?"

He closed the door and locked it, pulling the curtain across.

"I know how much you like her, Jake, that's all."

He picked up the fruit bowl and tugged a few grapes from their stalks. "I know we're complicated, but so is she."

"Ah, so this is about Bradley?"

He didn't say anything.

"I knew it, Jake. After the pub, you didn't say a word and, to tell you the truth, I don't know what's going on there either. I mean, she says they used to go out back in London, but from what I saw he wants it to go back that way, and I mean, well…"

"Go on."

"Well, you don't turn up thousands of miles across the other side of the world for just anyone, do you? There must be more to it than a friendly visit."

Jake thought back to the way Bradley's hand had guarded Tamara from anyone else. He thought back to that night outside the station when she had obviously been with him – her face had said it all.

"She didn't look overly happy about him touching her, though, so perhaps she isn't interested." April motioned for Jake to push the fruit bowl towards her before he took all the grapes.

"She's too good for him," he said.

"For what it's worth, Jake, I agree. I didn't like him at all. Or maybe I'm biased, seeing as you're my brother."

He perked up. "Come on. I'm off to the pub for a quick one, before the storm really gets underway. It's driving me insane being stuck in here with nothing but my own thoughts for company."

"Yeah, you're pretty damn boring." She ducked as he aimed a grape for her head. "And you can't fool me."

"What do you mean?"

"You're desperate to see Tamara, and you're hoping she'll be at the pub for once."

"Just get dressed," he grinned, picking the grape up off the floor.

"Okay, but only for an hour." She patted her baby bump. "This little one will be doing gymnastics all night and I need my sleep."

Jake smiled. April was right about his motive. He didn't want to give up on Tamara, not yet, not when there was still so much he had to say.

***

212

"It's really coming down out there." Len took a bottle of apple juice, twisted off its top and handed it to Bobby.

"I'll take one of those, please," said Jake, as April made her way down the bar to chat to Hugo. "May I?" Jake indicated the empty stool beside Bobby.

Bobby nodded.

"Listen. I–"

"Now don't start, Jake. We've cleared the air, and I think you did me a bit of a favour anyway."

"How do you work that out?"

"I'm planning to retire. Not immediately, but soon, and it would never have happened if you hadn't come to Brewer Creek. Oh come on, don't look so guilty, lad." He turned on his stool to face Jake. "It's about bloody time. Tamara has helped me see things a lot more clearly let me tell you."

"She's a great girl."

Bobby smiled.

"Do you think she'll stay here for a while?" Jake did his best to look nonchalant, but he could tell from Bobby's eyes that he'd failed miserably.

"I don't know. And remember, she's living with two OAPs, which I think is cramping her style."

Jake didn't want to think about the possibility that he may never get to tell Tamara how he really felt, about who he actually was. "Do you have plans for this retirement of yours?" he asked, steering the conversation away from his feelings which ran deeper than he had thought possible.

"Not really, at least not yet, although I'm sure Katherine is planning it for me already. But the people of this town need someone reliable to look out for their animals, and I believe that that person is you."

"I don't know what to say." Jake pulled his hand through his hair. "That's the last thing I expected you to say to me tonight."

"I've got a new perspective these days. I'd also be willing to sell the surgery on to you – it's bigger than yours, and you'll need

213

somewhere to accommodate a larger client base. I can also give you first refusal on the equipment that I've got, medications and the like."

Jake exhaled slowly, excited at the prospect of really building a life here in Brewer Creek. "Can I take a look at my own books first? To see what position I'm in?" he asked, wondering what that life would be like without Tamara, if she refused to ever give him a chance.

"No rush." Bobby threw back the rest of his apple juice. "Now, I'd better be off. Miss Tamara will not be happy if she has to wait outside the station in this rain. She walked this morning, but I doubt she'll want to walk home with that lightning looking like it's got something bigger planned." He shrugged on his raincoat, and his eyebrows arched in good humour. "I thought my years as a taxi service were long gone."

"You'll miss it when she's gone."

Bobby patted Jake on the arm. "You're right, I will."

The lights in the pub flickered. "Drive safely," Len called, as Bobby pulled open the front door of the pub and hurried towards the car.

***

It was only when they went through the foyer at the hotel and took the lift that Tamara realised what a colossal mistake she had made. She should've realised that Bradley wouldn't take this break-up in his stride; to him, it wasn't the end.

"I'll wait outside," she said, when they reached his room, but he pulled her inside. He stripped off his wet shirt and made no effort to find another, then he was against her, his lips on her neck as he pressed her against the wall.

"Bradley, stop." She swallowed hard, trying to ignore the softness of his lips making their way across her collarbone as he used his hand to tug her shirt collar out of the way. Her hands pushed against his biceps as his fingers expertly popped each button of her shirt in turn. It was then that she found the strength and pushed harder.

"I'm serious, Bradley, stop!"

"What's wrong?" He moved towards her again, but she held him off.

"We're friends now, nothing else."

"So was I mistaken that your body responded to me just then?"

He wasn't, but she wasn't going to admit that.

"Bradley, this is what has always happened. I've had my say, told you things aren't right between us, and somehow you convince me that you've changed and we end up back together. It can't happen any more."

"Stop fighting it, Tamara."

He moved towards her again, but she was ready. She pushed him hard and she didn't mistake the fire in his eyes. Her mind flashed back to the moment he had pushed her in her flat and she'd hit her head.

His shoulders slumped and he backed away this time. "Oh God, you think I'm going to hit you, don't you?"

Her breath caught in her throat because that was exactly what she had thought. He turned and walked over to the window and stood staring out through the lopsided, yellowed net curtain.

Tamara hoped that she was making a good judgement when she moved towards him. This time it was she who took his hand and pulled him over to the bed so that they were sitting next to each other. The gesture spoke of friendship rather than the lust that had so often brought them together in the past.

"I forgive you for everything that happened," she said. "I forgive you for the way you treated me at times, but now you need to forgive yourself and move forwards."

"Is that what you've done, with Jake?"

Her feelings for Jake were none of his business, and he didn't need to have his nose rubbed in it either. Jake had climbed unexpectedly into her heart, and it had helped her to realise the end of her relationship with Bradley. But even if there was no future with Jake, there was still that hope of finding someone else.

Tears pooled in her eyes as Bradley looked at her, and she desperately fought them off as she pulled him into a final hug. He clung to her as tight as a little boy holding onto his mum after being lost in a crowd. When Tamara finally pulled away, neither of them said a word. She got up and walked over to the door, clicked it shut behind her, and said goodbye to her past for good.

Chapter Twenty-Six

The city centre was emptying fast, the rain falling heavier. Tamara's umbrella had died – no sooner had she put it up than the wind had dragged it out of her hand and along the walkway, bending the spokes and tearing the canopy. Drenched, she reached the station in time to hear the announcement that all trains going to the Central Coast had been cancelled until further notice. A storm passing through had caused major problems on the line.

She pulled out her phone and noticed that the battery symbol was red with a figure of nine per cent beside it – she could thank the overzealous use of the maps function today for that.

Please, please, oh please, she willed, hoping that this call would connect before her battery went dead.

"Where are you?" said Katherine. "Are you on your way home?"

The wind whipped up around her legs as she explained that there were no trains until further notice. She swiped a tear from her cheek, a tear that had appeared not because she was upset that her train was cancelled, but because of the emotions that had tumbled out of her that afternoon. She finally had the closure that she had needed for such a long time.

"There's a major storm, Tamara, has it reached the city?"

She looked at the dark skies hanging overhead. "Not yet, but I'd say it's almost here."

"I'll call Bobby and he'll come and get you."

"Don't do that," she said weakly, although all she wanted tonight was to be safe in that annexe. "I can call a work friend, spend the night here, and get a train out tomorrow. Bobby won't want to be out in the storm."

"Nonsense," Katherine insisted. "Now where are you?"

**

Jake sat with April in the pub. "You know, I really do think Marty was in Sydney on one of his dodgy deals. If he knew where we were, he would've found us by now." He looked at his sister. "Are you even listening?"

"Sorry, I'm tired, that's all."

He knew the feeling. "Would you listen to it out there?" The wind rattled the pane of glass in the window beside their table.

"I'm happy here, Jake."

April's words took him by surprise. "Are you really? You're not pining for the big city?"

She thought for a moment. "I do still dream about big cities: London, New York, even Sydney. Who knows, maybe I'll go and live in one for a while? But for now, I feel settled in Brewer Creek and we're starting to make friends."

He tore at the corners of a beer mat. "I like it here, too, but I don't know what these people will do when they find out that we're fakes."

"You always were a bigger drama queen than me, Jake. You sound like a big girl. I think the residents of Brewer Creek could surprise you one day. Talking of which, are you putting your name down for the darts tournament that Tamara is organising?"

He listened as April rattled off a list of prizes, including dinner for two, champagne, and a month's supply of eggs. It was good to see her happy, to hear that she felt settled. He wondered how much of that was to do with the pregnancy hormones and how much was to do with Hugo, the man she couldn't stop staring at every chance she got. It looked like he wasn't the only one having to keep a lid on his feelings.

"You like him," he said.

"Jake!"

"What? You quiz me about Tamara, why can't I ask you about your love life?"

"What love life?" She patted her belly. "I've got plenty on my plate for now, and who would want to take on this little one anyway?"

He looked over at Hugo, who was moving a glass skilfully beneath the Guinness pump to draw the shamrock. "Hugo doesn't seem like the type to be put off by the fact that you're about to be a mum."

"I doubt that."

"Now who's the drama queen? Now who's underestimating the people in this town?"

"Touché," she grinned.

"You know you'll always have me around, don't you?"

"I know, but remember you have your own life to live, too. You can't put yourself last all the time."

He leaned in conspiratorially. "I wasn't going to say anything, but Bobby is retiring. He wants me to take over his surgery, his clients, everything."

"Jake, that's awesome." She kept her voice to a whisper. "And you know I'll pay you back every cent I've borrowed these last few months, and then some."

"Yep, you'll owe me forever." He rubbed his hands together.

"Hey, why don't I take a look at the books for you, see what your financial position is with regards to Bobby's proposition? It'll be a good opportunity to put the theory of my course into practice."

"You're on."

"So what are you going to do about Tamara? Are you going to tell her everything?"

Jake shook his head, sitting back in his chair. "I thought about it. But that was before the boyfriend turned up. I'd say it's pretty obvious they've got unfinished business, wouldn't you? Tamara's big enough to make up her own mind, and from what I saw she wasn't exactly sending him packing." He tried to erase the unwelcome image of Bradley touching her like some highly prized trophy that he was afraid someone else was going to put their paw prints all over.

Jake was about to launch into more Bradley bashing, when a gust of wind carried Bobby back into the pub, drenched from head to toe, his raincoat next to useless in the storm out there.

"Is everything all right?" Jake called over.

"Here, take this, it's clean." Len appeared with a towel as Bobby walked over to Jake.

Bobby wiped his face, but it didn't erase his concern. He told them the whole disastrous story: his car had broken down; Katherine's car was stuck in a garage across town, waiting for its service; all the trains were cancelled up to Brewer Creek; and Tamara's phone must have died, and he couldn't reach her to tell her to get in touch with a work colleague and stay put for the night.

"Of all the times for *both* cars to be out of action," Bobby said, "it had to bloody well be tonight."

Jake picked up his keys. "I'll go and get her. Where is she?" He memorised the intersection and made a note of it on the back of the torn beer mat just in case.

"I'll come with you," said Bobby.

"You stay here. There's no point both of us going. Can you do me a favour?" Jake looked directly at Hugo. "Look after April for me?"

"I'll go one better than that," Len interrupted, before Hugo could agree. "It's quiet now, so I'll take April home and she can get herself to bed. You need to look after yourself, young lady. And Hugo, can you mind the bar until I get back?"

Jake gave April a reassuring glance as he left the pub. She wouldn't want to be in the house all alone, but it would only be a few hours until he brought Tamara home safely.

***

The rain pelted down horizontally and Tamara huddled shivering in a shop doorway, her fists clenched into tight balls with her nails digging into the palms of her hands. Cars zoomed past with windscreen wipers viciously swiping from side-to-side to let them see the road ahead. Forty-five minutes later, a horn beeped and Tamara ran out from her hiding place.

When she looked into Jake's eyes and not Bobby's, she felt an overwhelming sense of calm as he explained why he was the one who had come to get her. Jake negotiated the traffic as they left the city and joined the freeway, and Tamara surreptitiously watched him duck his head, raise his head, any way to try and gain some visibility through the storm. He slowed for the tolls as they approached the Harbour Bridge, and Tamara jumped as they emerged the other side and the rain unleashed its force at the windscreen as though someone had flung a heap of gravel down from a great height.

Her teeth chattered and she pulled at her top, which clung to her skin like clingfilm. Jake turned the heater dial up to full without taking his eyes off the road.

When they veered left and took the next exit, Tamara asked, "Where are we going?"

As soon as it was safe, Jake pulled over beneath a street lamp and leaned into the back of the pick-up and pulled out a tartan, woollen blanket. "Here, take this. I'm sorry if it smells a bit." He waited for her to take her seatbelt off and lean forwards, so that he could drape it around her. "It belonged to Waffles, and I haven't got around to washing it since she went to Mr Wilson's."

Tamara didn't mind the smell, it was comforting.

"I thought you could use a bit of time out before we head back to your place," said Jake. "I'll send Bobby a text so that he won't worry." He fired off a message and then fumbled around in the back of the pick-up again.

"Thanks," Tamara said timidly when he passed her a small towel to use on her hair. She rubbed and squeezed the drips from the ends, and as the radio signal crackled its last breath Jake switched to the CD player and the soothing sounds of *The Fray* echoed around them.

"Do you want to talk about it?" he asked.

"About the trains being cancelled?" She knew full well that wasn't what he was asking, and she had a sneaky suspicion that he knew who she'd been with today. Her eyes stung with the tears that she thought she could keep at bay, but once they began to glide down her cheeks she buried her face in the towel and her shoulders shook along with the rest of her body.

Jake pulled her into him and, exhausted from the emotions that had finally come to a head since leaving the UK, she rested her head against his chest. She breathed in the intoxicating smell of him, that mixture of soap and the hint of woody aftershave that had become so familiar.

Still cradling her in his arms, he said, "You owe it to yourself to be happy, Tamara."

She wanted to scream at him: "What would make *you* happy, Jake? What are you hiding?" but she didn't say a word.

Eventually she stopped shivering and Jake turned the heat down. "You can talk to me, Tamara."

She looked at her nails in the hope of finding a jagged edge that she could fiddle with to preoccupy her while she told him the whole sorry story. Instead, she stared at the raindrops ganging up on the windscreen, as she started at the beginning: from the moment she met Bradley Cox, right up until the day she left the UK. When she hinted at what had happened the night she went back to Bradley's hotel room in Sydney, she noticed Jake fidget in his seat.

"Bradley doesn't have anyone apart from me, and that's the way it's always been," she justified. "I wanted to give him a chance to explain, to apologise even, but I realise now that whatever is going on in his head isn't something that I can fix; it isn't something that I can ignore either."

Jake gripped the steering wheel, stared straight ahead, and bit down on his lip before he said, "Do you still love him?" She didn't answer immediately, and this time he looked at her. "It's a simple question. Do you love him? And I'm not asking if you feel sorry for him, or if you want to be his friend. I'm asking you whether you see your future with him."

Tamara wiped the back of her hand across the steamed-up window and stared vacantly at the dark grey buildings. "No, not any more. I'm not sure now that I was ever completely in love with him. I think that we had a lot of fun, he swept me off my feet at times, and I cared about him. But real love?" She shrugged. "Real love shouldn't make you feel like that; not ever."

"Like what?"

"Worthless, like you're not good enough. The problem was that I couldn't see it. I couldn't see that we weren't right together. I spent two years with him, listened to everything he struggled with, stories about his family that I wouldn't wish on anyone. But we're over now and after today, saying goodbye to him, I feel that I can finally move on."

"Does he accept that?"

"You know, I think that he does this time." She shook her head, letting out a long breath. "I bet you think I'm crazy, don't you? Putting up with being treated like that. To my friend Beth, it's simple: a guy treats you badly and he's out the door pronto. But take it from me; it's not always that simple."

"I don't think it's ever that simple."

Her heart jumped as Jake's fingers lifted her hair behind her ears, and he looked at her with an intensity that she mirrored. "Men like Bradley are controlling; they're manipulative. It's only when you're in too deep that you realise, and then it's not as simple as walking away. By that time, you care, and that's nothing to be ashamed of."

His understanding took her by surprise, and when he pulled her close Tamara wondered what she would have thought if anyone had told her when she arrived in Brewer Creek that Jake would become a confidant, someone to whom she could pour out everything without judgement.

***

Right here, right now, in the car with Tamara snuggling into him as they listened to the rain dancing on the roof of the pick-up, Jake couldn't imagine being anywhere else. He stroked the soft skin of her forearm as he felt her breathing slow down and settle into a steady rhythm. He knew now that he wanted to tell her everything, but as he watched a sleepy smile creep across her mouth, he knew that it could wait until the morning.

He cupped a hand under her chin as she looked at him in the dimly-lit vehicle and he felt her lean into him. His thumb ran across her mouth, across her lips. "We should get you home," he said, and reluctantly touched his lips to her forehead. He breathed in her floral perfume and the fruit-scented shampoo from her hair. He wanted to kiss her properly; he never wanted to stop. But with everything going on in his head and hers, he was willing to wait for that perfect moment.

Jake followed the lights of the freeway blended in amongst the mixture of tail lights and headlights finding their way home in the rain. His forearms tensed against the wheel at thoughts of Bradley, and of Marty: men who treated women with such contempt when they felt like it. His body brimmed with anger, which only subsided when he looked across at Tamara with the blanket pulled all the way up to her chin. She had a look of contentment, and her eyes held that just-about-to-drift-off look that flooded him with relief. He wished he could make this moment last longer, pull over and watch the rise and fall of her chest, the gentle softening of her face and lips that had been through so much in one day. But that would have to wait.

Once Jake dropped Tamara safely home to her parents, he decided that tomorrow, as the saying went, was "another day". Tomorrow he would tell her everything; he would tell her exactly how he felt. Satisfied that his life was about to get back on track, he drove on towards home. By the time he pulled up outside, the sky had cleared and only a crescent moon and a dusting of stars remained. He turned his key in the front door and hoped that April hadn't put on all the usual security measures or he'd be spending the night in his pick-up.

Luckily she hadn't, but when Jake stepped inside the front door, a familiar surge of dread pervaded every part of his being.

Two ornaments lay broken on the hearth, papers were scattered across the wooden floor, and the ottoman was up-ended. He ran to April's room; the bed was perfectly made. He ran to the lounge room and there was a half-drunk hot chocolate on the side, with her coral-coloured lipstick staining the edge.

He ran to every other room in turn, then called out into the back garden.

But she was gone.

Chapter Twenty-Seven

The heady summer storm in Brewer Creek had passed, and left in its wake were leaves that clogged up the gutters; branches strewn across roads or walkways making them impassable; and enormous puddles that doubled as mud pools.

For the small community of Brewer Creek, it was time to show their strength and solidarity, and already Jake was floored by how many people had turned out in the middle of the night. When he couldn't find April, Jake had driven to the pub in the vain hope that she was with Hugo, but the place was draped in darkness and his frantic knocking at the door was finally answered by Len. Jake gave Len a garbled account of what had brought him to Brewer Creek, who Marty was, and the reasons why he wanted to hold off on calling the police. Len hadn't even hesitated in helping him, and had taken the friendship tree down from its position next to his telephone in the hallway of the pub, and called each and every resident.

Now a sea of faces filled the pub: some in pyjamas; some in gumboots; others fully dressed with wax jackets to battle the rain. And it was time to come clean.

"I can handle this for you," Len told Jake, as the town's residents huddled and speculated as to what was going on.

"Thanks, Len, but I'll take it from here." Jake looked out at the faces of the people who had grown to like and trust him. There were the Jacksons from the dairy farm, and next to them Derek, the mechanic. Mr Williams and the Turner family had turned out; the twin sons of Mr Lee, who ran the bottle shop, looked ready for business with their shirt sleeves rolled up revealing a myriad of tattoos. And there were people whom Jake didn't even recognise – a lady in a khaki wax jacket beside Len and his wife, a tall man who reminded him of the actor, Edward Woodward.

Jake had never seen anything like it.

He cleared his throat. "April is my sister." There, the first admission was out, but there was no time to waste. "We came to Brewer Creek to get away from our stepfather, a man who made our lives a misery, a man who hurt my sister." The gasps from the residents didn't deter him and neither did the stunned faces. "We felt confident that by pretending to be a couple and by coming to a remote town so far from home, he would never find us. But a few weeks ago April saw him in Sydney, and now she's missing."

Denise Jackson gasped. "Do you think he has April?"

Jake met her gaze. He was willing to face any retribution for the lies that they had told, but his only concern right now was for April. "When I got home, it was clear that someone had been inside the house and that April didn't leave of her own free will. My guess would be that, yes, he has her."

Conversation erupted, and tears pricking Jake's eyes and the catch in his throat stopped him continuing. Len picked up the brass bell that stood at the end of the bar, its patina the giveaway of the pub's history, and when it rang out silence fell.

"Listen up, everyone," Len boomed across the pub. "I'm sure you all have plenty of questions but for now we need to focus. April Manning is missing. Each group will be assigned a small area on the map to search. Leave no stone unturned. We're a small community and we look after our own." He patted Jake's shoulder. "No matter what April and Jake have done, what they may or may not have told us, April is one of us now."

Arthur Seymour, who owned a cluster of holiday cottages on the outskirts of Brewer Creek, stepped forward. "Why can't we call the police?"

Agreement surrounded his question and Len had to call order with the bell again as Jake looked on helplessly at people who understandably wanted answers.

He found his voice. "This man is scum. He did his best to drag April and I into his life of dodgy dealings and when we refused, he did what he knew best – he used threats and violence. He's threatened to implicate us in whatever crimes he's committed, but I don't care about that now. My worry is that if Marty gets wind of the police being after him, he'll hurt April or the baby." All it'd take was a swift kick to April's stomach, and Jake didn't even want to think about what the ramifications would be.

Jake's spirits lifted when the pub door opened, but sank when he saw that it was only Bobby arriving to help.

"I know it's a big ask from you all," he turned to the crowd again, "especially now you all know that April and I haven't been honest with you. But I really need your help." If the residents wanted to hang, draw and quarter him after this, then so be it. As long as April came home safe and sound, he didn't care.

Len deployed project management skills fit for an Army base, dividing the town into sections on a map, designating them to the eagerly awaiting search parties.

When Bobby was given a search area, he joined Jake and placed a hand on his arm. "Don't worry, lad, we'll find her. Most of the town is here tonight, thanks to the friendship tree. It would've taken us forever to drive around and wake everyone up if we hadn't had that to help, and the phone book would've been useless as most residents have mobile phones – saves paying landline rental," he winked.

Jake appreciated Bobby trying to reassure him. He watched the good people of Brewer Creek failing to yawn; failing to complain about their phones ringing at some absurd hour of the night. His dishonesty didn't appear to have fazed a single one of them, unless they were too sleepy to say. Not one person had turned his or her back. Everyone had come together, not questioning the why so much as asking the how: How can we help? How can we find her?

As groups set off on the search, Len took Jake out into the hallway that doubled as the entrance to his living quarters. "Do you really believe that this Marty is still in town?" Len asked.

Jake harrumphed. "Marty wouldn't have access to a car unless it was stolen, and he doesn't have the guts to do that himself." He scraped both hands helplessly through his hair.

Bobby joined them out back as Jake pored over a map of the town in the hope that it would trigger something. Anything.

"Is it true what people are saying?" Daphne Abbott was the next to appear. She was the last to arrive in the pub, a waterproof jacket covering her quilted dressing gown.

"Is there any news?" It was Mr Wilson's turn to gather with the group out back, with Waffles in tow.

Jake began to feel stifled; he desperately needed air to breathe, and luckily Bobby was one step ahead.

"How about you take Daphne, Mr Wilson, and organise some food for everyone?" Bobby suggested. "There are plenty of supplies in the kitchen, so grab anything. It would really help. We need to keep up people's strength."

"Right you are," said Mr Wilson. He settled Waffles into the corner of the pub and then guided Daphne's arm towards the kitchen with a wink at Bobby that let him know he was in on his plan.

"Thanks, Bobby," said Jake. "I know she means well, but I don't really need anyone else in my ear at the moment."

A short while later, platters of simple sandwiches – cheese, vegemite, ham and salad –were laid out on the wooden tables alongside pots of tea and coffee.

Bobby confirmed a section on the map, grabbed a ham sandwich, and was off.

"Wait, I'll come with you," said Jake.

Before they could escape through the front entrance, Mr Wilson chimed in. "Take these and eat while you drive." He bundled some sandwiches into a serviette and gave it to Jake. "You'll be no good to us or April if you collapse somewhere and we have to get a search party out for you, too."

Jake graciously accepted the tiny parcel and, before they left, he nodded to Hugo. He saw the worry, the fear in the poor boy's eyes.

"We'll go to the disused sheds first," said Bobby, as they climbed into the pick-up and Jake flicked the headlights onto full beam.

"How the hell did this man know where to find you?" Bobby asked. "This town is off the radar for most people; we're not exactly famous."

"Mum's house was trashed last week. The only thing missing was her phone." Jake shook his head, unable to believe that such a simple mistake had resulted in this. "Mum isn't one for technology so had the most basic phone, didn't use a password, rarely deleted anything."

"Ah."

Jake's hands tightened on the wheel. "If that arsehole has done *anything* to her, I'll—"

"Take it easy, Jake. We'll find her."

The pick-up bumped over the uneven dirt road towards the outskirts of Brewer Creek. Both men jumped out and made their way to a disused barn, quiet in case they'd stumbled upon the right place. Jake switched off his flashlight as they tried to listen in the still of the night for any telltale signs, but nothing. Creeping around the outside of the barn into the thicket, Jake ignored the scratches against his arms, and flinched when a sharper branch tore at his neck.

By the time they trudged back to the pick-up, it felt as though they'd searched each and every blade of grass.

Bobby pulled a clean tissue from the pocket of his raincoat and passed it to Jake. "Here, you're bleeding."

Jake held it against his neck and let it soak up the blood. The smell of rain lingered and the mud squelched beneath their feet as they slouched against the muddy, once-silver, bumper of the pick-up.

"I know you don't want the police involved yet," said Bobby, "but they'll probably handle it a bit better than a bunch of amateur locals."

Jake watched the glow from the moon shine across the field, casting shadows from the tall, imposing trees framing the land. "He's the lowest of men, Bobby. He's nothing like you; he's nothing like me. He wasn't that bad when he and Mum first started going out together, but then he started to get involved in petty crimes, even a bit of drug dealing on the side of his building job. And then he got greedy. He started robbing a string of homes on the outskirts of town. You know, far enough away so that the locals wouldn't get wind of it."

"Why didn't you report him from the start?"

Jake recalled the first time Marty had swiped him around the head, the way he'd manipulated him and played mind games to make up for what he lacked in physical menace. "He changed a lot over the years. We were trying to protect Mum, so when he told us that he'd cleaned up his act we tried to give him the benefit of the doubt.

"He caught April at the house once with Adam, the married man she'd fallen for, and he told her that if she wanted a roof over her head then she would have to play by his rules. He threatened her and told her that if she didn't help him out in his dodgy dealings then she could leave and never come back. He told her that if she breathed a word of his threat to Mum, he'd make her sorry she was ever born."

Jake cleared his throat when his voice began to wobble. He pulled a water bottle from the back of the pick-up and offered Bobby a swig. Bobby shook his head and Jake gulped most of it as he sat back on the bumper.

"Marty started targeting small shops but he wanted to take bigger things; things he couldn't manage on his own, and he wanted April to drive the car. When she said she didn't want a part of it, Marty turned nasty, pinned her up against a wall and threatened to tell the police that both April and I had been in on the robberies all along if she didn't help. He said that he'd plant evidence, too, and that we wouldn't be able to stop him."

"What happened then?" Bobby's gentle voice echoed in the still of the night. "Go on, lad."

"He turned on April. He demanded to know where this *Adam* was, so that he could drag him out of hiding and give him a talking to for taking advantage of someone half his age – Adam was much older than April; it didn't take Einstein to work that out, with his paunch and his thinning hair. I never knew what April saw in him, but that's beside the point; he was her choice." With formidable tension set in his jaw, Jake continued. "She said nothing, so Marty waited for her to come home one afternoon when neither Mum nor I were there. He punched her in the face, and somehow she managed to get away and run up the stairs and lock herself in the bathroom."

Jake felt Bobby's arm across his shoulders as he fought to keep his voice under control. He pinched the top of his nose to fight the tears that didn't feel normal for a grown man to shed. "She couldn't hold him off, Bobby. The lock was only a sliding bolt, and one shove from Marty and it flew open. She tried to run past him but he grabbed her again, and after calling her all the names under the sun, he gave her one last shove down the stairs."

Jake sniffed. "Where's a woman with a packet of tissues when you need her, eh?"

"Sorry, you took my last one earlier."

"He didn't stop there, either." Jake continued. "He gave her a good kicking as she lay helpless on the floor, the gutless prick. He left her there until I came home." Jake put his head in his hands at the memory.

"He sounds quite a piece of work."

Jake knew he had to pull himself together; falling apart now wasn't going to help his sister. "Mum eventually saw Marty for what he was and threw him out. I'm surprised he was clever enough to keep up the pretence with her for so long, but mind games were his forte. The physical violence came at the end when his brain seemed unable to cope with anything else."

Jake lifted his palms from the bumper, rubbing the mud from

them onto his jeans. "We should get going." He climbed into the pick-up. "You know, I never thought Marty would fork out for a flight to Sydney all the way from Perth, just to find us; it looks like I underestimated him." He poked fun at his own stupidity.

"Don't be too hard on yourself, Jake. It sounds like you did the best you could under the circumstances. May I ask if this Adam is the father of April's baby?"

"He is. April knew that he had a conference in Sydney late March – they had already planned to meet up there for the entire weekend – and because we'd left Perth so quickly, she felt she owed it to him to give him a proper explanation. Goodness knows why; the guy's married. Anyway, I guess what did happen that weekend was a final goodbye shag, because bam, pregnant."

"Does he know, about the baby?"

"He knows, but he has no intention of leaving his wife. He says he'll support April and the baby financially, but apart from that I think he wants the whole mess to magically disappear."

"Big man," Bobby sighed.

"Even April sees the affair as a big mistake, and she doesn't want the financial help either. But she doesn't regret being pregnant." His voice shook. "She can't wait for this baby to arrive."

Jake stopped the pick-up beside the orchards at the far end of town, and they desperately scoured the fields and abandoned barns along the perimeter. But their search was futile, and before long they drove silently back to the pub hoping that someone else had better news than them.

***

Rugged up in a fleece and a pair of jeans, with her hair pulled hastily into a ponytail, Tamara pushed open the door to the pub.

"I wish you'd stayed in bed, love, this is no place for you right now," said Bobby, as soon as he caught sight of her.

"Let me be the judge of that."

When she had wakened and seen the light streaming under the

door of the annexe, Tamara had known that something was wrong. Her mum had filled her in on everything and she'd come straight here.

"See if you can try to get him to have something else to eat and drink, would you?" Bobby urged when Tamara's eyes fell on Jake. He was sitting at the far corner of the pub looking helpless, head in his hands, going through utter hell.

"I'll do my best. Has anyone called the police yet?"

Bobby's look told her that she was about to open another part of this frightening mystery. "I'll leave it to Jake to explain," he said.

Jake sat hypnotised by the green, gold and russet tones of the stained glass window looking out over the street, and he squinted as the sky outside gradually emerged from the depths of darkness. The sudden light accentuated the dark circles beneath sunken eyes, and the pallor of his skin. He looked up when Tamara sat down, and his eyes came alive for a second before they plunged back into despair.

"I heard what happened." Tamara gently touched the cut across his neck as tenderly as he had touched her face last night, as carefully as he had tucked the wet strands of her hair behind each ear. That felt like a lifetime ago now. "Bobby told me everything," she said.

His whole body collapsed with a mixture of relief and hopelessness.

"Jake, you must call the police. You'd never forgive yourself if something happened to April and you hadn't done everything that you could."

He didn't put up a fight. It was as though he'd been waiting for her to come to the conclusion for him. "Marty's gone too far this time, Tamara."

She tilted her head to indicate they should go out the back of the pub to make the call, then hooked an arm through his as encouragement.

"I don't care what he tries to pin on me now. I'd sooner go to jail than lose my sister."

Tamara didn't press him for more information, even when the word "jail" sent a shudder through her entire body. She had no idea what he was tangled up in, but right now finding April had to be their only focus.

"I would've told you everything in the end," he said.

"I know." She wished she could take away some of his pain. Even though he had lied to them all, Jake had every right to stand tall and proud as a man who had put his family and loved ones first, no matter what the consequences were for him.

He slumped down onto the telephone stool out the back and lifted the phone to his ear, then jumped at the sound of a voice.

"Sorry to interrupt." It was Daphne Abbott, doing the rounds with refreshments to keep up everybody's strength. "I was wondering if either of you wanted something to eat? Or can I get you a cup of tea?"

"Thanks, Daphne." Tamara took the tray of sandwiches. "I think we're fine for now."

Oblivious to the tension in Jake's hands or the distress in his voice, Daphne shuffled over to the bag sitting beneath the telephone table. "Excuse me, I put my bag here for safe keeping but I need some tablets. I've got an awful headache. Oh damn." The contents of the plastic container flew out across the floor as Daphne succeeded in prising off the top; to make matters worse, she dropped her handbag and its contents followed a similar pattern.

"I'll do this, Daphne." Tamara did her best to keep the annoyance out of her voice and bent down to pick up the bag's contents. She shoved everything back inside as Jake recounted his story to the police.

"Thank you so much, my dear." Daphne took the tablets and her handbag from Tamara.

"Don't forget these." Tamara retrieved a bunch of keys that must've fallen out.

"Thank you," Daphne tutted. "I'd forget my own head if it

wasn't joined to the rest of me. I should wear these on a chain around my neck." She put two tablets on her tongue and swallowed them with the remains of her cup of tea which was tucked between the pumps on the bar. "I've no idea how I misplaced my other set."

"They're on their way," said Jake.

Tamara gripped his hand.

"Who are?" Daphne asked.

"Actually, I think I will have that cup of tea please, Daphne?" Anxious to get the older woman away and allow Jake to pause for breath before he faced the police, Tamara steered Daphne out towards the bar, but the old lady was in for the long haul.

"Heaven knows where my other set of keys is. I even have a special hook underneath the till where I always hang them so that I don't lose them. When it was time to go home that day, I couldn't find them; most peculiar." She shrugged then collected a few stray mugs and teacups from the bar ready to take to the kitchen for washing up.

Jake stepped past Tamara, his whole body braced expectantly. "Is there anything else you can remember about that day, Daphne?" Tamara shot him a bewildered look. "Was there anything out of the ordinary?" he persisted. "Anything at all? Think really hard; it's really important."

Daphne took a deep breath and shook her head slowly. But before she left, she said, "Actually there was something. It was very strange but there was a customer asking if we sold those giant scourers – you know, the ones that are about so big–" She gestured with her hands. "I could've sworn there were some on display but there weren't, so I had to search through the storeroom for another box, and when I came back into the shop the customer had gone. Why he'd ask for something so specific and then leave, I'll never know."

Daphne tilted her head to one side. "The funny thing is I saw those scourers beneath the shelf where they should've been when I locked the shop up at the end of the day. If I didn't know any better, I'd say that someone had hidden them on purpose."

"Daphne, I want you to think really carefully now," said Jake.

"I'll try."

"Can you describe the man?"

She cocked her head and thought for a second. "Scruffy he was. A bit dirty-looking and he had a way about him that I didn't like. Oh, I know you can't judge, but he made me uncomfortable. He was polite enough, but even the tattoos on his knuckles–"

Tamara put her arm around the old lady and steered her to sit on the nearest chair.

"Oh my Lord, it was him, wasn't it?" Daphne clasped a hand to her chest. "That man has April."

Tamara ran after Jake, out of the pub, and across the road to his pick-up.

"Wait up." It was Hugo. "Do you know where she is?"

"Get in." Jake barely waited for him to shut the door behind him before he drove off down the street.

Tamara's heart beat furiously. Nobody spoke; nobody dared to breathe. Less than two hundred metres away, April had been right under their noses all along.

Chapter Twenty-Eight

"You should wait for the police, Jake." Tamara pulled at his arm, but he and Hugo leapt from the car despite her pleas. As they marched away, she blocked them – arms outstretched – imploring them to listen. "You said yourself, Jake, he's nasty. He could do something to hurt April if he panics, and that would be down to our own stupidity."

Jake hesitated then seemed to see sense. Instead of facing Marty head-on, all three of them slipped down the side of the brick building where the shop sat at one end. They crept down the narrow path, the weeds and debris snapping beneath their feet, until they reached the back of the shop.

"I think that window up there is to the storeroom," said Jake, pointing. "Let's see if we can at least suss out what's going on. I need to know that she's alright, Tamara."

"Wait." It was Hugo this time. "I think we should leave it to the police, like Tamara said."

Jake shook his head. "They could be ages yet. Tamara, I'll put you on my shoulders and you tell us what you can see through that window." He had already crouched down for her to climb onto his shoulders.

There was no time to be embarrassed at having her legs wrapped round his neck, as Tamara allowed Jake to lift her into the air. Level with the window, she had no qualms about using her fingers to break the empty cobwebs that clung in a mass and impaired her view.

"Can you see anything?" Hugo whispered anxiously, jumping

when a rat scurried across his path and through a dilapidated wooden fence.

"Stop moving around," Jake growled. "The last thing we want is for Marty to hear us."

Tamara moved her head a little to the left to where the glass was clearer. She gasped. "April's in there."

"Is she okay?" Jake tensed beneath her.

"I think so. She's curled up on the floor with a bottle of water. I can't see Marty. Maybe he's gone, or he could be in the front of the shop."

"Try to get her attention, ask if she's okay," said Hugo.

"Quietly," Jake urged.

She made a fist and knocked gently on the glass, but April didn't hear. "I think she's asleep."

"Try again," said Jake. He groaned subtly with Tamara perched on his shoulders, and she could feel the strain in his arms as they gripped her thighs.

She knocked again and this time April turned around, her hand flying to her mouth to quieten the gasp of shock that must have escaped.

"Are you okay?" Tamara mouthed.

"She's alright," she repeated to the others when April nodded.

"Where's Marty?" she mouthed this time, although it took three attempts to get April to understand.

April pointed to the door of the storeroom that led to the shop. Then she got onto all fours, pushed herself to her feet, and disappeared into the tiny bathroom to the side of the storeroom. She came out with a long black pole which stretched up to the strip window and opened the slats.

"Can you hear me?" April stood back.

"Yes," Tamara whispered. "Is Marty in the shop?"

"He's out front, and he locked me in. God, I've never been so frightened in my life," she hissed, the tears welling in her eyes.

Tamara felt her pain and pressed a hand against the window, even though it was too high for April to reach and barely big enough for a small animal to pass through.

"Where are the police?" Hugo stiffened. "They should be here by now. This shouldn't be up to us."

"Calm down." Tamara shot him a warning look. She knew they may not have long until Marty appeared.

April got down to the floor the best she could with her pregnant belly, and peered under the door. Satisfied that they were safe for now, she came and stood under the window.

"You okay?" Tamara touched Jake's head as she asked the question.

"Yes." His strength must have come from the adrenalin of finding April and the determination to keep her safe.

"It was awful, Tamara." April began. "I opened the door thinking it was Jake. I'd fallen asleep in the armchair, and then I was confused when I woke and didn't think to check." Her body recoiled.

"Did he hurt you?" Tamara felt Jake tense up even more.

Shaking her head, April said, "No. He just kept going on about me, about how it was my fault that Mum didn't want him, how pissed off he is at Jake."

Suddenly April froze with a finger to her lips.

Tamara held her breath, and when she saw the door opening she ducked to the side of the window so that she couldn't be seen. Jake staggered beneath her but held strong.

She heard a creepy laugh, which had to belong to Marty, and then, "Ha, that stupid brother of yours still hasn't found ya, has he? Ah, don't look like that now..."

Tamara moved her head enough for her to see into the storeroom again. She cringed when she saw Marty, every bit as nasty-looking as she'd expected. She knew Jake had heard his voice, too, because his hands gripped her legs even harder.

Marty had April up against the wall, his hand holding her jaw in a vice-like grip.

"Poor, innocent April; sleeping with a dirty old married man. Tut-tut, naughty girl. And as for that brother of yours, he bottled it. All he had to do was to drive the fucking car for me and keep his mouth shut, and we could've kept playing happy families." His mouth was close to April's and Tamara held her breath. She could almost smell the stale, trampy odour that she knew would come with him.

"You both screwed things up good and proper for me and Deborah." Marty's face took on a sneer, his lip curled up on one side as he leant harder against April's stomach. "Where's your knight in shining armour when you need him? Where's pretty-faced Jake hiding tonight? Got himself a good woman to keep warm and left you out in the cold?" He pushed April's head back harder against the wall and smiled as she whimpered.

Tamara held her breath, knowing that if Jake could see the scene unfolding he would be breaking into that shop right now.

Where were the police? Where were they?

"Now we've got ourselves a little problem, April." Marty backed away from her and motioned to the open door of the storeroom as he picked up an empty carrier bag. "I need money, and until I get it you're stuck with me."

Tamara moved so that she could see through to the main part of the shop and watched as Marty stuffed the bag full of items from the shelves. He forced the till with a crowbar and emptied that, too, then shouted to April, "Get out here!" He sniffed, wiped his nose on the back of his sleeve and grinned, showcasing two rows of violently nicotine-stained teeth.

Without daring to look back at the window, April did as she was told and Tamara watched Marty pace back and forth at the front of the shop.

"Should've fucking well made you walk last night when it was still dark," he yelled.

Tamara hurried Jake to let her down, amazed that both he and Hugo had been silent through the whole event. She wondered how much of Marty and April's exchange they had heard but they didn't have time to dissect it now. "It looks like he's getting ready to leave," she hissed at them.

The trio walked as quietly as they could down the side of the shop but froze at the unmistakable sound of the shop's bell tinkling as the door opened. There was a rustling noise – perhaps the carrier bags that Marty had filled – but no voices. Tamara's heart felt as though it were thumping outside her chest, and when a twig snapped beneath her shoe they all froze.

As Jake moved one step closer to meet whoever came out of the shop first, Tamara saw a burly figure leap out from nowhere. She heard a scream – April – then saw two men brawling on the road, one of whom was Marty. Then suddenly sirens were blaring and police officers descended from everywhere.

Jake and Hugo ran out from their hiding place but Tamara could only slide down the brick wall, crouching down with her head between her knees. The drama had unfolded as though she were part of a movie set, but all she could hear was an echo, an eerie sound of what had taken place. She felt an arm around her and looked up to find a policewoman who helped her to her feet and walked her out to the front of the shop.

Marty had been bundled into the police car already and only April, Jake and Hugo remained with the other police officers. April was screaming and clutching her swollen belly, and looked even more terrified than she had in the storeroom. Hugo clutched her hands and desperately tried to reassure her.

When April screamed louder, Jake yelled, "I need an ambulance, now!"

Tamara stared open-mouthed at the pool of blood on the pavement where April sat, and then watched her friend double over with pains that seemed to come hard and fast. Tamara felt nauseous. The immediate danger from Marty may be all over, but had he hurt April in the ultimate way by making her lose the baby?

Chapter Twenty-Nine

"I'm sorry I won't be here for the darts tournament, Daphne." Tamara pulled a jar of mincemeat from the shelf in the shop. It was Christmas Eve and her mum was paranoid that come tomorrow morning – she always liked everything to be baked fresh – she would run out of filling for the mince pies.

"Don't be silly. I'm just sorry that we didn't manage to organise it before. What with all that trouble nearly three months ago, having a big knees-up seemed the furthest thing from everybody's minds."

Tamara opened the chest freezer and took out a Magnum. She was making the most of craving ice-cream; in less than a week she would be back in the UK, where winter was already in full swing.

"All that trouble", as Daphne put it, was a bit of an understatement. Tamara still woke at night in a sweat when she remembered Marty's face and April sitting in a pool of blood. But April's baby had shown strength and resistance to Marty – just as Jake and April had done – and after a few nights in hospital, Aprill had been discharged and told to rest until the baby arrived.

Hugo had barely left April's side since that day. He had claimed to be her fiancé in the hospital, to gain prime bedside position, and the couple were now happily ensconced in the cottage that brother and sister had once rented.

Jake had left for Perth two days after the showdown and, apart from a brief goodbye at the Harding property while his mum waited in the car, Tamara hadn't seen or heard from him. Apparently Marty had done more than break into the family home over in Perth; he'd smashed the place up good and proper, and it would be quite a job to put it back to rights. The ever-supportive family man, Jake had gone back with his mum to fix the place up and a locum had stepped in at his practice for the time being.

Tamara often found herself wondering what might have happened had Marty not turned up that night. She still remembered the way Jake had looked at her, the way he'd held her in the car as they talked, everything that remained unsaid between them. She wasn't sure whether it was his being on the opposite side of the country or whether it was the closure with Bradley, but when her contract finished with Carter Brown Tamara had the overwhelming urge to go home to the UK. She needed to go back and see whether her life was still there, or whether she wanted it to be in Australia.

"April was in here yesterday," said Daphne, interrupting Tamara's thoughts.

The tension across Tamara's forehead lifted and she smiled at the thought of her friend, now rapidly approaching her due date at the end of December.

"She gave me some books for the mobile library. They were brand new," Daphne continued.

"That's lovely. We must have quite a collection now. When are you hoping to launch the library?"

"By the middle of next year, fingers crossed."

Tamara smiled, a little sad that she wouldn't be there to see the project launched and in operation. Some of the neighbouring towns had also been roped in when word got out. April had taken over the co-ordination of the friendship tree – although Daphne was to look after it during a "maternity leave" period – and had already organised the long-awaited darts tournament, plus a fete at the local church to raise funds for a mobile library van.

Tamara cupped her hand beneath her ice-cream in time to catch a shard of crisp chocolate. She had been hoping April would have the baby before she left Australia. Perhaps it would bring Jake back, even temporarily, and at least she would get to say goodbye to him properly. From their brief conversation before he left, Tamara knew that he wished he had gone to the police sooner. He blamed himself for putting April's life, and that of her unborn baby, at risk. He had been a mess the last time she saw him, and she hoped he had worked through what was going on in his own head, especially since the police had charged Marty and were content that neither April nor Jake had had any involvement.

"I'd better get back, Daphne." Tamara pulled open the door but Daphne stopped her. In her hands lay a small package.

"Is that for me? Is it a Christmas present?"

"It's a little something for you," said Daphne, patting the bottom curls of her hair. "You'll always have a place in Brewer Creek, no matter where you are in the world."

"I don't know what to say, I—"

"You can open it now," she smiled, as though encouraging a child to open one present before Christmas Day.

Tamara pulled off the wrapping and opened the humbug-striped box.

"It's Brewer Creek, fifty years ago," Daphne explained proudly, as Tamara pulled out the six-by-four inch classic black and white print showing the town's main strip.

Unexpectedly Tamara felt tears well up. Her words fought to get out. "Thank you." She wrapped her arms around the old lady.

As she walked home on Christmas Eve beneath the Australian sun, the reality of leaving hit Tamara like a mallet driving the final peg into the ground. Her job and the bad relationship habit with Bradley had carried her along on a current that had once seemed impossible to break. But since she'd come to Brewer Creek, Tamara had opened her eyes to everything around her. She would never forget this place, not ever. She would never forget the people she had met, who had once been sown like small saplings, but had since grown into fully fledged, lifelong friends. Each of them, in their own way, had been part of her journey over the past year; her journey of getting to know herself and who she wanted to be.

Chapter Thirty

On Christmas morning, Tamara pulled on a red fitted dress. Ever since she was little, her family had made an effort for the big day and even the forecast of thirty degrees did little to deter from their traditions of a real tree and a roast dinner with all the trimmings.

A wolf whistle greeted Tamara at the foot of the stairs, and there stood Bobby, dressed smarter than usual in a pair of grey trousers with a light grey polo shirt. The only flaw in his outfit was that ridiculous Santa hat, sitting skewiff, just as he always wore it. But it made Tamara smile; it was Bobby all over.

Katherine floated past her in a green wraparound dress, with familiar white, dangly festive earrings in the shape of snowflakes. A Christmas mix played on the iPod from the corner of the lounge, and in the kitchen Tamara watched as her mum filled mince pie bases, put the tops on, and brushed them with egg.

"Have you heard from Jake?" Bobby asked as Tamara stood adjusting the crooked snowman ornament on the Christmas tree. She breathed in its pine scent and let it send nostalgia cascading through her body.

"I think Jake has his own problems, and I've definitely had mine." She sat down on the arm of Bobby's chair and they gazed at the tree together, its twinkly lights barely visible in the Australian summer. "Who knows? Maybe in a different place or at a different time, it could've all worked out perfectly."

He grinned. "I knew it."

"What?"

"You like him."

246

She smiled and nudged him before walking away to take charge of the champagne.

The table looked like something out of a catalogue. A holly-berry red runner stretched down the middle, and on top sat a turkey large enough to feed them for the next week. Carrots, pumpkin, and peas sat in one bowl; roast potatoes in another; and pigs in blankets lay in a tray next to the gravy boat.

"It's a shame Mr Wilson couldn't join us." Bobby twisted the salt shaker over his dinner as Katherine exchanged a knowing glance with Tamara. "What? Is there something I don't know?"

"Mr Wilson has been invited elsewhere," said Katherine diplomatically, and Tamara stifled a giggle.

"Come on, don't keep me in suspense," Bobby begged.

"Daphne Abbott invited him to her place," Tamara revealed.

"Well I never. The saucy minx," he chuckled. When he'd recovered, he asked, "Is everything sorted with your new place, Tamara?"

"Yep, the house is mine for six months at least."

Tamara and her mum had viewed the photos of the exquisite, English country cottage on the internet, marvelling at its idyllic proportions. Set in a tiny village not far from Norwich, the cottage was the end one of four, chocolate-box fronted, and with red roses climbing around the front door when the seasons allowed. Beth's cousin owned the property, but a secondment with her work would take her out of the country for a while.

"Beth's driving up on New Year's Eve," said Tamara.

"Watch out, Norfolk!" Katherine giggled, as she spooned out some sage and onion stuffing which had crisped on the top.

Tamara grinned. Beth had been disappointed that she wouldn't be returning to London, and had already begun to take the mickey out of the sleepy Norfolk village. Apparently there was no local talent – especially of the vet variety – but Tamara decided that wasn't necessarily a bad thing.

"You'll find Norfolk a lot different to London," said Bobby.

"I know, but after being in Brewer Creek I've seen another side to the world; a less barmy side." In many ways she was going back a changed person with a more definite sense of who she was.

"Careful now, love, or you'll be starting to sound old," said Bobby.

She poked her stepfather in the ribs. "I've got a long way to catch you up, *Dad*."

As they finished lunch, the phone sprang to life and Bobby debated who it could be to wish them Christmas cheer as he went to answer it. Tamara couldn't help but reach out and touch the fresh holly arrangement in the centre of the table. Her mum had insisted Christmas wasn't Christmas without it, and had found it at the markets and kept it fresh in the laundry trough for the last few days.

"It's a girl!" Bobby bellowed excitedly when he reappeared. Tamara jumped and pricked her finger on the end of the holly. Relieved that the baby had been delivered safe and sound, Tamara could hear her mum asking questions: the weight, the name. But all she could think was she might see Jake again before she left, and then maybe she would know; she would know if she still wanted more than a friendship with him, or whether she had missed her one chance.

***

Tamara raced to the hospital with Danielle, and Katherine's legendary Christmas pudding with spiced brandy butter was put on hold until she returned.

At the hospital April was sleepy after her labour, but Hugo was there, unable to tear his gaze away from the beautiful girl lying in the bassinet beside the bed. With a full head of dark hair and swaddled in a baby pink blanket, Jasmine Manning was gorgeous.

When Tamara arrived home to the smell of Christmas pudding mingled with the pine tree standing tall in the lounge room, she showed her parents the photos taken on her phone.

"She's beautiful," said Katherine, a hand clasped to her chest.

"We didn't stay long. April was drifting in and out of sleep and the room was so peaceful, we thought we'd better let her make the most of it."

"Good idea. It won't be long before Jasmine keeps her awake at all hours demanding attention." Katherine cut the Christmas pudding and the air filled with the fruity-brandy smell.

"I deserve a medal for waiting for this," said Bobby, his eyes widening like saucers at the pudding set down in front of him.

"I appreciate it. Thanks, Bobby." Tamara giggled. She was going to miss him more than he knew.

"So is Jake on his way?" he asked, another spoonful poised and ready to go.

"He arrives on the morning of the 27th." Tamara had asked April while Danielle and Hugo were busy cooing over Jasmine, but that had been the only mention of him. Instead, Tamara had said her goodbyes to all three of them, and baby Jasmine had taken centre stage, her tiny, beautiful face preventing the moment from being too sad.

"I might have to go for a walk after all this food," said Tamara, as she followed Bobby into the lounge room. She plucked a chocolate snowman all the way from the rear branch of the tree.

"Not fair! I thought we were all out." Bobby smiled when Tamara passed him half – the snowman's head. "Thanks."

"Come on, you only put them on there for me anyway."

As Bobby settled in the armchair, she realised that there was no chance of getting him out for a walk. She estimated about five minutes before he fell asleep.

"Tamara, phone," Katherine called from the kitchen.

"Who is it?" she mouthed, padding into the kitchen. But Katherine left, shutting the door behind her without saying a word.

"Hello?"

"G'day, Tamara." Her stomach lurched at the sound of Jake's voice, as rich and thick as their Christmas dessert.

They chatted about April, about the baby, about the work he

had been doing at his mum's property, about the ridiculous heat in Perth over Christmas. And then they chatted about her impending return to the UK.

"I'd really like to see you before you go, Tamara," he said.

"I'd like that, too. I leave on the afternoon of the twenty-seventh."

She waited for the awkward silence to pass.

"I'll be there," he said. "But are you sure you're making the right decision? To go back, I mean."

She had doubted herself a million times already, but never so much as she did now. "I think so."

"I wish things could've been different."

"I do, too."

The phone call had come too late for anything to happen between them. In less than forty-eight hours she would see Jake again, but only to say goodbye. And this time it would be for good.

Chapter Thirty-One

Len's voice boomed across the pub in true landlord-style as the residents of Brewer Creek crammed inside the pub on the sweltering thirty degree day.

"I think we're all agreed, Daphne, that you have given so much to this community in the sixty-five years that you've lived here. The friendship tree was your family's legacy and, while some of us resisted it," – a few friendly giggles were heard amongst the crowd – "you have proved that what the friendship tree really represents is the sense of community. And in this day and age, that is a rare thing. So I want everyone to charge your glasses again to this wonderful woman who brought Brewer Creek together."

"To Daphne," the voices chorused through the room as Len presented her with a bouquet of pink and white lilies.

Len held up his hands to stop the crowd dispersing. "And now, this town wants to say thank you and goodbye to someone who hasn't been here quite as long as Daphne, but who has slotted in and kept the friendship tree going. Come on, Tamara, up you come."

Bobby winked at Tamara as she reluctantly left her seat to a round of applause.

"Now we can't give you flowers – you'll never get them past Border Security," Len chuckled. "But we do have something for you to remember us by." He handed her a gift.

Tamara's hands shook as she tore open the silver wrapping. She hadn't predicted this goodbye ceremony, and it was taking all her strength to get through it without breaking down. She looked around the crowd, hoping that Jake would push the door open and join them. But he still wasn't here, and with only three hours to go until she had to leave for the airport, she had no idea whether he would make it.

When the wrapping fell away, it revealed a framed friendship tree in Daphne's Mrs-Pepperpot-style handwriting. Tamara clutched it to her chest, a wonderful reminder of a place that felt like home in so many ways.

The crowd clapped when Tamara stepped down, and Danielle swooped in beside her. "Is he here?"

She shook her head.

Danielle clutched her arm. "He will be. He won't let you leave without saying goodbye."

Tamara had confided in Danielle soon after Marty had been arrested. And now her friend seemed as obsessed about Jake turning up as she was.

"I can't believe you're going." Danielle sipped her beer and Tamara shot her a warning look. "I'm sorry. There's no point saying that is there?"

They moved to a table at the far end, away from the main crowd.

"You will keep in touch, though, won't you?"

"What do you think?"

"Good," said Danielle. "And you never know, maybe I'll come over to the UK once I'm qualified. I could even work there for a while."

"That would be fantastic. It's better to try something even if only for a short time." She couldn't describe her own experience here in this town any better.

"It's been a privilege knowing you, Tamara Harding."

Tamara rolled her eyes and sipped on her lemon, lime and bitters. "I'm not dying, you know," she giggled.

"That did sound a bit melodramatic, didn't it? Seriously though, there was always a nagging feeling in the back of my mind that leaving Brewer Creek and the farming life behind to pursue nursing was like turning my back on everything I knew. But you've helped me to see that it isn't closing the book on the past; it's about finding out what's the right fit for me."

Tamara couldn't wait to see Beth back in the UK, but at the same time she realised that the length of a friendship didn't mean it was any more superior to the relationships she formed with new people along the way.

"So come on," said Tamara, as her eyes glistened with expected tears, "what's happening with you and Will?"

With a naughty grin, Danielle filled Tamara in on her whirlwind romance which had already reached the stage of discussing sharing a place in the city when she started her studies.

Before she left the pub, Tamara felt a light tap on her shoulder and turned to find Mr Wilson, trusty navy cap in hand. She hugged him tightly; the unlikely friend whom she respected and thought of as a grandfather figure. "I'll miss you, too, Mr Wilson. Look after him," she said to Daphne, when they pulled apart.

"I will, dear," she said. "And you look after yourself."

Mr Wilson leaned closer to Tamara as he pulled on the familiar navy cap. "Remember, true love isn't easy to find, but don't you ever settle for second best." And with that he kissed her on her cheek, tipped the brim of his cap, and went on his way with Daphne's arm looped through his own.

Tamara looked around the pub one last time and waved goodbye. This was it, time to go – and Jake still wasn't there. She had run out of time.

Chapter Thirty-Two

At the check-in desk, Tamara swung her suitcase onto the conveyor belt and watched it zip off into the unknown maze behind the scenes. She stashed her boarding pass and passport back in her shoulder bag, and joined her parents.

"I got a window seat so I can loll against it and hopefully get some sleep."

"I don't know why you insisted on being here so early," said Katherine.

Tamara had come early because it was better than sitting around looking at everyone, waiting for the off, wondering whether or not she was doing the right thing. If Jake had shown up today, would she have known one way or the other?

"We'll be over to see you in July," Katherine rambled. Tamara could tell that her mum was struggling to hold in her emotions. "It'll give us a good excuse to miss winter here. And we can stay for a while – if you'll have us – now that Bobby is retiring."

Tamara turned and hugged Bobby. He held her for a long time while people bustled past them as though they were part of the fixtures and fittings.

Tamara's parents knew what was coming before she said, "I'm going through now." She hugged them in turn and tried not to think about the look on her mum's face, as though she was committing her daughter's face to memory. "I love you both." She adjusted her bag, lifted her shoulders bravely, and walked towards Passport Control, knowing that if she turned back she might just change her mind.

Chapter Thirty-Three

Jake caught his breath as his head darted from side-to-side, taking in the masses of people crowded in the International Terminal at Sydney's Kingsford Smith Airport. He did his best not to shove a stroller out of the way, instead smiling meekly at the young mother trying to negotiate the airport with four kids in tow.

He spotted Bobby in the distance, holding a takeaway coffee, with Katherine by his side. He'd made it in time. He shook out his t-shirt, which clung to his chest after the marathon sprint he'd made all the way from the car park.

But he couldn't see Tamara anywhere.

"Jake?" Katherine turned in her seat.

His heart sank. "I'm too late, aren't I?"

Their faces said it all. He was too bloody late. He'd missed his chance with her for good this time.

Bobby took control. "I'll call her phone."

"She left the phone here, Bobby," said Katherine. "She said she'll get another one when she's in the UK."

Katherine patted the chair beside her but Jake didn't seem to notice. He was still pacing on the spot trying to figure out his next move. He raked a hand through his hair more fiercely than usual and left a red mark on his forehead. "Why the hell did she go through so early? Her flight isn't due to leave for almost two hours."

Bobby sighed and tapped the chair beside him; this time Jake obliged. "You see, Jake, Tamara hates goodbyes. Always has, and her mother," he looked directly at his wife, "well she doesn't take them well either."

Jake looked at Katherine with the balled-up tissue in her fist. Her eyes were red-rimmed and she looked tired but calm as she sipped her coffee.

"I wanted to see her again before she left," Jake told them. "My bloody flight was delayed from Perth, then the car rental place didn't seem to have a record of my booking, then I stopped at the hospital to see April and the baby, but ended up in a huge tailback. My phone ran out of power, too, and I don't know any of the numbers off by heart." He was babbling, but the longer it had taken him to get here, the more he knew that he had to see Tamara; he had to tell her that he was in love with her, that being without her wasn't an option any more.

Jake had stayed away after all the trouble he'd brought to Brewer Creek. He thought that Tamara would be better off without him, especially if Marty followed through on his threat to implicate him in his crimes. But the police had carried out a thorough investigation and cleared Jake of any involvement, and he'd had time to process everything that had happened. He soon realised that it was time to break away from the past and do something that he wanted for once.

Now all he wanted was to see Tamara, to beg her not to go. But it was too late.

He thought of the tiny bundle waiting for him over at the hospital: Jasmine, wrapped in a pink cotton blanket and whose finger grasped his own as though he could keep her from all harm. He thought about how happy his sister was with Hugo. He thought about his mum, starting over with her life in Perth and urging him to do what was best for him.

As he left the airport, Jake knew that the Brewer Creek he had come to love would be a very different place without Tamara. And even though he had so much to be thankful for now, in many ways his life suddenly felt discernibly empty.

Chapter Thirty-Four

Inside the tiny Norfolk cottage, Tamara sank into the plump sofa cushions. She'd been back in the country for three days, but amidst the thrill at being back on familiar turf and the over-excited conversations with Beth, the regrets had started to seep in, exacerbated by the lull that usually followed Christmas.

It was New Year's Eve, and with the sounds of the season blaring from the iPod as ABBA belted out *Happy New Year,* Tamara was at least content. She might not know what would happen next week, next month, next year even, but for now it actually felt right to take a step back and let life unfold.

Tamara had deleted Bradley as a friend from Facebook, and she hadn't heard from him since he left Australia. She hoped his future would be a positive one and that he would find the person who was right for him. She also hoped his family would find a way to work through their history, but knew that it wasn't her place to worry about any of them anymore.

As ABBA came to an end, something out of the window caught her eye.

"It's snowing!" She leapt up to watch the soft white flakes fluttering delicately down from the sky, disappearing almost as soon as they landed. She imagined the neat, white layer that would form if the snow persisted long enough, and felt as though every worry she had ever had could be blanketed over to allow her to start afresh. In a couple of hours Beth was due to arrive, and Tamara couldn't wait to see her oldest and dearest friend. But her time in Brewer Creek had also taught her that with friendship there were no rules; no age limits; and, if sown correctly, the roots of friendship would forever remain strong.

Tamara perched on the windowsill, the warmth of the radiator seeping through her jeans, and she looked up at the picture of the friendship tree hanging above the mantelpiece. Below it was the framed picture of Brewer Creek all those years ago, and next to that a photograph of her, Danielle, and April, grinning like Cheshire cats in the pub, making a toast towards the camera. A photograph of Tamara and Beth, sipping colourful cocktails with luminous umbrellas poking out at angles, had travelled all the way to Australia and back again, and sat on the windowsill where Tamara perched now. She looked around the room at her memories of two very different lives; it felt good to have known both.

The snowflakes became larger as though the window was a magnifying glass, and Tamara hopped down to follow the enticing warm, sweet smell snaking through the air from the kitchen. It wasn't even midday, but right now she didn't care. Skilfully avoiding the cinnamon stick, she ladled out a glass of mulled wine and took it back into the lounge. She swapped the main light for the miniature white twinkly lights on the Christmas tree. Beth had arranged for the tree to be there to welcome Tamara to her new home, and she smiled as she remembered the note pinned to the angel at the top: *Sorry it's not a real one but couldn't be bothered with pine needles in the car!* Typical Beth.

Tamara sat mesmerised by the tree lights and sipped on her mulled wine until the gentle squeaking of the letterbox made her jump. An envelope floated down to the mat.

As she picked up the delivery, she thought about how many times she had sneaked out in her pyjamas to get the mail in Australia from the box at the end of the driveway, battling cobwebs and plunging her arm in, hoping for the best.

Warmed by the memory, she set her glass down on the hearth of the inglenook fireplace and ripped across the top of the envelope. Inside was a single sheet of paper, folded neatly into thirds. But instead of a letter, there was a picture. It was the outline of a tree trunk and its many branches, but the branches had no leaves; nothing. The trunk was coloured in brown, but when she turned the paper over there was only white space. She peered inside the envelope, in all corners, to check that she hadn't missed anything.

It had to be the kids down the road, surely? Well, whoever had taught them to draw such dull Christmas trees needed to be educated in the joy of the season – there wasn't a single stroke of colour, not a single bauble.

She shrugged and peered through the window, then poked her head out of the front door to see if she could spot any of the children to thank them for what must be a belated Christmas card. But the street was abandoned as the snow fell harder, and the road, pavements, and parked cars were covered in their fresh undercoat of white emulsion.

Retreating back inside to the warmth, she took a swig of mulled wine and pulled out a woollen jumper from the cupboard beneath the stairs. She was about to ball the picture up and use it as kindling on the fire, when there was a firm rap on the front door.

"Hang on!" she shouted, barely able to contain her giddiness at the thought of Beth waiting on the other side. "I'm coming!"

But when she flung open the door, standing beneath the outside lamp that lit up the porch wasn't the face she had been expecting. In a chocolate brown, shearling leather coat, covered in large white flakes, Jake was as gorgeous as she remembered. She watched more flakes settle on top of that delicious mixture of blond and brown in his hair. This time she didn't feel the icy bite of the wind; she didn't register the frosty doorstep nipping at her toes through her thin socks.

"Aren't you going to let me in?" Jake's voice tugged at her belly. "It's damn cold out here, and us Aussies aren't used to it, you know."

She stepped aside as he came in out of the cold and pushed a pot plant into her hands.

"What's this?" He may have travelled ten thousand miles to find her, but those were the only words that she could think of right now.

"It's a jade plant," he grinned. "A symbol of friendship."

She looked past the smooth, rounded, rich green leaves which, according to the accompanying label, held the promise of surprise flowers come spring, then set the pot down and picked up the ball of paper. "Did you do this?"

"It's pretty bad, isn't it? It's my attempt at a friendship tree, but I'm a terrible artist, as you may have already realised."

"I thought it was supposed to be a Christmas tree." She felt her mind begin to relax, but her body was still on high alert. "I assumed it was the kids who live down the road. I was going to tell them they needed to add a bit more colour; give a bit more Christmas cheer."

He laughed, but then turned serious. "I'm in a bit of a predicament."

Her heart pounded and she was pretty sure it was at risk of stopping if he stepped any closer.

"April's latest venture as the friendship tree co-ordinator is to organise a Winter Ball, of all things."

"Sounds fun," she said, holding her breath as he closed the gap some more.

"It would be, but I don't have a date."

His familiar aftershave and the warmth of his body as the gap grew smaller sent her into panic mode. "Why did you come, Jake?"

His hand lifted to her cheek and then to her hair. She wanted to turn her mouth to his wrist, close her eyes, and spiral into heaven at the scent of the man she had kept at bay for too long.

"You didn't say goodbye." He took both of her hands in his. "You ran away. When the going got tough, you left."

He was right. That's why she'd upped and left the UK in the first place, and when things didn't go perfectly in Australia, she had done the exact same thing. She'd thought she didn't have a choice; she'd thought that running away was the solution.

"Life's full of challenges, Tamara." His fingers lightly rubbed hers. "I wouldn't have come here if I didn't think you felt the same way about me. I've wanted you ever since the day we ended up covered in mud, trying to escape Fergus. I think that was the moment I really started to fall in love with you."

The corners of her mouth twitched at the memory, but then she snapped out of it and stropped into the kitchen. "I didn't need rescuing then, and I certainly don't need rescuing now."

He followed her and grabbed her hands in his again to make her listen. "Stop being so defensive; stop walking away when things don't work out as you expected."

She whipped her hands away. "If you'd told me the truth sooner then maybe I wouldn't have walked away. Maybe I'd still be in Brewer Creek. Maybe I would've admitted that I love you, too."

He moved perilously close, his face inches away. "Say that again."

Were her legs about to buckle? Tears welled in her eyes. She couldn't say it again, not out loud. That would make it real, that would leave her vulnerable, and something would happen to ruin it all, she just knew it.

When he spoke again, she felt the gentle air from his mouth against her face. "I knew you felt the same way about me, Tamara. And that's why I had to come. Without you in Brewer Creek, it makes me not want to go back there. Streuth! April is all lovey-dovey with Hugo and the baby, Danielle goes all doe-eyed when she talks about this Will and... what?"

Tamara failed to stifle a giggle.

"What? Why are you laughing?"

"I've never heard you say 'streuth' before. You sound so Australian when you're in one."

"What does that mean?"

"Never mind." She grinned. "It's an English expression."

He wrapped his hands around her waist and pulled her to him.

His mouth locked with hers and he kissed her with an urgency that showed how difficult it had been to contain his feelings for so long. This was real; this was really happening. And Tamara was giddy with longing.

They tugged at each other's clothes and she fumbled with his belt buckle, stumbling through to the lounge and onto the rug in front of the fire, unable to wait a moment longer to feel their bodies touch.

They lay on the rug, far enough away from the fire that it wasn't too hot, and their urgency settled to a slower pace as their laughter stopped. Jake kissed her face, her neck, holding her gaze in between. His tongue trailed down her skin and over her breasts, and her body responded. He met her lips again with his, his tongue gently probing, and she moaned when he pushed himself inside of her. She wrapped her legs around him, pulling him deeper and deeper. She never wanted to let him go again.

***

Tamara pulled on her black, woollen coat, and a burnt-orange beanie, scarf and gloves, as she and Jake stepped out into the magical white world which had fallen silent. Beth had called from the motorway services to say she was stuck in traffic and would be at least another couple of hours, so Tamara seized the opportunity for a romantic walk in the snow until her friend arrived.

"What are we going to do?" Tamara couldn't help herself. Old habits die hard, and she was trying to plan the future. "Do you want me to move back? Is that why you came, to get me? Do you want to move here?" She listened to the snow squeak beneath their feet.

Jake pulled a snowflake from her eyelashes as it settled. "I don't have all the answers, Tamara. Nobody ever does. But for now, Bobby has stepped in to look after the practice while I'm away, and while you and I make some decisions."

"So my parents are in on this, are they?"

"They were sworn to secrecy. I think your mum was desperate to tell you. The jade plant was her idea, by the way. I think it's her way of giving you a gardening lesson from a distance."

Tamara's head tilted back and her laughter echoed around the deserted street. "Let's hope I can keep it alive then." And she added, "Bobby would've found it much more difficult to keep it from me. I bet he's been desperate to say something."

"Well, I guess they both have an incentive for me to come here," said Jake.

"You mean so that you can persuade me to move back to Brewer Creek?"

"Not necessarily. But I'd say you hit the jackpot with your family. Parents who let their kids follow their own path in life and support them all the way are the best people in the world. If I end up being anywhere near as good a parent as either of them, I'll be stoked."

Her heart skipped a beat at the thought of Jake considering parenthood, but as a distraction, she asked, "Stoked?"

"Happy."

She shook her head. "I don't know. You and your Aussie-isms."

"Get used to it." He pulled her beanie down so that it covered her ears, and tucked the dark wisps of hair beneath it so that they wouldn't flap into her face. "I'm not playing games, Tamara. I'm in this for keeps, even when the going gets tough. I'm not running away and I won't let you run again either."

She stared back at him. She had literally never felt as happy as she felt right now. His words were exactly what she needed to hear. Running away wasn't the answer. It hadn't been the answer for her and Bradley; not for Bobby trying to escape his past; and certainly not for Jake and April, who had almost paid the ultimate price.

"Could you see yourself living here?" she asked, as their feet spoiled the pristine coating of white against the black tarmac.

"I'd be willing to give it a try. I've got a six month visa, and Bobby has Kenny Jackson on standby to help him out should he get really busy at the practice. But Bobby reckons six months is as long as he wants to be working. After that, he says that your mum is due a retirement fit for a queen. I think he made some joke about taking her to Buckingham Palace and seeing if they could stay there for a while."

"That sounds like Bobby. So what happens after six months?"

"After six months, we make a decision. We can move back to Brewer Creek, together. Or, I sell the practice and relocate here, to the UK."

"You'd do that, for me?"

As Jake nodded and the snow continued to fall, Tamara realised that this was it. She and Jake were permanent, no matter where they decided to live; they were going to be together from now on.

A smile to match Tamara's played on Jake's lips and she brushed a snowflake which landed on the tip of his nose. As he stooped down to pick something up, she looked behind them at the way they'd come, smiling at the two sets of footprints – one much larger than the other – leading from her cottage; footprints that would tread through life side-by-side, no matter what it threw at them.

As she turned back towards Jake, he caught her with that familiar warmth of his lips. His tongue gently explored her mouth and, although her cheeks were freezing and her nose tipped with cold, she felt as though porridge oozed through her veins, warming her from the inside out. She had never felt so cosy in her life.

Then her hat whipped off, and a firm thud triggered wetness through her hair, down her face, and slithered inside the neck of her coat. She gasped as the cold trickled down her breasts and she looked at Jake – another snowball in his hand – laughing so hard that he almost couldn't breathe.

"Oh, two can play at that game!" She scooped up a generous helping of snow and pummelled him with one snowball after the other. He was quick, though, and fired snowballs back at her in quick succession.

"Okay, I surrender!" He was on the ground now, holding his hands up. "You've had more practice than me, you win!"

She held out a hand to help him up, but instead he pulled her down on top of him. They lay there giggling, ignoring the kids from the end of the road who looked at them peculiarly as they ran past dragging plastic sledges, heading towards the fields.

"I hope Beth makes it before the snow gets too heavy." Tamara rolled off.

"What *are* you doing?" Jake watched her, as she swished her arms and legs out to the sides simultaneously.

"I'm making a snow angel. Go on, give it a go."

Obediently, he mimicked her motions, and when they'd finished they stood and admired their handiwork before the snow had a chance to rub it all out.

Jake's arm pulled her in close as they walked slowly back to the cottage. "Maybe we could start a friendship tree here in this village, become part of the community."

Tamara wrapped her arm around his waist and hooked her fingers through the loop of his jeans. "That sounds like it could be dangerous."

His eyes twinkled mischievously as the snow fell around them. "Or it could be a lot of fun."

Grinning, Tamara pulled Jake inside the cottage. "Now I like the sound of that."

THE END

**Fantastic Books
Great Authors**

Join us on facebook:
http://www.facebook.com/crookedcatpublishing

Find us on twitter:
www.twitter.com/crookedcatbooks

Lightning Source UK Ltd.
Milton Keynes UK
UKOW02f2128170516

274404UK00020B/159/P